The Ship's Cat

The Ship's Cat

ALEX HOWARD

Black&White

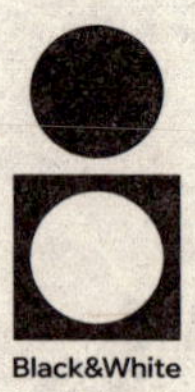

First published in the UK in 2026 by Black & White Publishing
An imprint of Bonnier Books UK
5th Floor, HYLO, 105 Bunhill Row,
London, EC1Y 8LZ

A CIP catalogue record for this book is available from the British Library.

HB ISBN: 978 1 78530 770 6
Export PBK ISBN: 978 1 78530 942 7
eBook ISBN: 978 1 78530 772 0

1 3 5 7 9 10 8 6 4 2

Typeset by IDSUK (Data Connection) Ltd
Printed and bound in Great Britain by CPI (UK) Ltd, Croydon CR0 4YY

The authorised representative in the EEA is Bonnier Books UK (Ireland) Limited.
Registered office address:
Block B, The Crescent Building, Northwood, Santry
Dublin 9, D09 C6X8, Ireland
compliance@bonnierbooks.ie
www.bonnierbooks.co.uk

To my brothers, Matthew and Robert

'A cat with polydactyl toes brings good fortune at sea.'

– Old Maritime Superstition

'A cat with polydactyl toes brings good fortune at sea.'

Prologue

HE HAD HELD ON FOR so long. So long, fighting the sub-zero temperatures and lace-thin air.

But now his thoughts began to stretch like a streetlight seen through wet eyes. A layer of frost coated his paws, which were polydactyl, each with an extra toe, giving them the appearance of a set of white mittens. His nose, long since numb to the reek of kerosene and ozone, twitched almost imperceptibly. In the half-light, he almost looked carved, except for the fur on his tail tip which shifted gently in the eddy of air that swirled up from the landing gear door. His paws were crushed against his belly, like a praying mantis, while a line of bolt heads pressed into the jagged edge of his spine. Numbly, a final thought twisted through his brain – a thread of ink in water.

Thought you were gonna make it, Archie old boy . . .

THUNK. A sound so loud it pulled the little cat back into consciousness. Dim shapes slid and locked. A knuckle joint straightened like a prosthetic limb. And then Archie, the four-year-old stray from Stepney Green, East London, opened his eyes, their lids cracking a thin film of ice. Beside him, a hydraulic piston extended, like a telescope, pushing out a great elbow of steel. He shook his head, sending thawed droplets of water flying from his whiskers and bitten-edged ears. It was the first time he had moved in over three hours.

Suddenly, the floor sank beneath him. Scrambling, on a final drop of adrenaline, he hooked his thumb-toe over a run of pipes as light began flooding the space – beautiful, yellow, life-giving light.

Then a blast of air, violent and deafening, tearing over his ears and flattening his smoke-grey fur against his face. He opened his mouth in a yellow-toothed screech.

What in the name of— HELP!

Prickling with terror, he watched the enormous landing gear wheel hinge out from the plane's belly like a hideous kicking leg. Sounds amplified – the rush of air and thunderous howl of the engine. He dug his claws in deeper. Somehow, and he didn't know quite how (but Archie was a jammy cat) his rear legs found a foothold on a lip of metal. This calmed him, momentarily, enough at least for another thought to enter his head:

How in the gull's gizzard did you wind up in here? You've really outdone yourself this time, Arch.

A tilt like a see-saw. Now the plane's belly became visible, stretching out and flashing metallically under a burning sun. Air filled the little cat's mouth, unswallowable, like a muslin-stuffed wound. A row of lights switched on above his head. Behind, the jet's hungry vortex sucked and sucked, pulling his bushy tail backwards, towards its ghastly mouth of spinning fins.

Oh dammit, I'm going here. Come on, boy, hold it together. What a story this will be.

His grip loosening, Archie hooked a foreleg around the landing gear's vertical strut and whipped his tail, monkey-like, around his body. The plane rolled to the left, then back to the right. A patchwork of fields revealed itself below, gliding serenely past. With a pinch of his nose, Archie suddenly realised that he could smell the land even from way up here – its arid earthiness and the resinous tang of sun-baked scrubland. Strange. Unfamiliar. The plane dropped, and levelled again, its long line of ailerons harassing the air this way and that. Archie's belly sank. Now cars flashed on a spaghetti of motorway. And now a train track, long and straight like a scored line. And now a mosaic of parked cars, their roofs flashing back the sun.

And now tarmac, getting closer and closer and closer and . . .

THUD!

'Mrrrrrroooooooooaaww!'

The claw on Archie's polydactyl thumb tore from its nailbed, its translucent talon remaining embedded on a bundle of cabling, like a stinger.

The runway raced below in a blur of lines. Brake pads clenched. The smell of hot rubber. Heat. Then at once, the engine's roar subsided. Relief rolled over Archie's fur in waves. He sighed, his ears pricking back up as he nursed his nail bed with an unhealthy-looking yellow tongue, one eye on the tyre under him as it rolled over tarmac and dashed lines.

Flipping heck, my ruddy backside is toasting here.

Eventually, Archie's eyes focused on the ground which was no longer moving. Engines fell silent. No more motion chaos. With ears still ringing, and a brain only half-awake, Archie unhooked his forelegs from their sloth grip around the telescopic wheel column. He twitched his tail as fear transmuted into the default setting of East London's most notorious stray – unquenchable curiosity and scowling suspicion.

And then, with the nonchalance of a gull strutting through Borough Market, Archie leaped down onto the warm tarmac and licked his leg, as if arriving in a hot land by plane was the most normal thing in the world for a London stray cat, and hardly worthy of a second thought.

Well pickle my paws and call me Sheba. What a palaver that was. Right, I'm peckish. Any caffs round here where I can get a bite to eat?

PART ONE

XENOS

(ξένος): 'FOREIGN; STRANGE; STRANGER'

1

Arrivals

OF COURSE ARCHIE HAD KNOWN leaping into the underbelly of the Airbus was probably a bad idea. He was a thinking cat after all, shrewd of mind and canny of paw. The problem wasn't Archie's assessment of a situation, but more the fact that the stray had grown to live by impulse; and that, all too often, was his downfall.

At four o'clock this morning, for instance, he had been prowling along Bow Road in the drizzling rain. It was a good scrap run, one of the East End's finest, and was guaranteed to throw up the odd mouse or kebab wrapper. But this morning it was the scent of a she-cat that was drawing him along its littered gutters. Equal amounts alluring and intoxicating, the scent drew him further and further east, away from his bed, which, for the last few months, took the form of a fly-tipped mattress dumped in an access road behind an Indian restaurant. Fly-tipped mattresses were street-cat gold, and this one had served him particularly well: sure, the extractor fan ducting above it was noisy, but it also doused him with delicious jalfrezi-scented air – warm air, the type of air that cancels out the chilly blasts that persisted up the Thames even now, in early May. And no cat, not even a hardened stray with a decent coat like Archie, wanted to be caught out in one of those bone-seeping easterlies. There was even a squat wall, just to the mattress's side, from which he could keep a weather eye out for usurping strays. No beast, not even a bellicose fox, was going to rob him of his memory foam palace; not after the frosts of last winter which saw the little stray's back frostbitten and red, his thinning tale wrapped desperately over his paws to keep them warm.

But back to this morning. Yes, he could remember the first red buses nosing along Bow Road; a spattering of partiers returning from a nightclub. But apart from that, all other memories of the morning came back in a knot of disconnected images.

That was, until the pigeon.

Dammit, that's where it all started – it was that ruddy pigeon's fault!

Hell-bent on tracking down the she-cat's scent, Archie had found himself on a station platform, scavenging around the base of a vending machine for a mid-mission pick-me-up. No sooner had he nibbled half a salt and vinegar crisp than the pigeon – the evil pigeon which had sealed his current fate – trotted past. Clearly hungry itself, it had hopped onto a waiting train, thrusting its silly neck back and forth, and set about pecking at the greasy remains of a sausage roll just beyond the doors. Now he couldn't explain why, but something about that bird gave Archie what he referred to as 'the 'ump'. And when Archie of Stepney Green got 'the 'ump', there was no going back. A fight was on the cards. There was no peace offering – no dangled Dreamie or shooing foot that cat, human or, indeed, pigeon could proffer, to pull the yellow-eyed East End stray back from the red mist of the 'ump.

Who does he think he is, trotting onto a train, givin' it all that? Archie had seethed at the bird.

Claws flexed (six for the price of five, on each paw, in Archie's case), the plucky stray had charged at the bird, ambushing it down the carriage and into an explosion of feathers under a luggage rack.

It put up a good fight, that pigeon; so good that, by the time the job was done, and Archie had quelled his 'umpiness with a mouthful of feathers, the train's doors had slid shut and it was hurtling eastward. He'd boarded the airport express.

Stepping out into the drizzle at London Southend Airport, he hadn't seen the plane at first. His first priority was to get home, as no self-respecting London stray found themself east of Dagenham of an evening without good reason. But he was so *tired* – so worn out from the trek and the fight. It was then he saw it – the cheerfully orange Airbus – and its circular windows glowing through the drizzle, like a taut string of lanterns. So ambient and welcoming. It was those windows which had lured him with their promise of warmth; made him concave his scabby back under the perimeter fence that ran the length of the airfield and clamber up into the peaceful, warm nook of the landing gear bay, the engine's heat still permeating from an earlier flight. And there, soothed by the whirring pipes and patter of rain beyond, he'd collapsed into an exhausted, heavy-headed doze.

And now here he was, in a heatwave, somewhere far, far away.

Archie, you total muppet, honestly, he thought now, swaggering out from under the plane's belly as a human foot kicked a rubber chock under the tyre. *Bleedin' could've snuffed it back there. You've had your fair share of bumpy rides, but that one took the biscuit. Worse than that Uber Eats rucksack you rode in to Shoreditch that time.*

The tarmac was sticky under his paws where the sun had made the bitumen gooey. It was an unfortunate predicament for the cat to find himself in, but a stray's luck comes from its confidence, and Archie had that in oodles. He swaggered across the airfield under the blistering sun, head low, like a Spaghetti Western gunslinger, and straight in through a set of double doors to arrivals.

He licked his leg and passed its damp topside across his head. His paws tingled, still recovering from the icy fractals that clung to them at altitude, but other than that he felt fine – good, even. He gazed around. He was in a corridor. Strip lights fizzled above and the wall was plastered with adverts depicting holidaymakers frolicking. Archie craned his neck up to the nearest one. His belly flipped. A rush of panic coursed along his back, making its wiry hairs stand on end.

Among a series of different foreign sentences, he spied English:

Welcome to Dalaman
Türkiye's Turquoise Coast

2

Concourse

HE STOOD FOR A MOMENT in horror, ears twisted back, and his forepaws performing a little anxious pad on the spot.

Christ, TURKEY?

Like many thinking cats, Archie was a decent reader of human letters, though he had learned them quite by accident. He hadn't so much studied as *absorbed* human language by casting his eye across the headlines of the newspaper fish-and-chip wrappers he would frequently lap grease from. Most East End chippies had stopped the old tradition of wrapping their cod in pages of national tabloids, but a few (the *good* ones) still persisted in this old custom, and none were greater, more flavourful of fillet and more generous in their scrap-offering clientele than The Cod Almighty of Wapping – the finest fish batter this side of Billingsgate.

Flipping heck, Turkey. This can't be happening.

With a sigh, he rose and pawed his way into an empty room divided by columns of queue barriers. He sat again and tried to gather his thoughts. Like any stray, he was accustomed to hitching lifts, be it in a van, train or Uber Eats rucksack, so the predicament he found himself in – having to accustom himself to a new location at speed – wasn't altogether unfamiliar. The big difference was that all these former locations were all still in London – Westminster or Monument or Cannon Street – a mere hop, skip and jump back home on the Circle Line.

Of course, he considered, now cavalier, licking down his grey side with big head movements, *it's not like this is unheard of. This ain't no more mad than when that mutt got in the Royal Mail van and posted himself Special Delivery to Dover. Or when that kitten flew from Greece to Switzerland under the plane. But you, Archie, ain't no kitten . . . and you* definitely *ain't no dog. How could you be so daft?*

Suddenly, a human in a bright orange jacket appeared clutching a radio. Archie reared up, his coat spiking into a huge pompom of anger, a guttural growl gathering in his throat. *WHATCHOO LOOKING AT? YOU WANT SUM? COME ON, THEN?!*

The human backed away, a mixture of surprise and fear on their face as they muttered something into their radio.

That's right and stay away.

That was another problem, you see: Archie didn't like humans. Hated them, in fact. In all his four years straying in East London, he had been largely alone. Not liking humans was tricky, because the East End was a place filled with humans of all sorts. He had, therefore, been a cat accustomed to the quiet moonlit street; the rancid back alley where rat-torn bin bags spilled their meagre offerings; the rusty tin roofs of the Mile End scrapyard, or the urine-reeking under-pass. Born in a storm drain on the lower Thames foreshore, he had never known the comfort of human for any length of time, and not even that of his fellow cat, save the odd frolic with a she-cat if the moon was right. And even when a human did attempt to offer a stroke (since some, of course, tried) their unexpected affection filled Archie with deep suspicion, his back concaving under their touch, ears flat, eyes flashing molten gold and his throat emitting his trade-mark guttural growl. Gestures of human love bounced off Archie like a spark from a heat shield. He was a cat hard-wired to live by his wits; a ducker, a diver, a right diamond geezer of a cat, crimped of whisker and jagged of ear. At his ankles, his grey fur ran so long that it fluffed out, like the fetlocks of a shire horse, eventually giving way to his most notable feature – his bobcat-sized polydactyl paws, his secret weapon in bust-ups when things, as he put it, turned *a bit pear-shaped*.

Like most strays, he had, of course, had brushes with the local authorities; the so-called 'cat protection'. One morning, a couple of autumns back, a well-meaning resident of a penthouse overlooking the Thames had spotted him limping along the mud and had called the Whitechapel Cat Rehoming Centre on Gunthorpe Street. Upon their arrival, Archie was distracted with a strategically placed cat treat as the deadly loop of cat-catching doom hovered down over his head, pulling taut a split second after he noticed it. Naturally, this sent him into a hissing scratching blur of limbs, whereupon he was sedated, placed in a cage, given the name 'Mr Lynx' (on account of lynx-sized paws), admin-istered with vaccines, cleaned, deloused, dewormed, combed and shampooed ready for adoption. Shortly thereafter, he had had one of his most famous outbursts; an episode often recounted with wide-eyed fear among cat-sanctuary staff all over London. It had happened as follows: a member of staff had decided to feature 'Mr Lynx' on the Centre's social media as 'Cat of the Week'. Archie had been taken from his cage and placed on a little plinth with suspiciously little resistance. But no sooner had the camera begun to roll, and the beaming staff member lifted Archie by the belly, declaring the immortal opening line, 'Here we have our gorgeously friendly Mr Lynx . . .' than Archie lost his nut, lashing out in a whirl of claws and yellow teeth, leaving the young handler yelping with a gash perilously close to his groin.

Thereafter, Archie burned through new owners at a rate of around two a month, each one marching him back to the rehoming centre in his carry box, their arms red with a lattice of scratches, a thousand-yard stare in their eyes.

'The cat's a psycho, mate, I can't have that around my kids,' he overheard one of them say.

And another: 'Mr Lynx? I'll give him bloody Mr Lynx! He tried to mount our toaster . . .'

So back to the streets it was; the dank, unsleeping East London streets, where he'd swagger bandit-style along the alleys, each scrapyard and rubble heap a stomping ground for his huge paws as he slashed at rodents and bewitched she-cats. And so the cycle ran on and on: Archie, 'that psycho grey street cat'; Archie the arch-spined bastet, canny of eye, matted of fur, his mangy spine showing its vertebrae under the Whitechapel streetlights. Grifter; lifter; pork scratching stealer at the Well & Bucket; a constitution of steel with the ever-present ruby-red glisten of recently congealed blood on his forehead.

Bollocks to them and their lot, he snarled whenever he saw a house cat preening itself on a gentrified windowsill. Suffice to say, there had been a time, one time *very* far back in kittenhood, when he'd craved the love of a human in one of these yuppy East End homes. But life – cruel life – had driven all desire for affection away.

You need one of three things to escape the ghetto, he often thought. *A pedigree coat, a knack for tricks, or a standout talent for mousing.* And he had none of these. Being a house cat would do his head in anyway. Legging it over every time his human knocked a fork against his bowl? His stupid brown bowl with 'CAT' written on it? *Nah, blow that for a life.*

Because believe it or not, there was an upside to being a stray. Archie was a free cat, always able to do his own thing, whether that be mewing at the Billingsgate fish traders until they flung him a mackerel or parking himself defiantly under the heat curtain of the cash and carry on Commercial Road. He used humans for what he could get, and nothing more. There was no point expecting more – they would only do what they always did. They would give him a taste of companionship only to abandon him when they learned of his true character. He would call upon this fact, regularly, when he felt himself warming to someone, to reinfuse his heart with an extra dose of protective bitterness. (*See? SEE? No one wants near me. Same old story.*)

But now here he was in Turkey – a predicament which tested even his hardened wiles.

Now, from down the corridor, he could hear the voices of disembarking passengers. *Sod it. Ain't no way I'm gonna get myself impounded out here.* He rose, and skittered over to a pedestal desk, well out of sight. In the gloom, his mind turned to the Turkish kebab shops on Whitechapel High Street, where bits of doner kebab spilt onto the pavements. *Ah, I could go some of the real stuff here,* he thought. The image of London in his current context gave him his first flicker of homesickness. It dissipated in an instant as he nosed his way up a set of stairs and past a couple of customs officers who chattered across the little gulf between their kiosks.

Easy-peasy.

Skirting the wall, his large paws kicking up the dust, he slipped past the kiosks to a set of automatic doors, which parted reverentially for him, revealing an enormous concourse, teeming with humans. *Oh, flamin' Nora!* He doubled back but the doors refused to open, even when he begrudgingly lifted his tail in greeting. *Damn it damn it damn it.* No sooner had he turned away than the automatic doors parted, sending forth a stampede of humans, sending him skittering, his tail spiked up and bottle-brush wide.

Nope, nope, nope. Nah, not keen on this.

Thinking fast, he noticed a bank of vending machines and darted behind the nearest. Like most strays, he had learned to harness fear; to redirect its chemical assault on the brain to precision of paw and limb. Cortisol was simply an aperitif for combat; adrenaline its muscular afterburner. In the gloom, he surveyed the blur of human legs, eyes saucer-wide.

He darted out. A parade of trolleys clattered past in a metal snake. Claws clicking against the tiles, he twisted his body in the other direction, flying head first into a parade of humans pulling suitcases, the synthetic stink of suitcase fabric overwhelming his nose. Everywhere a swarm of eyes . . . everywhere a kaleidoscope of semi-alien colour, sound and cologne.

Archie broke out into a gallop. *Don't let 'em catch you, Archie boy. They'll know you're on the trot! They'll lock you up!* Turkish cat prisons; he'd heard stories.

He raced past an information desk, a bureau de change and a strange machine that was wrapping a suitcase in clingfilm. *Where the frig's the way out?* Feeling short of breath, he swerved into a coffee shop, his tail swishing, cheetah-like, and squeezed in unseen under the countertop. He sat for a moment, his muscles aching deliciously.

Mroooooaw!

A heel sank onto his tail. Red-hot pain. An explosion of chaos. His yowl sent the barista shrieking and letting slip her stainless-steel beaker of steaming milk, which sailed to the floor with a clang. Another human attempted to clamp hands about Archie's midriff. *Don't think so, matey,* he growled, squeezing free. This was the chase – the life Archie was used to: wheeling, dealing and ducking among human enterprise. The constant pitting of wits.

He came to a stop in a quiet spot by a travellator. *What the bejesus is that? An escalator with no steps?* Unable to quell the curiosity, he leaped onto the travellator's rubber handrail and glided sideways. He began to walk along it in the opposite direction, moving and yet standing still. He could now see a floor-to-ceiling window, and beyond it, a line of taxis shimmering in the sun. *The outside! Looks bloody hot. This must be one of those places Londoners go to put their trotters up,* he thought, taking in the action beyond the window as if it were a portal to a strange universe. The idea of a 'holiday' was as alien to Archie as it was for all cats. Why wait for only certain times of the year to do what you want?

The travellator finished and he plopped off the end of its handrail in a limb-flailing thud, turning to glare up accusingly at it. *Ya bastard, why did you do that?* A few humans had seen the spectacle, one young woman pointing her phone in his direction and laughing. Eyes were beginning to swivel his way, peering at him, gnawing into him – ogling, cooing.

Oh get lost the lot of you, he seethed. Sprightly of paw, he managed to zip out through the doors.

Back outside, the sun was as punishing as ever. Buses and cars nosed around in a heat-dulled creep, as humans struggled with stacks of luggage balancing on trolleys. Everything seemed to glimmer and flinch under the sun, which shrivelled in the middle distance into a wobbly haze above the roofs of parked taxis. Archie felt his mouth turn dry and his belly wage a renewed assault on his tastebuds. *Strategy, mate, strategy. You'll be back in London with your trotters up on your mattress before you know it.*

But first, just one Turkish kebab . . .

3

The Sting of Salt

*F*LIP ME SIDEWAYS. *Hotter than a pie house oven out here.*

As he stepped out beyond the shade of the terminal roof, the sun seemed to burn far hotter than it did when he had emerged from under the plane's belly. And that was surely ... early afternoon? Maybe he had still been thawing out back then, or perhaps the reflecting roofs of taxis, here in the drop-off zone, supercharged the sun's energy somehow. Either way, the heat stunned Archie and shot darts of pain from the tarmac into his paw pads.

All along his body, his pelt seemed to crisp up and his whiskers drooped so much that they entered the corners of his vision. It was an oppressive heat, and he could feel it ricocheting like a bullet off the objects around him. Families stood bewildered, fanning themselves with their passports, and Archie's ears pivoted off in the direction of voices, trying desperately to detect traces of English. All it would take was someone he could flank, cling to, a spot of derring-do, and he would be home. But all he heard was foreign tongues. He flumped down under the awning of a taxi rank. *Better watch it, ya know, Archie boy. Things can get tasty in this kind of heat.*

A few summers back, he had got locked in a garden shed. He'd been sniffing down a she-cat (of course) and her scent had taken him to a line of elegant townhouses in Hackney, and eventually into a garden shed. Disappointed at finding nothing, he curled up under a cobwebby workbench between two tins of fence paint. He'd drifted off to sleep, during which time a human had re-bolted the door. What followed was one of London's intense heatwaves, and he was stuck for a good two days in the fertiliser-reeking hell-sauna, subsisting only on the juice of spiders and beetles. It had very nearly killed him.

Trying to relax, he attuned his nose to a bouquet of nearby aromas and let his ears twizzle to the buzz of strange insects, the likes of which he'd never heard before. A suitcase *gff-gff-gff-gff*-d over the paving slabs, accompanied by the greasy smell of grilled sausage. The smell reminded him with a pang of the Cornish pasty stand outside West Ham station. He blinked slowly. Those were the best times to be a stray cat – night-time, when the humans were gone and feelings of loneliness were dulled under hunger and fighting: foxes, badgers … crepuscular owls. Any species was fair game at 4 a.m.

Crikey, I ain't half parched, he thought, his thirst tugging him back to reality. A little way off, he spied a shady spot alongside the terminal where a bin was oozing a puddle of fluid at its base. He ambled over, wading into the moat of juice, enjoying its warm stickiness under his paws. He sniffed and lapped. *You know what, not bad, that, as bin juice goes.* Rising on his hind legs, he tugged at a bag stuffed into the bin's mouth. Its contents duly spilled – a pastry, half a cookie, a carton of juice and (unbelievably) a kebab. He tucked in wildly, smacking his lips, before he licked in and out of his polydactyl paw pads, enjoying the follow-up course, pastry flakes.

But he didn't purr.

In fact, Archie had never purred in his entire life. Perhaps he had when he was a kitten, but then he – like all cats – couldn't really remember that far back. He quite simply didn't know how to purr. He'd heard other felines do it, of course; that velvety, contented rumble emitting from somewhere deep within – house cats, tucking into their food as he surveyed them at the cat flap threshold, ready to wage a blitzkrieg for their bowl of Whiskas. But for wire-furred Archie, for whatever reason, purring just didn't feature. *Jus' ain't in my make-up,* he'd think, glaring jealously at other cats. Occasionally, when a human deigned to offer him a bowl of something, he'd overhear them say, 'Ah he must like it, he's purring!' But what they'd *think* was a purr was in fact his unique guttural 'eating growl' as he wolfed the meal down. A chewing grumph, yes; a *purr*, it most definitely wasn't.

There you go, you've had your kebab. Job done, mate. Now no messing – get back home. That London pigeon population ain't gonna control itself.

It was then it happened. The smell. The intoxicating odour that would change the course of his trip, and life, forever.

Ooooh hello, I've not smelled that before . . .

Something about the smell immediately tugged at him, at his spirit and innermost core. It caught him off guard, in a way no smell ever had before. Automatically, he rose and followed his nose. The smell of she-cats had a similar pull on his olfactory system, but this was different. This struck him like a smell from a different world; a world once experienced in another life, all but forgotten. It was an eye-widening smell and immediately set him flicking through his mental Rolodex of memories. *Dockyard? Canal Basin? Salt barn? Garden centre?* He knew it was none of these, and yet somehow it was a mixture of all of them. It tugged with its hefty organic warmth. It made him feel wonderful.

What was *that scent?* He trotted on, keeping the smell locked in the cross hairs of his nose, his scraggly whiskers whipping to and fro. Occasionally he lost it under the tapestry of competing odours – jet fuel, eucalyptus, hot soil and taxi fumes. But the smell always returned, relentlessly tugging at his nostrils. He crossed beyond the car park, past an air traffic control tower and up past a hotel, his paws spongy on the surrounding grass. Finally, in front of a field, he stopped and flared his nostrils to their fullest extent, eyes pinched shut. Cats pride themselves on their sense of smell, and Archie's was particularly respected among the London caterati. Despise him or fear him, the Stepney cats prized Archie for being able to sniff the arrival of an invading alley cat gang from as far away as Aldgate, or sometimes even St Paul's if the wind was favourable. It had saved his life on several occasions – most noticeably the year before when he detected the teeniest soupçon of poison, artfully concealed in an appetising treat out the back of a well-regarded restaurant. That one very nearly got him.

And he could smell absence: the disappearance of pollen as spring turned to summer, or cardamom being gradually replaced with starch as Diwali celebrations came to an end. There was always a sadness when a comforting smell vanished . . . like the heart lurch he felt as he entered the Stoke Newington library one morning to the tremulous absence of Mr Sanjit's aftershave the week he was made redundant (an incredibly generous treat-giver) or how the aroma of Mrs Colwell's Sunday roast was missing, two days after she collapsed on the Shadwell Estate, her heart having given out. *Dear Mrs Colwell. A proper East Ender. She could've understood me, in time. She came the closest . . .*

He shook his head as a seagull squawked overhead, pulling him back to the moment. Beyond the airport, the smell hung heavier, shouldering past the aromas of olive groves and the tang of rosemary. It pulled him yet further into the depths of his past – to a time before the streets of the East End; to kittenhood, mudflats and the fleeting recollection of the face of his mother. No amount of bolshy airport aromas could squash its majesty.

Then the word dropped into his head, clear and fully formed as if it had always been there.

The sea.

4

The Trek

THE SEA LEADS EVERYWHERE.

So reasoned Archie as he licked a pine needle from his paws. He had found his way to a bank of trees at the far end of the terminal. Needles littered the ground, catching in his toes as lizards darted around the dusty roots, their tiny chests pulsing. The humans were small dots now, way off to his right where he could still spy the car rental kiosk queue of exhausted adults and sun-hatted children.

If I can get to the sea, I can get to the Thames and back to Blighty. Job done! God, it really is proper scorchio out here.

The sun glinted through the canopy, imbuing the little patch of ground with a woody, herbal odour. He began to spot other cats. Here and there, they sprawled in the shaded warm dust at the foot of trees in a little clearing. *What are these mogs? Do they have humans? Or are they all on the trot like me?*

He edged over, head low and tail upright in greeting. He figured he might as well be civil while he was here. Who knew, they might even help a fellow stray out. Like many strays, Archie was able to turn on the charm, particularly when in the presence of, as he termed them, 'brothers from other mothers'. But as he approached, he was shocked by the cats' indifference – no meowing, no spiked tails, no flat-eared growl of warning. Instead, as he meowed they simply continued to lounge, flicking their tails through the sandy soil, slow-blinking, dozing.

Archie struggled to practise civility for any length of time when not taken seriously. It gave him 'the 'ump'. He began to feel put out when his greeting didn't garner a response. He headed to another gaggle, this time under a bush by a chain-link fence where the hot whiff of cat faeces hung in the air.

'Meooow … ?'

This time, one cat did deign to raise its head, looking over its shoulder at Archie before uttering a chirrup and rolling in the soil, paws hooked in the air. A she-cat.

Nah, nah, I ain't up for any of that, thought Archie, turning away, ears flattening. *Sorry, love, I've just spent four hours under an Airbus.*

He sidled away, head lowered grumpily. *Bet they all have owners*, he thought as he stepped beyond the canopy of trees. It occurred to him that the draw of London wasn't just the familiarity of the food, streets and sounds, it was the temper-ature. He simply couldn't exist in such a hot land; he didn't have the coat for it. These cats had narrow, heat-dissipating bodies, and fur so short and fine it looked almost like human hair. He sat at the chain-link fence, buoyed only by the magical smell of sea that continued to hang on the air.

Beyond, a scrubby tract of land stretched, seemingly to infinity, bubbling and squirming in a heat haze. It was from out there – *that's where the sea is, out there!* – beyond the shimmering lip of the horizon. Archie squeezed under the chain-link fence.

Come on, old boy, let's get ourselves back home.

Back under the sun's torch, his greasy coat flinched and squirmed. He began to trudge determinedly forward. Out here, everything was throbbing, flickering … clutching at life's outermost strings. Plant life sprouted up through the soil in spiky fronds, while the air buzzed with the sound of insects which kept Archie's ears flicking. After a few minutes, he caught sight of his huge paws leaving sweaty prints on the cracked soil, prompting a panicky feeling to wash over him. Heavily, he placed paw in front of paw, pulling himself across the scrub in the direction of the scent, clinging to its hopeful promise of home. Soon his head began to pound with dehydration, his tongue turning rough and dry, like a husk. Huge ants burrowed at the sight of his approaching face, which had turned grim and panther-like as the land turned from scrub to a high-grassed meadow. Occasionally, a jet tore along the runway behind him, its engines throwing up clouds of dust. Then the salty smell would wash back like a balm over his nose, impelling him with its promise of a cooling wash, and home … teasing him like a lure to a fish.

His legs started to buckle. Suddenly his thoughts turned to a swirling hallucinatory refrain: *home, home, home*. As a stray he'd never seen the sea for real, only seen it depicted on the side of buses in the form of a package holiday advert; and like many cats, despite having partaken in the odd bout of fish-gazing, he tried to keep that habit to a minimum. (An old mate of his from over the river, Saaf Landan Tom, claimed to have lost the best years of his life to fish-gazing in the London Aquarium – *Mate, you watch 'em and you can't stop; they're right there . . . just glistenin', innit.*)

He looked back across the field. He had come too far to make it back to the airport without collapsing. Strange thoughts of home rose and fell, bubble-like, in his head. Despite having the ruggedest constitution of any cat in East London, Archie knew he was reaching his limit. His toes had long since desensitised to the burn from the soil and his breath was rasping in bursts. *This hill . . . I just . . . need to make . . . it over this hill.* Or was it a hill? Why did its rippling edge keep receding? Soon the carrion crows would start eyeing him, their beady eyes sensing imminent death. *Come on, boy, don't conk out now.*

Then he heard it: the crash of waves on a beach. *There better . . . be a . . . ruddy . . . boat going to England,* he thought woozily. He dragged himself for the final few feet, his breath still scratchy as he crested the top of a line of boulders. Beneath, the land opened out into an endless blue-green of glittering waves.

Blue. Archie had never seen so much blue. Perhaps it was the exhaustion, or the sudden breeze which rolled over the hill, but all that blue rendered him immobile with awe. *Stone the crows, this view's something.* He tucked his tail tight around his body and gazed out in narrow-pupiled euphoria, his senses seeming to revive under the sheer sight of ocean. Below, a little cove cut in between two headlands, which jutted out into the water, covered in olive trees and pines. In the foreground, the sea was calm, moving in satin bands of blue, while beyond the headlands it glittered and danced. Here and there, tankers scored the horizon, their funnel smoke becoming indistinct with the atmosphere.

Over and over, in the tufty cavern of his ears, the sea whispered its call in an endless *ker-sssssshh*.

Blow me down, honestly, thought Archie again. *This ain't real. I didn't know these colours existed. Am I even alive right now? What a belter of a trip home this is going to be!*

Turkey's colours were in a different league to the greys and mud-browns of London. Everything looked vivid and blazing. The silver-green of olive trees; the plants with their fiery orange flowers, and the sand in the bay down below – dazzlingly white, like cotton. It was all a far cry from the pebbly grit of the Thames foreshore. It was the palette of a whole other world and, while the little cat didn't know it in this moment, the beckoning light of home faltered for a moment in his head, like a torch's beam dimming under a low battery.

There'll be Adam's ale down here, surely, he thought, raising his tail as he scanned the beach. Unsteady, he traversed the craggy hillside between fig trees and fragrant knots of rosemary. He could see humans now, clinging round the edge of the beach like greenfly around a rose stem. And boats – plenty of boats. Boats bound, no doubt, for all manner of places. The crisp snap of a sail cut through the air, reaching Archie's ears a little late as sound dragged its heels in its race with light.

Then a hiss rose up behind a beach café, where a tap gushed water into an stainless-steel bowl. *Thank gawd for that,* sighed Archie. *Music to my ears!*

5

The Fisherman

'GLUG-GLUG-GLUG-GLUG.' *AHHHHH, THAT'S GOOD.*
Archie gulped the water like he always did, with little growls gurgling at the back of his throat.

Sweeter than any Mile End shawarma, that. No half-binned bargain bucket comes near water when you're a parched cat.

He didn't know it yet but witnessing that view had changed him. Something had begun to shift in his soul and he would never know that it was this very moment where it all started, in the same way that one never knows the exact moment they fall asleep or when a bud cracks out of its tight green capsule. For now, home still resonated within his belly, like a habit, and his resolve to get out of the heat and back to East London, with as minimal human contact as possible, drove his every glance and thought.

Never again will I take you for granted, oh ale of Adam, he thought, smacking beads of water from his mouth. He trod away from the steel bowl, already feeling the water course through his blood, enlivening it.

Suddenly a large golden retriever meandered past. It noticed Archie and let out two sharp barks.

YOU WANT SUM, MATE? hissed Archie, arching his back and skittering sideways, his tail quadrupling in size. Startled, the dog yelped and doubled back. *Yeah, that's right. JOG ON, little doggie, jog on!* growled Archie under his breath as the huge dog flailed on its paws. It walked off to rejoin its human, who clipped a lead round its neck. Once or twice, the dog looked back warily only to see Archie still puffed up, eyes flashing, pupils thread-thin like a lizard's. *Stupid mutt,* he thought as his hairs settled. *Thinks he can take me on? Archie of Stepney Green? I've had mutts twice his size for breakfast down Millwall way.*

Archie, of course, despised dogs, but he particularly despised dogs on leads. It wasn't fear that drove his animosity so much as jealousy. Oh, he could duck, weave and make general mincemeat of any East End dog – be they a whippet or Weimaraner. That wasn't the problem. It was sheer green-eyed jealousy. A lead meant an *owner*, a human; a metaphor of acceptance and love. *That's* what made him see red. These pets had humans who cared for them, and while he could convince himself the straying life was a good one, seeing these leads would bring the reality of his own loneliness crashing down. A dinner was waiting for them, sure as clockwork; walks twice a day, and a pelt skin free from the gnaw of mites and mange.

At that moment, the air shook with a noise. All around the bay, a human cry rang out, long and mournful. Half song, half chant, it seemed to give strange meaning to the setting sun, and volleyed around the buildings and earthy hills. While another cat would've darted under a sun lounger on stumped legs, Archie recognised it immediately. *It's the old call to prayer. They must be Muslims in this land!* A calm fell over him as he twitched his tail with newfound curiosity. He had passed many a chill evening at the great mosque on Whitechapel Road. The imam had grown accustomed to his visits and would greet him smilingly as he ambled in beside the worshippers and took up a napping position beside the doorway. The thick carpet against his belly on cold days felt luxuriant, as did the prayers of the imam which would send him into a trance-like calm.

Turning, he leaped up onto the sun lounger, his belly dripping with sand and watched the worshippers thread into the mosque. Just like at home, the sound had a calming effect on his soul, and as he gazed out at the ocean ahead, a breeze ruffled the long fur around his ankles, which had taken on a russet hue under the orange of the setting sun. *If the sun's right ahead at this time of day*, he mused, *then that must be west – home!* He settled, and tucked his paws under his front. *Mind you, this is actually a bit of all right. Could get used to this.* But as the thought took hold, his stubborn alley cat resolve bulldozed back to the fore, snuffing out any prospect of a different life. *Humph! It ain't no effing better than the sunsets over Hackney Marshes, though.* Like many Londoners, both human and cat, Archie found himself getting oddly defensive of his city when it was faced with criticism, and this peerless subtropical sunset – believe it or not – constituted a form of criticism.

He rose, shaking his head. *Right that's it. Home time. I've had my fill. That's west over there. If I set my pins that way, I've got a fair crack of getting out of this pie oven, and back to the lovely East End drizzle and mist.*

Ker-flump!

Archie's head spun away from the sea. With the mosque now silent, little noises were cutting through the air again. Off to his left was a jetty and a little boat. Archie's eyes followed its sailor as he ambled to the boat's stern, paused, and took a swig from a flask cup, in the way of a human having one last moment of calm before getting on with a job. The boat was almost toy-like, so small that it heeled under the sailor's weight as he strode back up the deck and into a little wheelhouse where he screwed the cup back onto the flask.

Archie wandered over until his nose was gripped by a tugging fishy smell, and when Archie's nose met the smell of fish, there was no breaking away.

Oh 'ello, NOW we're talking, guvnor!

He broke into a trot, his polydactyl paws leaving odd-shaped prints in the sand. The fisherman was now lifting nets from the jetty and rolling them around a spool with the lackadaisical ease of a human who had done the same job many times. He was a littlish man with a peaked cap, and a bushy black moustache which seemed to outsize the features on his face. He wore shorts, stopping just below the knees where his nut-brown legs extended spindle-like into a pair of beaten-up trainers.

Experience meant Archie was naturally suspicious of all humans. Typically, he only entered their orbit for food, snatched their proffered scrap, before scampering away, his bounty clutched in his jaws.

Slowly, nervously, Archie lowered a paw on the lip of the jetty, his eyes glued to the fisherman in deep-rooted mistrust. *If I'm gonna sail home on this thing, I'm going to need to trust this bod,* he thought. He froze, his second forepaw raised mid-air. *But how do you trust a bleedin' human?*

There was something charming, and even magic, about the boat and its variety of coloured nets which the fisherman now arranged in its belly. As Archie lingered, one of the boat's winches caught the sun, flashing infinitesimal texture into the gold of the little cat's eyes, deep and layered like pouring desert sands. The boat's wheelhouse was tiny, hardly big enough for the fisherman himself to stand in, but the whole thing seemed welcoming. Still on the jetty, frozen with one paw raised, Archie began to wonder whether it was merely the promise of fish that was drawing him. *Gotta watch it, Archie,* he thought to himself. *Never let your tum cloud your judgement. Not when the stakes are this high. Just 'cause he's got tasty nosh, don't mean he's cat-friendly.*

He caught a glimpse of the fisherman's eyes – deep, trusting blue. Archie lowered his paw onto the jetty. Then, as the fisherman turned to hurl a little marooned crab overboard from his deck, he spotted Archie. His moustache lifted at the sides in a smile, the leathery brown skin around his eyes creasing. It was a kindly and gracious face, enough to give Archie confidence to instruct his paws to advance and reluctantly raise his tail in greeting. The fisherman wore a checked shirt with its sleeves rolled up and salt stains sending little fissures of white across the chest. Now nearby, Archie could tell he was older than he originally thought as little grey hairs sprouted within the moustache and escaped out the side of the peaked cap.

Gentle-looking bloke, Archie considered with a twitch of his tail tip. The cat's track record on the split-second judgement of a human was good, but he had made mistakes. Bad mistakes. And the criss-cross of scar tissue under the fur of his flank was a lasting testimony to one particular bad error. In his experience, a cruel human took two forms. First, there was the lout who roamed in a gang. This human was often young and took foul delight in using animals as the victims of pranks for their twisted entertainment. Their cruelty was sharp but nascent … a seed of evil which might or might not blossom into a career sadist. *I don't think this bloke is one of them*, Archie considered. *You can see that type coming.*

But the second type of cruel human was harder to detect. Cruelty in this type of human had wormed its way into their soul, like a parasite that hijacks the shell of an insect. They were controlled by cruelty; driven by it. These humans, though rarer, had built up a back catalogue of lifelong wickedness … and were better at covering their tracks. These were the ones you didn't always see coming.

And believe it or not, it wasn't always humans. Archie had learned, for instance, never to take on a Tower of London raven. You just didn't. They were forged in steel. They'd undergone years of training as tower-guarding mercenaries since the days of King Charles II. They would raise the alarm and attack you on the ramparts like a horde of piranhas, leaving you little more than an outline of a cat.

Ultimately, Archie had developed his own crib sheet of red flags. It had served him well over his years as an East End stray:

1)   *Never trust a human with a heavy step.*
2)   *Never prowl an estate where juvenile humans are at play.*
3)   *Avoid humans carrying string or rope.*
4)   *Always give humans on liquor a wide berth.*
5)   *Never follow a lone human into a warehouse.*

He scrutinised the fisherman's features once again – his hands, his muscle tone, the way his eyes moved and fell upon objects.

Hmmm, you've got me foxed, mate, he thought, padding up and down on the scorching wood as the fisherman clutched his flask from the wheelhouse. *Sod it, I'm going in! I'm gonna speak.*

'Mroaw?'

The fisherman looked up. A wry smile formed as he wiped his moustache with the back of his hand and placed the lid back on the flask again, sealing in its steam. He leaned against the bulkhead and chuckled.

'Pisi uşağum, atla gel, gemide fare vardur da!'

I don't have the foggiest what you're saying, matey, thought Archie, though he understood the gesture which followed – the inward sweep of the hand. The man shifted some crates with the side of his heel. Archie jolted in shock at the sound. Then, carefully, the fisherman knelt down, and stretched his finger and thumb out to Archie. He giggled, sending his black moustache bristling, and his wrinkles creased across his weather-beaten cheeks. A bassy liquid growl formed in the back of Archie's throat. *You better behave, mate!* The fisherman grinned wider, a metal filling in a back tooth flashing. Now only a cleat lay between cat and man, its double outstretched prongs dribbling rust down the boat's side.

The fisherman's smile held, almost robotically.

Archie curved his back downwards.

And suddenly, Archie felt himself becoming weightless.

6

A Stroke of Luck

'M RROAAAAAAAAAAAAAAAAAAAAAAAAAAAAAAWWW!'
Ouch, you IDIOT, put me down!
The fisherman had lifted Archie by his scruff, pulling his skin tight around his body like a cord-tightened laundry bag. He thrashed his legs, his eyes flashing like coals. *I knew it, I knew it. You can't trust a human. NEVER.*

Quite how the fisherman had got his scruff was a mystery to Archie. Maybe it was an expertly timed sleight of hand, or the heat had dulled Archie's reflexes. Either way, Archie found himself hovering above the boat's deck in the fisherman's clutches, before being lowered over a hatch which the fisherman raised with his other hand, revealing the dark innards of the boat's bilges.

What the bejesus?

'Burada, burada!' yelled the fisherman, pointing into the hatch.

Suddenly Archie spied his moment.

Take that!

The fisherman recoiled, dropping Archie as if he had become suddenly hot. *And that, and THAT!* The fisherman sucked air through his teeth, letting out a curt 'urgh!' as blood plumed into the sleeve of his shirt.

Yeah damn right, growled Archie. *Thought I could trust ya. Thought you could get me home, and out of this hot mess. Should've known, shouldn't I?*

Archie had landed awkwardly, his paws skidding across the gut-strewn deck, tail coiling in the air like a snake charmer's cobra. *You utter muppet. You're a blooming Judas, mate.* He leaped onto the side bench which ran the length of the foredeck and bobbed his bum up and down, preparing to leap ashore. But the boat had drifted away from the jetty – too far to make the leap successfully. Trapped, Archie glowered back at the fisherman, who approached him cautiously. Archie hissed. *Come closer, you plonker, and I'll have your lugs off! You're dealing with Archie of Stepney Green . . . iron of claw and forged in dirt, not some sun-seeking house cat. Now let me off!*

A moment's silence – that awkward calm that follows a cat and human not having seen eye to eye. The fisherman surveyed Archie with a sad look. In the olive groves ashore, cicadas buzzed restlessly in the newfound silence. Archie thumped his tail against the boat's wooden bench. The fisherman scooped up some sea water which he splashed onto his arm wound. He muttered to himself, and loosened a mooring rope off a jetty cleat with a flick of the wrist. *I know what he's up to,* seethed Archie. *He wants me to deal with the rats down below. Or cockroaches. Or whatever else they have out here. I've 'eard of this caper. Bleedin' typical.*

The fisherman started the engine, drawing the throttle knob astern so the mooring rope fed smoothly out the cleat.

He strode gingerly past Archie to the bow to pull aboard the rope, the cat's back concaving as he passed.

Well, here you go, Archie, you daft ball of fat. He was on the move, sailing out into a wide sea, and with a human to boot. And he hadn't even got any fish into the bargain.

The little boat cut a silver curve around the bay as blue-grey diesel fumes filled the air with their industrial tang. In the wheelhouse, the fisherman spun the wheel one-handed, glancing over his shoulders and muttering something into a radio mouthpiece until the vessel was nose first to the ocean. Already the swell was growing larger and more boisterous, and with the disappearance of sunlight overhead, there came an inky darkness. Archie's stomach churned; but examining his paws, he was surprised by how steady his extra polydactyl toes made him in the swell. *Other cats would have stacked it by now,* he thought, splaying his toes as he skulked along the side bench, perfectly balanced against the pitch and roll.

He climbed up to the prow and looked out. Foreboding filled his belly at the sight of the murky water, resurrecting images of London in his head – its squares and red-bricked Georgian townhouses. *At least I'm heading in the direction of home. A dodgy start, maybe, but it's out there.*

He began to feel less anxious; calm, even. The rocking of the boat had a hypnotic motion, and the warm evening air pinging against his whiskers wasn't at all unpleasant. A couple of times he caught the fisherman's eye from behind the glass of the wheelhouse. While it was a solid 'one-all' in this game of cat versus man, Archie was starting to conclude that the fisherman was probably not a malevolent type, just a quick-thinking opportunist who saw in Archie the solution to a problem. And after all, what was Archie himself if not a quick-thinking opportunist?

We're gonna be cooped up, mate, best get on as best we can, he thought. *And I ain't no sulker. Sulking is the house cat's game.*

Part of him even had a quiet respect for the fisherman – a hard-working human plying an honest trade – and Archie could tell, with the benefit of proximity, that he was poor. His shirt, more than just salt stained, was tattered, with buttons missing, and his left shoe had a sole which flapped up when he walked. And as for the boat itself? It was so small that even if they *did* land a huge catch, it couldn't amount to much more than one market stall's worth of fish.

Thinking of fish, ain't you gonna fling me something mate? Ain't that a mackerel head over there?

He climbed onto the boat's sheer balustrade and padded to the back, his claws pinching into the wood, and his lithe feline body moving with the sea. Finding himself at the stern, he came across a scattering of fish guts and began tucking in. It was not *fresh*, as such, having spent the day toasting under the sun, but it was still succulent – ideal for a stray who, for reasons of fate, providence, or God knows what, had found himself on a Turkish fishing boat in the Eastern Mediterranean. *Mmm, pretty decent fish brain, that. Could do with being jellied, but can't have it all ...* He whipped his tongue around his mouth, his mood buoyed, and celebrated the meal by sharpening his claws along a wooden flagpole which extended out diagonally over the propeller-churned water. From it, a handsome Turkish flag fluttered, its tip dragging in the foam. *When I'm back in London I'm gonna ride the Thames boats more*, thought Archie. *Fish tastes better when you share its postcode.*

Night fell. The boat's engine upped its revs as yellow light from the wheelhouse cast out over the blackening waves. Whistling through his moustache, the fisherman ducked out, nibbling something between his fingers. He turned and looked at Archie nervously. A wry smile formed on his moustache. Softly, gently, like a slow-rolling film, he tiptoed forward before crouching down to the deck, his mouth making little clicks. Gradually, he extended an oil-stained hand, half lit under the light. It contained something fragrant.

Now, now, eeeeeeasy boy, easy, Archie intoned, tiptoeing forward. He tweaked his jagged whiskers, lowered his sore-lined back. Slow, slow, slow – one paw, then the other, then the other. Gradually, Archie met with his cross-species nemesis, ready to pounce or dash at the first sign of danger. *Eeeeasy boy ... Still can't trust 'im. (God that smells good, whatever that is.) He's still human! He still can't be trusted. (God, what is that AMAZING smell?)*

The fisherman whistled again. Archie read the script of his eyes: deep, pale, tired-looking, sharp, instinctive, a touch of hunger ... kind.

The last thing Archie remembered of that day was looking back to the lit mosque on the shoreline – a dot on the horizon – as the fisherman's hand lowered gently upon his crown ... and flinching; but for the first time in his life, letting it remain there.

7

Open Water

MILE END, THOUGHT ARCHIE, gazing wistfully over the azure sea, the perfect warmth of the morning sun on his back. *It's out there somewhere . . . over them waves . . .*

He thought he might feel different: last night, he had let a human pat him on the head for the first time ever. But he felt, remarkably, much the same cat. He stood on the prow as the little boat bounded over the waves, his two forepaws poised on its varnished front like a bare-chested figurehead on a Napoleonic galleon. Why had he let a human touch him? Was he turning soft? Was the sea affecting him with some strange influence? Or maybe heatstroke? Perhaps on some level, he knew he *had* to get on with the fisherman . . . after all, with just a flick of the scruff, Archie would be overboard, tossed into the deep water. *Easy does it, boy,* he thought. *Play it cool.*

Around a year ago, Archie had nearly 'accepted' a pat from a scaffolder at the Well & Bucket pub while snaffling the carpet edges for pork scratchings. He had been eyeing Hugh for several days: there was something kind about his angular face and Adam's apple, his rabbit-caught-in-the-headlight eyes that'd sink when his drinking mates made him the butt of some ribald joke. His movement was gentle compared to his pot-bellied compeers who guffawed on the neighbouring bar stools, and Archie felt safety exude off Hugh like a radiator. 'Don't encourage that thing!' the bar lady would screech in a Cockney drawl, seeing Hugh discreetly drop a pork scratching past his jeans. 'It'll have your guts for garters, that thing! Hangs around 'ere like a bad smell!'

But even Hugh I didn't let pat me on the barnet, thought Archie now, bemused. A little blast of sea spray caught his cheek. He shook his head and lumbered down onto the deck, slippery with morning dew. More than surprised, he felt slightly worried at himself. It didn't do a stray well to be so trusting: it could get him into all sort of bother. Suspicion was healthy – it kept him out of harm's way. What's more, letting in, dare he say it, *affection?* It'd only lead to a deeper level of emotional hurt he wouldn't know how to handle.

So why had he been so affable now? And so soon after the fisherman had manhandled him aboard?

Another strange thing: he had slept long and deep, right through the early hours, on a little blanket the fisherman had laid down for him in the corner of the wheelhouse. He couldn't remember the last time he had slept so heavily. And right *by* him. Perhaps it was all the commotion of the airport, or maybe a strange insect had bitten him on that scrubland, causing him to contract some kind of fatigue sickness.

I tell you what, I ain't done, he thought now. *I ain't had a proper bath since arriving.*

With the fisherman out of sight, Archie leaned his back against the bulkhead, lifted his leg, and gave his nether regions a thoroughly good sanitising.

Humph, all fine and dandy down here then, he thought, smugly observing that all was still intact. *I've heard of moggies going daft because they've had their bits lopped off in a trance. But that ain't happened here.*

He licked down each leg, the boat rocking gently under him, and across each polydactyl paw, his toes spread wide. An ache hung around his left flank probably from the sprint through the airport after hours of immobility; but apart from that, nothing. *Fit as a fiddle. Archie, you're on top form, mate, top form. A cat of steel. What other cat could survive a plane trip like that?*

The sun peeked over the horizon and onto the damp deck, making its moisture rise. He stood and ambled over to a drainage hole along the boat's side. What he saw surprised him, making him almost nervous. The sea had become mirror-flat with a sheen upon its surface like enamel. It spread far out under the sun, in perfect, uniform smoothness. Poking his head further through the hole, he saw the water churn up cleanly under the bow, like a spoon passing through warm butter. He backed away, feeling a little unsettled at the water's glassy perfection.

Where's the skipper? he wondered. *We really are miles out. Hope he knows what he's doing . . .*

He scouted round the corner of the wheelhouse and found the fisherman standing there, one tanned hand upon the wheel, looking directly ahead, his pale eyes bloodshot with tiredness. Behind, the nets dragged through the water. *This poor bloke don't half work hard for his grub*, Archie thought.

Archie mewed at the fisherman, tail high. As was typical for the stray, a decent sleep had sandpapered down the roughness of his mood. Seeing his earlier foe standing there, plying his trade so tirelessly, made Archie feel a stab of admiration. Suddenly, a peculiar notion caught him.

Maybe he's the one. Maybe he'll be the human I eventually stay with.

The thought swirled its way across his mind like a dust devil, departing as quickly as it arrived. It hadn't been the first time such a thought had struck him when beholding an okay-seeming human; someone who might, for once, get him for the sort of cat he was; respect his space; and find the warmth underneath his terse language of scowls and hisses. But something, deep within his brain, had programmed him to push these hopes aside. Even Mrs Colwell's kindness, in the brief time he knew her before she died, was warped beyond recognition by the self-doubting skirl in his brain. (*She would've left too, in the end.*) What he could always count on, though, was another wet London night and its foetid stench of bin waste. *Come back!* it beckoned facelessly. *Getting ideas, are you, junkyard mongrel? You'll never amount to more than this.*

And so the little stray sat at the threshold to the wheelhouse in the wide Mediterranean, not knowing where he was, or where he was going, or who he really was any more, his scabby grey tail raised in its pathetic bid for food.

'Mroaw?'

Unhearing, the fisherman looked ahead, whistling through his teeth. Archie entered the wheelhouse and sashayed his scrawny rear against the fisherman's ankle.

'Ah kedi, kedi!' said the fisherman happily, lowering his hand to tickle Archie behind the ear. Archie growled quietly, his ears flat. But he allowed it. *Don't you think I ain't still got my peepers on you, matey Jim!*

The man muttered something in Turkish and held his hands in the air in a faux 'I'm innocent' pose, giggled, and returned his gaze to the sea. He picked up a mobile phone which lay on a little shelf and began filming Archie as he leaped up to the dashboard and stretched his body, long and majestic above the boat's instrument panel.

Oh for God's sake WHAT WILL IT TAKE to get this guy to know I'm hungry?!

The rustle of a polythene bag. Food.

Oh thank you, about flipping time!

Archie's eyes tracked the fisherman's hand like a laser as it lowered several slices of Turkish sausage in a cupped palm. He chowed the meat, almost theatrically, the throb of the engine beneath vibrating his whiskers. As he ate, the fisherman used his index finger to lift a string charm from a hook on the wheelhouse ceiling, where it dangled beside a compass. It was a string bracelet, the type found in Arabic countries, with a little pendant depicting the Islamic evil eye. Deftly, he slipped it over Archie's head with a little tickle as the cat munched and munched, too lost in the moment and his little bassy grunts of satisfaction to notice his new garment. It fitted perfectly ... like it was made just for him.

Honestly, it's worth international travel just for the decent grub. Top work, guvnor, top work.

'Su, su!' said the fisherman, pouring some water from a crinkled plastic bottle into a cup.

Without realising he was doing it, Archie coiled his tail around the fisherman's bare ankle, though its root remained stubbornly puffed up like a bulrush at being *this close* to a human – a human who, despite making sound progress, was still in the quarantine zone of the cat's mental estimations. The man chuckled, his eyebrows rising with surprise. Lapping the water felt amazing, particularly since Archie's recent bath had dragged numerous burr seed pods off his coat which had lodged in his teeth and dried his mouth out again. Tentatively, the fisherman once more lowered his hand onto Archie's back, which flinched as if zapped with electricity. Changing tack, he moved his fingers in a tickling motion towards the uncharted outback territories of Archie's lower spine.

Hmm, actually . . . you know what . . . that's actually kind of nice. That's really nice, actually. Flip me!

Squatting, the fisherman continued to tickle, causing Archie to lift his rear in a kind of involuntary, sumptuous bliss.

Flipping heck, mmmm! What . . . FLIPPING HECK . . . what the hell's going . . . Mmm. Okay, OKAY STOP NOW!

The fisherman retracted his hand as Archie attempted a viper-like bite at the man's wrist. The fisherman looked at his arm. No blood. He rose, giggling at Archie with a shake of the head, his little moustache pulling into a smile.

'Izmir!'

Archie's ears swivelled. A voice blared loud and intent from the ship's radio. It was in English.

'Izmir, Izmir, reports of extreme—' A static hiss. 'Report to channel sixteen immediately for—'

Casually, the fisherman twisted the radio's volume knob, silencing the crackly voices. Archie cowered in the corner of the wheelhouse, a knot forming in his tummy. *Nah, mate, turn that up. That was English chatter, that was. And it sounded proper serious . . .*

Like all cats, Archie was exercised most by what he was able to infer from a human voice – and the voice on the radio didn't *feel* right. Beneath them, the engine growled, and it suddenly occurred to Archie that the fisherman, with his inferior human hearing, probably hadn't picked up on the tone, let alone understood the English. Or perhaps the fisherman could tell the cries or the radio weren't intended for him? He did, after all, seem to operate to a pleasing degree on instinct, much like a cat. Despite this, an unease grew in Archie's belly as he crumpled himself backwards against the wheelhouse bulkhead, his thick paws skidding on the slimy residue of blooded guts. *He should've 'eard that. Swear that was meant for him.*

Suddenly, and he couldn't tell quite why, Archie had the urge to look out to sea. Rising, he turned and poked his head out of the wheelhouse but caught sight of the sky before he managed to. Huge puffy clouds raced in frightening lines. They charged almost eerily, like a silent conveyor belt that had been sped up. It was peculiar, and made him feel strange – this disconnection between the energy in the sky and the calm of the water.

A soot-black bird landed on the prow. It turned to face Archie, staring him straight in the eye, its aperture eyelids blinking. With an uncanny chirrup, it rose into the air like a flake of ash on the heat of a fire.

Archie raised himself up on the fisherman's leg, mewing intently. *Turn on the radio, pal. Just turn the ruddy dial!* But the fisherman merely rustled in the polythene bag, dropping more sausage at Archie's heels, before extracting a wrinkled tomato and some bread for himself, popping both in his mouth together, his moustache bouncing as he chewed. But now he too was looking upwards. With a strange sort of relief, Archie could see a change come over his face. Above, the racing clouds had turned from white to gunmetal grey.

Gives me the collywobbles, that sky, thought Archie, unable to take his eyes off the clouds churning in great black rolls, their edges gilded in yellow.

Little blusters of wind; just enough for the fishing gear to thrash the hull. Like an orchestra tuning up, the sea drew together its energy until individual waves broke out with crimped white peaks. A swell licked under the boat. For the first time, Archie wobbled on his paws.

It was at that moment that Archie was struck with an intense and unquantifiable feeling of dread. It was unlike anything he had experienced in his life. It was a terror in the air, in the *atmosphere.* He had a decent nose for changes in mood around, say, a glaring of cats; that ineffable moment when friendly sniffing and nuzzling turns into a flurry of claws. But this was something else; a depression that punctured the skin and twisted a barbed hook right into his brain. *Where* it came from, Archie couldn't tell. It seemed to come from the very sea itself, like a portent of doom that only he could sense.

All of a sudden, the fisherman's eyes darted. He swung his head over his shoulder to look at the nets. Muttering something, he spun the wheel to starboard, sending the boat in an ungainly curve through the water. Spray rained onto Archie's back and a hydraulic whirring shot through the air as the fisherman retracted the nets. It made Archie shudder, bringing to mind the plane's landing gear and his untimely arrival into this madness.

The barbed hook inched deeper into his brain, twisted his neurons like spaghetti. *Something's off. Something is seriously wrong.*

'Mroaw. Mrooooooooooaw!' Archie raised himself against the fisherman's legs again.

'Kedi, shhhhhh!' said the fisherman.

Bewildered and sick with dread, Archie ventured towards the deck. While scared, he was a fighter, and something was drawing him into the eye of this feeling. Whatever it was, he wanted to meet it, square on. But as he neared the wheelhouse doorway, a wave pulsed under the boat sending a crate scudding along the deck, causing him to rear up. Above, thick clouds were shutting out the light, making the surface of the sea inky black. Water splashed over the deck more frequently now, one wave carrying with it a tendril of seaweed which looped over Archie's head. He flicked it off, giving it a sniff. It exuded an odd, methaney smell.

Another wave. This time the boat rocked like a knocked pendulum, before righting itself. Archie flailed, scurrying behind the wheel column with a growl. A hum came through the air: the wind vibrating the netting cables like the strings of a huge cello. All thoughts deserted him, save for one repeating ribbon that circled his head: *Get me out. Get me out. Get me out.*

The fisherman tutted, releasing the wheel for a moment to secure the crates. But the second he did so, the wheel spun chaotically. He continued anyway, heading forward up to the crashing prow, his checked shirt snapping in the wind. Archie surveyed him tensely through a little air duct at the foot of the wheelhouse. Each roll of the sea sent him staggering.

'Mayday Mayday Mayday!'

The radio was turned right down, its speaker dangling on its coiled cord down beside Archie's ear. It was difficult to hear what was being said, and when he did pick up the odd word, it was in Turkish. But he recognised the word 'Mayday'. Suddenly, an English voice:

'Mayday! Mirabella Five. We've crew overboard! Mayday, pan-pan medico, three six degrees …'

The message cut out.

Archie forced his head round the wheelhouse bulkhead to witness the ever-rising tumult, letting out a cry to the fisherman. *Flamin' Nora, come back, mate! Stuff's getting tasty, we're gonna die if we're not careful.*

As if hearing Archie's thoughts, the fisherman doubled back, holding a hand over his face against the spray, the boat rearing up like a bucking horse on the water. He rounded the corner of the wheelhouse gasping, his knuckles turning white as he struggled to hold the wheel steady.

And then Archie realised: it was the storm. He could feel it in his belly. It was the storm's malevolent tendrils clutching at his soul across the wide expanse of ocean. A great spiteful octopus of a storm. He turned to read the fisherman's expression. All cats are sound readers of human emotion, but Archie was especially adept at reading a human's thoughts when they didn't know they were being watched. For the first time, he spied the fisherman's teeth gritting behind his moustache, a tinge of panic in his eyes and his white knuckles trembling upon the wheel.

It happened in an instant. The wave didn't strike with a hiss like the others, but more a deafening thud. The kind of crash that a truck makes when colliding with a wall. It was the sort of noise that neither cat nor human thinks is possible until they hear it. Water engulfed the wheelhouse up to its roof. The last thing Archie remembered seeing of the fisherman was his lank body thrashing in a grey soft focus.

* * *

It doesn't feel like a struggle for long, drowning; more a panic followed by a quiet slipping away. A mute surrender to a growing whiteness. Sounds turned woolly as Archie, the little stray from Stepney Green, found himself submerged in ocean, his paws beating in a futile doggy paddle as stinging sea water deluged his lungs. His polydactyl toes beat against the current as his grey fur beat this way and that, like the fronds of an anemone. Then a back-suck as the huge mass of water began to drain out of the wheelhouse, pulling with it the little cat. Across his blurred eyeline, the orb of the boat's compass glided in a surreal diorama.

Sound became a blobbing roar. The fisherman continued his submerged thrash, engulfed in bubbles. Quite how long Archie was underwater was difficult to say – it felt like hours. The final thing he remembered was the fisherman's body twitching and turning sluggish, his shirt billowed out and his head collapsed back, like a ragdoll. Archie's vision became murky, as he fixed his gaze fiercely on a chink of light above the cabin door. Visions took on a beautiful ethereal form; discomfort started to ebb away. And then, in that small boat in that odd faraway sea, Archie began to detach from reality. Time turned to treacle. His pedalling legs slowed, spasmed, then stopped altogether. He was entering the great plateau of peace, known only to those mortals who have glimpsed beyond the jaws of death.

A final thought, oddly lucid, drifted through his brain like a wind-carried web:

How strange that this is how it ends for Archie of Stepney Green. All the fights, all the rotten food. And this is how it ends. How strange. I never once purred.

8

The Lull

THE BOAT'S GUARD RAIL WOULD not have been strong enough to hold back a human being sucked overboard.

But it was just about strong enough to hold back a cat.

Archie's mind fell blank as the huge wave drained through the wheelhouse door, bearing on its white frothy back his little feline form.

And yet it transpired, by fate or sheer luck, that a stretch of netting, which had snapped adrift at the stern, had wrapped itself around the starboard guard rail just at the point Archie had been hurled against it. Under the force of water, his limp body spun in the snagged net, the sea twisting him in it tighter and tighter, like a spider wrapping up its prey.

A dying cat is an awful thing to behold. Archie's eyes glared lifelessly upwards, their golden hue turned muddy, his mouth agape – the eyes of a fish lying dead on a fishmonger's ice tray.

And then, almost as suddenly as it had arrived, the wind vanished. The sea fell calm. Sunlight broke through cloud and the horizon came into focus again, the crinkled water turned smooth. Only the seaweed and spume remained, slathered over the deck, glistening in the fresh sun. The change in the sea was so sudden as to seem almost insincere. Any human witnessing a sea fall from tempest to calm in such short time would never look upon it in the same way again. Trust in nature would be forever besmirched, like a friend whom you'd inadvertently spied being unkind to a cat under the belief of privacy. All anger and fierceness had dissolved. The sea was almost coy, pulling itself up here and there into dainty little crimps, like it had been given a stern telling-off.

A few moments passed, as Archie and the fisherman remained motionless. Fortunately, the boat's hatches had held firm, keeping the water from deluging the hull. And Archie, the four-year-old stray who had found himself in Turkey, alive against the odds, flicked an ear. It was the sun that roused him, burning corrosively hot upon his head. All around him, vapour lifted from the deck. All was silent, save for the gentle kiss of the water against the hull and the *eeeeek uhrrrrrrrk* of the wheelhouse door on its hinge, opening and closing in the roll.

Then, without warning:

'Bleeeeeeeughhhh!'

A green-yellow streak of cat vomit projected into the air as Archie reanimated like a vacuum cleaner after a power cut. Every limb tensed, convulsed. Salty bile coated the inside of his mouth, making it burn.

What in the absolute bejesus was that all about?

Shell-shocked, he began to disentangle himself from the netting and set to staggering across the deck. He'd known some frightful storms in old Blighty, but this had been on another scale. Was this normal in these lands? Surely not – he couldn't imagine the fisherman would have set out if . . . *THE FISHERMAN!* Archie scrambled to the wheelhouse, pain smarting through his legs.

And there he was. The man lay twisted and still. *Roadkill* shot into Archie's head as he sniffed his bare foot. His shirt had ripped along the sleeve and down his arm a rope burn had lifted a red patch of flesh. The other arm was hooked around the wheel column, as if he had lunged for it. Maybe he had. He was still aboard after all. *How?* Then Archie saw the thread of blood trickling down from his forehead onto the wet deck. In a strange moment of numbness, Archie just stared.

Dead. You're dead . . . Mate?

A blink. Archie raised his tail automatically. Hope. Still half-closed, both the fisherman's eyes lolled towards Archie, a weak smile forming under his wet moustache. It was a quivering smile. A weak smile. But it was the most warming and reassuring smile Archie had ever known.

'Kedi?'

You're alive, thought Archie with a sudden mew, lifting his tail even higher. In spite of himself, he did something he'd never done before: he biffed the weak man's hand with the top of his head. *How did we make it through that?*

The fisherman lifted a hand, sucking through his teeth and touching his scalp, looking at his hand for blood. For a moment he stared around, blinking, as if having awoken from a strange dream. Then, wincing, he pulled himself up agonisingly slowly. Archie could almost feel the pain searing along the man's nerves where his spine had contorted against the wheel column. But gradually he unfurled. He twisted to face Archie, who had managed to clamber onto the boat's dashboard. Man and cat surveyed each other, drenched and beaten.

If there was one thing – the *only* thing – that could bond an alley cat like Archie to another being, it was shared trauma. Misfortune obliterates fronts and exposes the truth; it lays bare all that the human or cat have to hide. As Archie and the fisherman eyed each other in silence, both thought the same thing in their own language: *How are we here? That should've been the end for us.* The fishing boat was so small, so light and cork-like atop those colossal waves. How had they both not been washed overboard? Archie thought of landing on the plane and how close to death he had come, and how this was, quite possibly, his last cat life if such things were true. So how was he still here?

One thing was sure: as Archie looked into the fisherman's watery blue eyes, he trusted him. Something about the experience of the last half hour had shifted something in both man and cat. Archie had never found himself willing a human to live before, but looking down at the Turkish man from the dashboard, a lurch tumbled through his belly at the thought that the man wouldn't live. He even felt a curious feeling of protectiveness over him; somehow, that poor man was more vulnerable to the sea's impetuous temper; her strange and pervasive mood – a mood which he, Archie, could *sense* prior to its strike.

'Ah, güzel kedi!'

The fisherman's voice was beautiful. Archie had, of course, come to assume that 'kedi' was Turkish for 'cat', and every time the fisherman spoke the word he did so in such a warm yet playful tone that Archie felt his eyelids turning heavy. Levering himself up, the fisherman pulled Archie in for a hug. The cat didn't refuse, though uttered a chirrup of surprise as he felt the man's shirt press against his side. Gently, the man stroked down his fur, squeezing out water from its grey tufts.

All around the little boat, the sea kept its composure. Above the dashboard, windows parcelled up a clear blue sky in oblongs. The fisherman clutched the top of the wheel and squared himself in front of it. Vacantly, he passed his eyes over the engine controls and navigation panels. He pressed a button on the GPS module. Nothing. Had the storm carried them nearer to shore or further? Finally with what seemed like a small breath of tense expectation, he pressed the engine start button. Black-green smoke coughed out of the exhaust, but each time he released the button, the engine snuffled into silence. He grabbed the radio mouthpiece, and twisted the little volume knob with a *click!* Nothing.

* * *

Two days passed. Two long days drifting on the electric-blue sea, mirror-still under sweltering air. Cat and man grew to understand each other's routines and habits. The fisherman learned the precise whereabouts of the sore spot on Archie's flank and his fondness for dangling off the stern and swiping for fish at sundown (a fried bream on the gas stove made for a hearty shared feast); Archie learned to sit respectfully as the fisherman prayed on a little mat up at the boat's bow.

So it was with a mixture of sadness and relief that man and cat heard the drone of the Greek patrol vessel cutting through the water towards them. It was an alarming sight, its megaphone blaring and its uniformed border guard standing at the bow waving aggressively. *We were going somewhere, him and me,* Archie thought. *Nearly played a right blinder, there. He could've been your human.*

And when finally the border guard scooped Archie up by the belly with unaccustomed firmness and lowered him onto the scorching boulders of Rhodes, the little cat turned back to the fisherman. Paws throbbing against the rock, he stared in numb disbelief as the man was escorted off his boat and made to walk over the beach to a police van, the two patrol officers each maintaining a firm grip on an arm as he staggered over tussocks of sand. And with his mournful blue eyes, the fisherman cast one final sad look Archie's way, before lowering into the metal stomach of the van.

And there, on the hot desolate beach, Archie cried louder and longer than he ever had before.

9

Rhodes

A Turkish fisherman rescued from Ialysos beach after his vessel lost power and drifted for days attributes his survival to the befriending of a 'magic cat' on the dockside at Dalaman.

Kasım Yılmaz of Kalkan, Antalya said the cat boarded the boat in Dalaman Bay before the vessel fell victim to Storm Scylla, losing both electrical and mechanical power. The extreme weather events of the last week continue to send shock waves across communities in both Turkey and Rhodes, with seventeen souls confirmed dead and three vessels foundered, all of which were significantly larger than Yılmaz's twenty-five-foot-long boat.

Yılmaz said: 'The cat was walking the dockside looking hungry. I took it on board because I'd seen a mouse in the bilge. The cat had unusual paws with extra toes; I'd never seen one like that before. But I know he brought me luck at sea when so many brothers and sisters died nearby. Blessings to Allah for bringing me that cat.'

Scientists continue to study the causes of Storm Scylla and its possible formation as the result of a once-in-a-century pressure event in the Eastern Aegean.

THE CORNERS OF THE NEWSPAPER fluttered in the warm breeze. Two gnarled hands clutched its edges, holding its broadsheet pages high so the reader's top half was completely obscured. Gradually, the reader lowered it onto a paper tablecloth, which was blue and white and clipped to the table at its edges. The face that appeared behind it was small, shrunken – an old man, in a fine cream linen suit that looked too warm for the weather. He giggled and slid the newspaper over to his friend – equally old, with slicked-back, thinning hair – his other hand clasped round a glass of lager. The friend paused, pushed aside his cigarette that smouldered in an ashtray and scanned the print of his companion's newspaper. After a pause, he giggled, mainly out of politeness, before looking away and lifting his beer to his lips.

To their left, and just out of sight, the rear end of Archie the stray from Stepney Green protruded from underneath a rubbish bin. Wasps buzzed around its lid which was tilted up from its overfilled contents of black bags, eggshells and polystyrene cartons. A sicky odour of rotting emanated, merging incompatibly with the scent of jasmine from a vine which flaked away from a crumbling stone wall behind.

The boulevard in front of the café was thronged with tourists. Legs rushed past in Archie's peripheral vision, along with bike wheels, moped tyres and even the occasional *clip-clop* of a donkey's hooves. Little carts trundled, fanning wafts of grilled kebab, their skewers sizzling like static, while along the street, awnings held off the beating sun and shaded their maîtres d' who enticed tourists with rings of *koulouri* on boards. This was Rhodes Old Town, alive with tourists: fathers in neon-coloured shorts, mothers elegant and lean, fanning themselves with maps – all shuffling cheek by jowl in the stultifying journey to the beach.

And who notices just another scavenging stray in the ancient old town of Rhodes?

Mmmm, I do like (gnaw-gnaw-gnaw) *a good rare bit of* (gnaw-tear-gnaw) *cutlet. That's just the ticket, that is. Just as good as Dala— wherever it was. Why do they chuck out the best bits of meat? Just like in London. Humans are all the same. God, my rear end is ROASTING.*

Archie reversed out from under the bin. Still chowing on a piece of marinated sinew, he pricked up his ears and observed the long boulevard. Of course, he was perfectly at home sniffing among the discarded scraps that the seagulls had missed. He looked scrawny and almost unrecognisable from the bushy-faced tom he had been all but one month ago; now back on land, his thick coat had continued to moult excessively to the point that his vertebrae nodules were clearly visible and poked up, dinosaur-like, through his wispy back fur. The sun burned unrelentingly overhead, while the winding streets prevented any offer of a merciful sea breeze. *Flip, my bum. Honestly, this heat. Sooner swim across the Thames in sleet than be in this kind of weather. Oh, hello, what have we here? Chucked-out meat tray. Oh, what a lovely bit of tendon! Nearly missed that, I did.*

At least in Rhodes he was in good company: street cats seemed even more commonplace here than they were around the airport in Dalaman. In Rhodes, the cats were bolder, however. Rather than lounge in the dust under trees, the Greek cats prowled the ancient streets with purpose, weaving their scraggly bodies in and out of tavernas, one after the other, eyeing their various waiters like mafiosi henchmen. Archie admired it. Sometimes they'd sit at the entrance to an establishment and look the street up and down, as if *they* were the maître d' soliciting for custom. Every cat seemed intent on business, whether mysterious or obvious, and their mouths hung perpetually agape in a sort of heat-induced grimace.

They don't half swan about, thought Archie, backing out of one's way as it patrolled by. *Why are they acting so hardcore? Do they all want some? Because if they want some, I'll GIVE 'EM SOME!*

But they were a peaceful race of cats, and seemed unfazed by Archie's presence – a standout visitor with his moulting fur and cat-about-town swagger. Their call wasn't a typical *meow* like a British cat, but a more growl-like '*mrrrraaaaarrrrr*', as they begged for scraps at the foot of café tables. In Turkey, the land was the humans'; in Rhodes, the cats were fully in charge.

Two nights had passed since Archie made landfall and the fisherman's vessel was intercepted by the Greek border guard, and his spirit had only today started to recover. In the hours that followed being lowered onto the harbour boulders, he had walked the marina walls crying hopelessly in long, baleful, husky mews. That first evening, his every thought seemed to recall the fisherman's blue eyes flashing across the beach as he was shepherded into the van – each reincarnated memory a new needle stabbing his chest. It would catch him off guard, the sudden absence – like a tongue that keeps finding the gap once occupied by a tooth. He began to feel hatred towards the sea; to resent it for bringing him towards the first human with whom he felt true companionship, only to tear him away within days and dump him back on the streets. Hunger, however, is a powerful motivator, and the growing need for food soon wrenched his animal brain back to the hunt.

Stupid, STUPID ball of fat, he'd think, eyeing his shire-horse ankles treading over the cobbles. *To think that could've been it. If he really wanted you, he'd have protested more. Told the harbour bloke to keep you and not sling you out.* Sometimes, his mind replayed this last thought when he felt especially low or felt he was due a dose of self-punishment. In its wake came memories from his past; tiny snatches of time when he'd come near connection – tailgating a house cat into a warm abode with a nice-seeming owner, staying overnight in the mosque ... Mrs Colwell. At each memory, a burning feeling struck his chest like battery acid as he remembered how he ruined all those nascent connections: a swipe because they attempted a stroke, or looked at him the wrong way. And then there he was again. Back on the streets.

You will die just like all the strays ... alone one day after a fight or in the gutter. Don't dream, old boy, it never does well to dream.

And so unfolded his time on Rhodes – not so much living, as simply existing in the way he knew how: begging for scraps, lapping water at the fountains, and sleeping in the shade. A house cat with a constant supply of dehydrated brown niblets has the luxury to worry and mope. He didn't. Add to this the fact that feline rumination is especially miserable under a hot sun and, by day three, he was a fully-fledged stray once more, the fisherman's moustache and soft eyes now only making a doleful appearance over his mind once or twice a day.

There was one other thing he thought about, however: the storm. How strange that whole thing was. Do storms really come and leave that quickly? He recalled how his 'sense' of the storm seemed to come from somewhere beyond his normal five senses. He could *feel* it approaching in the same way he could feel the insidious tendrils of hunger clutch at his belly, or the ballsy testosterone of a new tom on his patch. It was just *there*. And then it wasn't. Why? He had always been famed for his sense of smell, but this was more than smell. *Maybe it's just the sea,* he thought finally, on the eve of day four. And with that, he put the matter to bed and wouldn't think of it again for many weeks.

* * *

Noontime was when the Rhodes sun beat hottest. Each day, at around two o'clock, Archie had taken to skulking down to the marina and dozing under an upturned rowing boat, whose nose jutted up and caught the breeze. There, he'd listen semi-consciously to the rigging of the moored sailing boats, letting his mind float off into images of the Thames barges of home. *Bet it's lovely and chilly back in London,* he'd think longingly. London nibbled at him in those moments; the smell of Arbour Square after a spring rainfall; the chaos of Brick Lane – a place where his coat and soul were at one with the setting. But just as often, he'd find himself thinking about the sea. *There's something about boats,* he'd think. *There's something about boats. Humans are better on boats. And so am I.*

Things felt less lonely in the evenings. Much like a cat, the old town of Rhodes revealed its true self at night. Walking the streets around six o'clock was dreamy, when the sun cast long shadows, bringing out the delicious Byzantine ambers and terracottas. The tantalising dart of lizards in the half-light. Much like at the Tower of London, the city walls had little gaps where windows once existed, and each little cell was typically filled with its own street cat. On one particular curved wall, Archie would look along at all the other cats doing just the same as him, and it'd give him a curious, habituated feeling.

Sometimes a human would lean down for a little tickle and, thanks to the fisherman's influence, Archie would occasionally find himself accepting it. But if the stroke exceeded more than a few seconds, he would raise his back into a hair-raising arch and offer two curt whips of his paw. *Got grub? No? Then scratch this itch and bugger off.*

But he was enduring human contact, for just that little bit longer.

When dark fell completely, he'd chum the accordionists threading between the restaurants in search of donations, pulled by the scent of grilled octopus. *You don't get accordions in Brick Lane,* he'd think, chewing on a tentacle accidentally marinated in a puddle of spilled sambuca. *Ooft, hello, yes! Taste explosion.* At this hour, the beach stall traders were away, but a handful of souvenir shops remained open with their carousels of fridge magnet souvenirs. Under their glow, Archie would slump beside the African braiding ladies and watch their fingers twining multicoloured treads through tourists' hair . . . tantalisingly close to a paw's swiping radius. Quietly, without him knowing it, Rhodes was making him question what a different sort of home might look like. On this, what would be his final evening on the island, he mooched back to his fibreglass boat, his mind swimming with contentment and sambuca. Crawling under the upturned hull, he was reminded of the time-honoured alley cat saying: 'Lose the claws, get indoors.'

Seconds later, his eyelids fell heavy under the distant drone of accordions and mopeds, but not before a final thought snuck in. *These silly paws and their extra toes. They've got a lot to answer for, I reckon.*

10

The Box

FLUMP.

Archie's ear swivelled.

It was early morning, just past five. Still sleeping, the scruffy cat's belly rose and fell under his fiberglass rowing boat, each exhale ending in a mini snore.

His other ear swivelled. A clanking sound from the marina. Persistent. Annoying.

He rolled over, resisting the tug of wakefulness, and buried his head under his huge paw.

Oh SOD OFF, beetle!

Archie sprang, hitting his head.

Twitchy blasted six-legged little creepy-crawly git!

With limp ears, he padded out from his shelter, feeling irritated. The sun was just rising, and the air was rich with the smell of damp vegetation. Archie stretched, butting his rear end in the air and sending bits of grit raining down from his fluffy underbelly. *Drink time. Ruddy parched, I am.*

Just as he started advancing towards the hosepipe, he froze in his tracks.

It was the *Calypso Spirit*'s anchor he saw first. It gleamed silver, distressingly bright. At first he didn't know what he was looking at. Only after several flicks of the head did he realise the great downward-pointing dagger of steel was *part* of something – a boat. A superyacht, in fact. It rose unnervingly out of the water like a sculpture, its bow curving sleekly and its decks layered with black-tinted windows. It was so big that he couldn't quite get a grasp of perspective; instead, he stood dumfounded, his tail tip twitching nervously.

Eventually, he tiptoed forward. *Flip me. The human who owns this must be minted!* He sniffed its side – plastic and seaweed. *Is it . . . a sailing boat? How do you get on the damn thing?*

He trotted a little inland and stared back. Now he could clearly see the boat's trowel-like bow thrust into the water, jutting like an angry chin, the deck pulled backwards and rising into an ugly, visor-like roof sprouting with aerials. It was clearly *meant* for pleasure but something about it signalled aggression . . . war.

Well blow me down, I've never seen nowt like this before. Where are they heading, I wonder?

The vessel must have arrived in the early hours, and with unnerving silence. Archie, like all cats, detested changes to his environment, particularly if they came unannounced. Only last month, Tower Hamlets council had changed the colours of its bins from blue to purple and he had found himself in an existential funk for half of the morning.

He tiptoed back towards the yacht, and let out a mew.

Hello? Anyone aboard? My God, is that a hot tub up on the deck? Flip me!

Towards its stern, he spotted a gangplank linking the gap between deck and shore. A young man appeared, in a pristine white shirt and khaki shorts, through a set of sliding doors on the sundeck. He began busying himself unfolding sun loungers, arranging them in a semi-circle, before placing a bucket stand for champagne between them. Archie drew in his features swiftly: lithe, cropped hair, earbuds firmly wedged, playing a tune whose beat he nodded along to. His muscles bulged against his polo sleeves and he reminded Archie of the sort of sporty human he would often see playing basketball in the East End parks. Shortly after, an older man appeared, looming up behind the first. Something about the way he approached, quietly from behind, made Archie think he might attack the young lad, and brought to Archie's mind the image of a predatory fish. This man was taller and less brawny, his shoulders curved forward in a skeletal stoop. He wore sunglasses that concealed his eyes, and that alone made Archie immediately wary of him. (Archie *hated* sunglasses, or anything that meant he couldn't see a human's eyes.) In a strange way, the taller man was like the boat itself: all angles, pointy, brutish . . . unnervingly silent.

Take those sunglasses off, mate, you look like a right muppet! thought Archie as the taller man rounded on the younger one and shouted.

'Oi. Oi. Er, *hello . . . ?*' he cried.

The younger man plucked out his earbuds.

'Sorry, Captain,' he said.

'No earphones on deck. And what did I say about these cushions? They can't be out now or they'll bleach in the sun.' He pointed and snapped his fingers. 'Let's wake up and get with it, Jake, yeah?'

The captain lifted the cushions and slung them at the younger man's feet. Dutifully, the young man picked them up and placed them in the shade of the inner deck.

'Understood. Sorry, Captain.'

Ah he's the guvnor, all right, thought Archie, stalking alongside the boat, his head craned upwards at the unfolding drama.

The captain wasn't done.

'Jesus H Christ, how many times do I have to tell you lot to close *and lock* the hatches when you wash down? Moron.'

The captain flung 'moron' over his shoulder, as if it was an apple core he'd finished with. He disappeared below decks.

He's a mouthy one, thought Archie. *I wouldn't let him speak like that with me.* The young man's treatment at the hands of the captain stirred a sudden feeling of injustice in Archie. Perhaps it was the sun, or his heart was going soft thanks to his time with the fisherman. It was definitely a *new* feeling. Either way, the exchange rocked him in a way his emotional constitution wasn't familiar with. *Bet that deckhand lad could get along with any Tom, Dick or Harry. I bet he'd get on with me, come to that . . .*

Archie scouted a little further along the boat, feeling a mixture of curiosity, exhilaration and bubbling animosity towards the captain.

Interesting that they're English, he pondered, reaching the boat's stern to find a Union Jack flag, its tip skimming over the water's surface. *I thought as much.* He couldn't deny it; hearing English being spoken gave him a pang of happiness, the same kind of joy he felt when he chanced upon a recently dropped jellied eel. England. That land far across the sea where it rains, and which had never shown him lasting love, suddenly seemed nearer and more reachable. *Damn you, London and your stupid drizzle. What do I owe you?*

It had been an epic trip. A great adventure. But this boat was clearly his sign – England was calling. He would sneak aboard, and sail back to London in style (for surely that's where they were bound?). And by the time he rounded up Dagenham Reaches, he would have forgotten all about these silly sentimental feelings towards humans and would be an angry plucky stray once again. He'd be back in cool, temperate London before the month was out, so long as he didn't do anything stupid like getting sidetracked or—

OH MY GOD, BOXES?!

Archie's fur prickled with excitement. A young woman of around twenty staggered towards the yacht, grimacing under the punishing sun. A loaded shopping bag swung from her hand, while under the opposite arm she clamped one of Archie's favourite things ... a cardboard box. It contained beers, but that was irrelevant. It was the box that counted. Struggling with her load, the woman waddled, duck-like, and her brown hair was greasy where it had escaped from her ponytail. As she approached the gangplank, Archie caught sight of her eyes, which were large and reflecting. The woman lowered the items to the ground before returning up to a car to retrieve another large box from the boot. Archie spied the brand on the side of the box: *Fosters*.

Oh gawd, not Fosters! I've seen many a human make a right show of himself on that stuff, he thought, recalling the brawls that often followed a home match when the scores hadn't gone West Ham's way. *Just a load of fizzy water,* thought Archie. *Gimme a rich stout any day. Far more flavour! And less gassy on a cat's gut, too.*

'Oi Georgie, get a move on,' yelled the captain, who had emerged again on deck. 'Where've you been?' He clapped his hands like a primary school gym teacher. 'C'mon, chop

chop. The helicopter's due at nine. What were you doing up there, checking out the handbags?'

'Sorry, Captain,' replied Georgie breathlessly, carrying one box up the gangplank and decanting the bottles into some kind of outdoor fridge. She spoke in a husky way with a hint of an accent. Norfolk, maybe? Archie couldn't quite tell. 'I couldn't find swordfish anywhere, and then the market seller only took cash so I—'

'I don't need the whole backstory,' barked the captain. 'Did you get what we needed?'

'Yes, I found a—'

'Good. Leave the box there and do the awning.'

Georgie obediently headed away, leaving the beer crates unattended.

Boxes, boxes, cor look at them lovely boxes! rejoiced Archie.

His heart thumped with rising ecstasy. His pupils widened. Even Archie, a cat hardened to a life of survival, much like his feline brothers and sisters, could not resist the whimsy, the folly and downright sense of entitlement that came with perching his fluffy posterior in a good box. An abandoned box called to him, like a flame calls to a moth, and set his mind a-racing with feelings of imperious box-dwelling grandeur.

But no, he mustn't. Not now. He had got himself into enough trouble. He needed to get home, and *safely*, and that meant not getting accidentally stowed in a fridge. He quashed his curiosity down, down, down, but like an insistent mole, it kept bobbing back up again. It called; it goaded. There was an unattended cardboard box but metres away, and no other humans currently with eyes on it.

Don't, Archie, don't. Don't look at the boxes. Don't—

But it was too late. Archie had started playing 'the game'. And when a cat starts playing the game it is nigh-on impossible for them to stop. Much like Jumanji, a cat must play the game through to its conclusion. Archie started to imagine all the bigger cats he'd feel like if he were to inhabit the cardboard fortress. *Panther. No, CHEETAH! God, it's perfect. Taut, high-sided … and still cool, probably, from the supermarket fridge. Jungle leopard? Cosier than any greengrocer's crate; cosier on the old bum than any Amazon parcel. This is it. The box you've waited your whole life for. LION!*

And so, with his mind drunk on ideas of box-borne grandeur, Archie trotted over to the box and peered in. There was room inside, good room. The other crate had been tightly packed but this one only had half a dozen bottles in it. He leaped in, the bottles sending out a little *clink!* as he did. His estimations had been right – inside it *was* deliciously cool and dark. He squatted, sending his pink, sandpapery tongue over the streaks of cool condensation. *Utter heaven,* he thought as he felt the sides of the box get taken, juddering him upwards towards the floating palace.

11

Zoomies

A SMELL OF POLISHED WOOD and sun cream sidled against the synthetic tang of PVC plastic – an expensive, regal smell. Archie was aboard the *Calypso Spirit*.

He felt himself get lowered, and the sound of sandals padding away to silence. It's always a risk, getting in a box: the chance of entrapment is high, but it's worth it for the pleasure.

He poked his head above the cardboard tabs. *Crikey O'Reilly!*

Sweeping away, the deck curved into an infinity of blonde teak planks. Archie raised his forepaws above the tabs before leaping neatly out of his cardboard fortress. He sniffed the deck, nostrils pinching, and trod reverentially over the sweet-smelling planks, feeling like a pauper in a sultan's palace. The deck planks felt dry and grainy under his toe beans. He reached the boat's edge and gazed down at his reflection in the green marina water. Feeling pleased with himself, he leaped onto the white raised foredeck, lined with square hatches. Gosh, it felt thrilling – a little meagre stray on a mega-yacht! Hitching a lift on the District Line rolling stock felt naughty, but this? This was gilt-edged weapons-grade naughtiness. And it felt *amazing*.

He smacked a beetle that landed in front of him, its red-black body hopelessly conspicuous against the white plastic. In front of him were a series of hatches. They were calling him, and he was desperate to glimpse the world below decks. Finding one, he peered down through its square pane. Below, a cream sofa curved around a table so highly varnished it looked like it had been drenched with honey. Spotlights, like tiny stars, ran down a set of stairs, ending on a final tread, where '*Calypso Spirit*' was engraved. There was even a grand piano. In the corner, beside an open cupboard, Archie spotted the young woman busying herself in a kitchen area, unpacking the lined-up shopping bags. And again, the unannounced head of the captain hovered into view, this time with his peaked cap removed to reveal a sunburnt bald patch.

Seriously, thought Archie, *this place is mint!* He turned in a vainglorious circle, tail high. *Talk about luck, Archie boy*, he thought. *Here you are, right as rain, with your health, your looks . . . a bit skinny on the flank and jaws, mind you; but with a belly full of beetle, and about to set sail on the plushest bleedin' boat in the world. Who needs human company when you've got LUXURY?*

It was then he spotted it. Around a corner was a wide-open hatch. Hawk-eyed for any unsecured means of entry, Archie was a master at spotting unattended entrances: all it took was one door momentarily on the snib or one up-and-over garage door not fully lowered and he had potential access to a bed and evening meal. Cat flaps, in particular, were vulnerable points of entry: a swaying cat flap often a telltale sign that the lock on it had broken. While a little ashamed, he had been known to devour an entire house cat's meal, growling his little growl, while the poor house cat stood by, too afeared to interrupt the infamous Archie of Stepney Green mid-feast. Such things were far from his mind today, however, as he crept towards the open hatch, the sun still pummelling his back. He peered down. A bedroom. His fur stood on end when he beheld what he took to be a family of swans at the end of the bed, only to discover, on second glance, that they were in fact a line of inanimate towel sculptures in the shape of swans.

He belly-crawled, snake-like, into the open mouth of the hatch. Soon, only his rump and haunches remained outside the hatch, his rear toes grabbing the hatch side firmly.

Okay, so it's the old grab-and-twist routine, Archie. You want to claw in with your left rear leg, snatch up the right fore and . . .

He lost grip. Terrified, Archie dangled, his whole body swinging like a fluffy pendulum and his entire weight held by a single claw. Awkwardly, he swung, letting out a small growl in spite of himself, his eyes flashing and his ears swivelling to and fro.

Bugger! Bugger! Bugger! You're gonna have to just . . .

Flomp.

The softest of landings. Of all the landings Archie had ever experienced – on water-butt lids and dumped settee cushions – *this* landing, on a queen-sized duck-down duvet, was the finest. He staggered up to his paws on the bed, shook his head, and gazed around.

He'd heard tales of places like this – the raffish homes of legendary London gangsters. He was in the lap of pure and complete luxury. *How the other side live . . . Good things come to cats who wait and you've sure waited, Archie boy.*

He sniffed the duvet cover – cotton, the finest Egyptian percale. Above, a gold-trimmed vent breathed down scented, nebulised air. He sniffed the tallest of the origami towel swans, arranged in descending height order. Feeling cheeky, he swiped at one, enjoying the endorphin rush that came with besmirching perfection. Then he made biscuits on the cushions, tearing up silk threads out of their hems. *I really could* [tear-rip-rip] *get used to* [rip-rip-rip-splice] *this.* His eyelids sank to half-mast as he shook out the dirt caked around his toe beans onto the pristine white sheet.

Through the hatch above, the sky formed a parcel of blue. The real world trilled its melodies at a blissful remove – the real world of suffering where loneliness counted: the seagulls (hungry), the accordion players (poor), and the woozy *phut-phut-phut* of motorboats around the marina. It was amazing how quickly they all seemed coarse and unpleasant. The squawk of a gull is remarkably unpleasant to a cat's ears when the cat in question is ensconced between two buxom duck-down cushions.

Twinkling in a corner, under a spotlight, was a bottle of Dom Pérignon champagne, comically large, resting in a golden bucket beside two cream leather chairs. Next to it, on an antique-looking ottoman, was an open copy of *Yachting Weekly* beside a pile of navy towels with '*Calypso Spirit*' stitched onto them. *Bet old balding boss wouldn't be best pleased to see me chilling out here,* Archie thought with a renewed thrill. It occurred to him now, with fresh irritation, how good house cats had it. Sure they didn't all live like this; but they lived as *worry-free* as this. They never needed to concern themselves over whether their bed would be warm. Stowing away on a superyacht was the best of both worlds – guaranteed splendour, but you didn't have to perform a schedule of forced cuddles or get anointed with monthly flea-repellent chemicals, just to earn your keep.

Suddenly, he began to feel delicious. Alarmingly delicious. Whether it was the scent of linen or the miasma of whisky, a tremulous thrill rose in his belly. He felt god-like and frisky.

And then it happened. His intrusive thoughts won. He started to zoom.

Tail swinging, he gambolled over the bed, and boxed the towel swans off it, one by one. Pausing for a snort, he resumed his zoomies by picking a fight with a daub of sunlight on the antique ottoman, leaving a colossal line of scratches down its front.

For the first time on his odyssey, Archie felt his mood transmute into the carnal, his self-aggrandising rapture switching into a familiar urge of the loins. And so it was that, with his tail fully spiked and his virility rising within him like expanding foam, Archie reversed his rear end to the oak cabin door, lifted his tail and sprayed. An iridescent trickle of urine dripped down the woodwork. He watched proudly as it seeped into the footplate, its pungent reek a gratifying *eau de toilette*; an anointing of his palace. *This gaff's mine now, and no one can evict me!*

Just then, from above, there came the loud stomp of footsteps.

12

Georgie

'GEORGIE? GEORGIE, WHAT THE DEVIL are you doing?' A cry came from the far end of the marina. Archie recognised it immediately as the captain's. 'I leave for *two* minutes. Oi, Georgie, the breather, *the breather*.'

Panic. Archie's head flitted left and right atop his percale cotton bedsheet. From the other side of the closed cabin door, a voice crackled through the radio.

'Captain to Georgie, Captain to Georgie . . . Georgie you airhead, you didn't open the tank breather. There's diesel spilling out the boat, you moron!'

Another set of footsteps bolting across the deck overhead. *Owp, it's all kicking off up there,* thought Archie, relieved that he wasn't the cause of the commotion. He attempted to follow the path of footsteps. Through the open hatch above, he caught sight of Georgie's calf, nut-brown and slender with a bracelet round it. Then a trainer, a shoelace, the metal nozzle of a fuel hose . . . and Georgie's voice, rasping with panic.

'Oh my God, please. No, no, no. *I'm on it, Captain!* Oh my God, this is bad.'

'Are you blind or were you painting your nails again?' retorted the captain.

Archie's ears lowered. The captain's voice was nearing, and had taken on a singsong, nasty sarcasm.

'Oh so that's only €300 of diesel there, you imbecile,' he said.

'Look, I'm sorry, Captain,' Georgie replied breathlessly. 'I … It was an accident, I swear. It really was, Captain. I'll clean it.'

'I mean, I know it's your first gig but I thought you'd have some *nous*. Your CV made you sound like a boaty bumpkin from Cornwall … who taught you to sail? Were they cross-eyed?'

'It won't happen again, Captain.'

'You had one job. Refuel a sodding boat. Align nozzle with hole. I mean, Christ, if you could do anything I'd have thought you could do that.'

A silence.

'I'll clean it up,' Georgie replied flatly.

'I'm *Captain!*'

Oooft. Archie scuttled for cover. The captain's response came in a juggernaut of noise.

'Now I'm going to go to the harbour master for the passports,' the captain continued, 'and when I'm back, that's cleaned up, the canapés are out, and that damn awning is out and open, or you're off this job. You can hang around here and get a job with the hair braiders on the high street. More your calling, I think.'

'Aye, Captain.'

'Don't tell me you haven't done the master suite? Christ's sake, please tell me you've . . .'

'Yes, Captain. Turndown's done, checklist complete. It's ready.'

'The seafood?'

'It's um . . . yes. Nearly ready, yes. Langoustines are marinating, just got to do the caviar. It's on ice.'

Archie heard the captain move away, muttering under his breath, 'Rule number one of refuelling a yacht, open the breather, princess.'

Archie's tail whipped against the bedspread. *What a nasty piece of work. He ain't half 'umpy. Who does he think he is, Ronnie ruddy Kray?*

Nervously, Archie traced his eyes around the cabin, scanning for places to hide, places to escape. If he was to be face to face with this human, he knew claws alone wouldn't cut it. What's more, he knew full well that a cat, when faced with a human like this captain, should *always* choose flight. It's not worth even threatening a claw – just get the hell out. A human like this would always be taller, stronger, angrier. There were many sizeable humans who Archie could, and did, duel with: the lardy oaf, the slowed-by-drink buffoon. But men like this? Never.

A knot pinched in his belly. He began to pace the cabin, suddenly conscious of his imprisonment. It was a familiar feeling, and its bite never grew old; being trapped in close proximity to cruelty.

And now footsteps coming. Louder, faster.

Suddenly the cabin door flew open. Archie raced on his paws, skittering in a blur behind the foot of the bed, his tail hair spiked like a porcupine.

A muffled sob.

It's not him, it's her, thought Archie with relief.

Archie inched forward and peeked out. Georgie sat sobbing on the edge of the bed in her white *Calypso Spirit* shorts, her head in her hands, too distraught to notice her surroundings.

The whole charade of a human being crying was appalling to Archie, as it was to many cats: a short sharp expletive of emotion, in the form of a meow, he could understand. But the ragged gasps; the intensity of emotion expressed to the point of *fluid gushing from the eyes?* It all seemed so ungainly and, frankly, bizarre. Archie watched in bewildered silence as Georgie snuffled, thick opaque tears blobbing onto her lap, one hand clutched around her belly as if she might be sick. Her big rabbit eyes blinked, sudden and aperture-like, and a vein stiffened against her temple. She cried in fits, like a toddler, pulling the back of her hand over her eyes. Now Archie could smell her scent like a unique ID – sun cream, biscuits, sugary chew sweets and, most noticeably of all, raspberry flavoured lip balm.

Surprised at himself, Archie felt an urge to stay close to this stranger; to listen and to tend. As with so many points over the last fortnight, had he dwelled, he might've spotted the beginnings of a profound inner softening in moments such as these. Only the week previous, he had mewed at his separation from the fisherman, and before that, when the fisherman lay hurt, had felt an emotion largely unknown to him – worry. But the tumult of life on Rhodes had over-written these upwellings, like a freshly dealt pack of cards. And probably for the best, too: after all, what use do feelings of care and pity have in the life of a stray?

We're both strangers on this boat, he thought, finally sitting down, still in peeking distance from Georgie. He looked at her neck, bowed forward, her taut white skin. Unlike him, this young woman was clearly a rookie to unkindness and its sudden aggressive presence was a shock to her system. And that made it a whole lot worse.

A smell gathered under Archie's nostrils. *Hang about, is that fuel?*

Suddenly, a primeval fear caught hold. He had witnessed first-hand how hungry fire was for fuel, ever since that stack of tyres he saw burning outside a tyre depot in Canning Town. *Flipping heck. I'd better warn her and FAST.*

He crept forward.

'Meow?'

Chaos. Georgie's every limb became a whirl of motion, as if being pulsed with electricity. Locking eyes with Archie, she reverse-scrabbled onto the bed like a puppy from the snapping jaws of a wolf. Startled by the pantomime, Archie scurried behind the champagne bucket, sending it teetering before hiding under the ottoman.

For a moment, the two surveyed each other. Georgie's face toggled through a mix of emotions: fear, incredulity, and finally mirth. She started to giggle.

'God! What the . . . ? Hey little fella! How'd you get in here, you cheeky lil' goblin?'

Goblin?

Archie inched forward, craning his neck. Tentatively, Georgie scratched his head between his ears.

'Aw, yes, yes, yes. You're a gorgeous lil' man.' Georgie's voice was soft and a little husky. 'Wow, you kinda look rough, are you a stray?'

Oh, thanks a lot, lady!

'Oh yes, yes, yes, yes. Lovely plumy grey tail, look at that!'

Beautiful, ain't it? Banksy's stroked that tail, ya know.

'Oh, yes, yes, yes. You're a wise old boy. Are you a wise old boy?'

I ain't old, bleedin' cheek!

'Oh you *are* cuddly, my darling. How did you get in, you naughty sausage, hmm? I bet you're a right little murder machine.'

Damn, right I am.

'You're a cuddly one. You gonna give me a purr?'

I don't do purrs.

'Come on, a little purr, Fluffkins?'

Fluffkins?! Oh, not there, not the flank. OI!

Archie swiped. The woman snapped her hand back.

'Okay, okay. Totes respect your personal space, boy. Touched out, hmm?'

'Touched out.' That's bang on, that. Couldn't have put it better myself.

'You have a collar, so you must have a home?'

She took a closer look at the string collar and evil eye pendant that still remained round his neck from when the fisherman fastened it there. Archie felt a sudden pang – he hoped the fisherman was okay, wherever he was.

'Wish I knew your name, little dude.'

It's Archie!

'Ooft, you sure are chatty. I'll call you ... Scruffs.'

Scruffs? What kind of bloody name is 'Scruffs'? Archie shot her a disdainful look.

'So, Scruffs, I'm having a bit of a day of it here. Oh ... oh my God.'

Georgie gasped. For the first time she clocked the decimation of the cabin – the bed covered in dirt, the torn silk threads on the cushion hems. She stood; paced the room in shocked dismay. Eventually, she spotted the mutilated towel swans lying misshapen on the floor by the bed's footboard.

'Oh Scruffs, not my swannies! I was up till like three on YouTube last night learning how to make the swannies. Oh, bloody hell, Scruffs.'

Sorry, lady. Didn't like them. Just sitting there, giving it all that. Gave me the 'ump. Had to be dealt with, they did.

'Georgie, get up here now!' From above came the muffled cry of the captain.

Georgie recoiled as if the voice had been a needle in her arm. She pulled herself up on the bed and released her hair from its ponytail, letting it pool on the pillow as she lay back, eyes closed as if in meditation. Slowly she made an 'O' with her lips and exhaled. Archie placed his two great forepaws up on her belly, making her flinch. Suddenly Georgie began to giggle, sending Archie's ears twisting in disgruntlement at the vibration beneath his paws.

'You know what, Scruffs?' she said between helpless giggles. 'The swannies are the least of my worries. Because I've just filled the boat with petrol not diesel. So that makes two of us who're completely doomed!'

13

Stowaway

ARCHIE AWOKE, CRAMMED BETWEEN a mega multipack of antibacterial cleaning spray and an even mega-er box of roasted peanuts.

The provisions hold aboard the *Calypso Spirit* was oppressive and sterile. A small room opened out behind a grilled wall, beyond which a corridor ran the length of the huge boat's lowest deck. Like the 'cells' at the Whitechapel Cat Rehoming Centre, everything was plain and functional. The only colour came from the orange cables which threaded down the walls, switching direction at right angles, running behind pipes and into mysterious boxes. A strange *rn–rn–rn* sound throbbed perpetually in the air, making Archie's vision slightly blur. The whiteness of everything was distressing; an unnerving antithesis to the gaudy colour and showiness of the world above decks. Down here, Archie was below the waterline, which meant no windows or natural light.

It was, however, the perfect place in which to hide a plucky stray cat prone to mischief.

'Hiya, Scruffs.'

'Meeeeow!' Archie's cries echoed long and doleful down the corridor. *About bloody time!*

Georgie appeared and slid the bolt across the grille door, a sad look in her large brown eyes. Cupped in her hands were two large langoustine shells, lined with white meat. 'I hate that you're down here, Scruffs. We'll find a better place soon. Meantime, wanna scoff on this?'

Ooft, these things taste good, murmured Archie in nibbling growls, ignoring Georgie entirely.

'God, you're inhaling that,' said Georgie eyeing him in a slightly worried way. 'It's okay, we have plenty of food on here, boy. You're pure acting like I'm gonna … wait wait wait … ' Archie was already nosing into the cellophane bag in Georgie's hands for seconds.

'Okay, so here's the thing, Scruffs,' said Georgie offering a second course of prawns. 'The owner's delayed and they've still not had to start the engines. So we're on borrowed time, shipmatey. Might as well live the good life for a bit, before they turn the engine key, eh? The evil captain's away at the minute, want to go up on deck? It'd just be us and Jake – and he's sound as a pound. You don't mind being picked up, do you?'

Owwft, don't you DARE! Archie swiped.

Georgie stopped; reconsidered. 'You don't like me touching that bit on your side do you. Shall I hold you here?'

Archie felt his paws straighten beneath him as he became airborne. His intestines redistributed mid-chew, but he resisted the urge to swipe. Georgie was, after all, taking pains to not hold him by his tender flank, and he had to respect that.

'Aw, you give me major homely feels, Scruffs,' said Georgie, scratching the back of his neck, taking swift steps down the corridor. 'This job has been the worst, but at least I'm not thinking about Fin. *You're* my new love, my boy. My VIP, my "Very Important Puss"!'

Being carried by a human felt immensely peculiar, but somehow Archie held off struggling. This was made harder by Georgie's cutesy chat (a hardened stray has little truck with saccharine babble). In an attempt at self-zen, he recalled Georgie's upset from yesterday afternoon, which had the effect of softening his irritation. He felt his claws retract from her white cotton polo shirt.

The pair circled up a metal staircase, Archie's paws now sticking out in front of Georgie like two fluffy prongs. They entered the saloon, which Archie recognised from spying down through the hatch from the deck the day before. Today its honey-varnished table was strewn with used plates, olive pips and twisted dirty napkins. A bank of computer screens glowed out weather systems, while the words '*Calypso Spirit*' glided across the screen of a cinema-sized television. Archie sniffed the open lid of the grand piano as they passed.

'Coast is clear, Scruffs,' whispered Georgie, pulling aside a sliding door to the deck. She lowered him before reaching into her pocket for her phone and filming him as he trotted ahead over the deck.

The sun never gives up here, does it? Bring on the drizzle, thought Archie, wincing as his pads smarted against the hot deck.

Georgie walked behind, gliding her hand along the guard rail smiling, her phone outstretched. Archie raised himself up the side of the jacuzzi and sniffed its turquoise water at rest.

'Jake to George, over.'

A warble on the radio clipped to Georgie's shorts. Archie recognised the voice as that of the muscular man he'd seen previously.

'Go ahead, Jakester.'

'So I'm going to start the engine to check the refrigerant is flushing under the new line. Could you do us a favour and check the exhaust outlet is clear off the port deck?'

Georgie froze, looked at Archie.

'George . . . ?'

She lifted the radio to her mouth, but lowered it again.

Could this thing properly blow with petrol in it instead of diesel? wondered Archie. He turned his head to the dockside and peered along the gangplank extending to the marina wall. *Maybe I should make a run for it.*

'Georgie, you there?'

'Uhhh . . . is that the pipe just forward of the saloon deck cabin, yeah?' replied Georgie.

'Yeah, that's the one.'

'Yup, okay. Bear with . . . '

Georgie bunched her fingers, showing all her teeth in a grimace. Clenching her hands in balls, she looked at Archie, half pathetically, half pleadingly. With nervous steps, she padded over to the edge of the deck and peered over before raising the radio to her mouth.

'Er yeah, we're good. No grime there, Jake. Go for it.'

Oh gawd, this is it then! Archie's ears twisted back in tense anticipation, his spine curving downwards. He could feel the blood in his ears. *Just run for it boy, why are you just standing here? Give up on getting home on this. Give up on her. Just leg it.*

Georgie made an 'O' with her mouth again, a habit of hers in moments of stress. She crouched next to Archie, looking it him with her big, scared eyes. 'This is it, Scruffs. I'm screwed. P45 here we come. I suppose working at the Truro Pizza Express isn't all that bad.'

A coughing sound beneath the decks. A gentle rumble. A deep long healthy purr.

'You're kidding?' Georgie rose to her feet. 'It's running. The thing's running!' She turned to Archie. 'Little bruh, the engine's only *running!* She furrowed her brow. 'Am I losing it?'

Well there ya go.

And much like the storm that hit the fisherman's boat and vanished in a twinkling, Archie thought little more of it. He was on a voyage; a strange cortisol-spiked existence – an existence entirely at odds with the thought-imbued dozes atop bar stools he occasionally took to set his mind right. It would be in those moments – rare as they were – that he'd dot the proverbial i's in his life; put to rights the injustices dealt upon him, and plot the necessary revenge. It'd be in those ponderous moments when he'd notice strange occurrences, contradictions … things that might require his attention lest he fall foul of a trick, or unexpected territory blitzkrieg waged by a rival cat. Out here, everything felt strange. A superyacht that suddenly drinks petrol when it usually drinks diesel? *What?* Had he been similarly reposed, he might even have connected the strangeness of this event with the strangeness of the storm, when a tiny boat he sailed on survived a tempest so huge that it saw other vessels in the area – much larger ones at that – founder with lives lost.

But he didn't. He couldn't. Perhaps it also had to do with the no-nonsense rationalism seared into him, something he had inherited from his ancestors, and which drove a stubborn refusal to accept anything 'magic' at play in the world.

Practicality dies hard in a stray cat, and Archie simply didn't countenance the spiritual. A cat was born, lived, and expired, ta very much. There was no hocus-pocus, no God and definitely no possibility that his meagre presence on earth could affect the elements, water, fire or anything else. A pompous house cat might entertain such notions, but not a stray.

And so the truth sat, hidden in plain sight, just beyond Archie's awareness. A boat suddenly developing a taste for a different fuel. That's just how things worked out here in this land of hissing cicadas and glittering seas.

What's more, it was only two events. And two events are not enough to constitute a pattern. Not yet anyway.

14

Siren Call

'WHEY-HEY UP SHE RISES, early in the morning!' Archie snuggled into Georgie's fleece, his head curled at 180 degrees back against his body. Above, the black sky twinkled with a litter of stars. Through it all, the Milky Way was visible in a carpet of yellow dust that twisted in swathes. Down the long side of the *Calypso Spirit,* the sea sloshed and hissed invisibly as the vessel's angry trowel nose cut through the satin-black waters of the mid Mediterranean. In half consciousness, Archie thought of the endless miles of dark water all around them, and him here, right in the middle of it all; a tiny spot of lights and noises. And his beating heart.

Occasionally, Georgie's arm glanced over his ears as she turned the huge, spoked wheel. It was 5.06 a.m., a good half hour before sunrise, and Archie was sitting in a human lap for the first time in his life.

Well how's about this for a slice of solid gold, he thought, twisting and hooking his paws in the air.

Now and then, a balmy wind whipped over his coat tousling the longer of his grey scruffy hairs. He moved in and out of consciousness in a delicious way – the type of symbiotic dozing reserved for two beings who feel entirely safe with each other. Behind the pair at the stern, the light from the lower cabins glimmered in the propeller-churned froth.

Yeah I reckon I'm about eighty per cent of the way towards pure happiness, prrped Archie.

Over the last few days, Archie had felt more connected to Georgie than he had any other human. This was the first time he had actually slept on her lap, however, and he rather wished he could express to her the gravity of this personal milestone. Georgie understood cat language in a whole new way: not only did she comprehend his mews, prrps, and body language (there is an entire vocabulary in a feline's tail-flicks alone) but she also seemed to anticipate his culinary needs before he recognised them himself. *Maybe this could be what love is,* he'd find himself thinking as the *Calypso Spirit* pounded its propellers through the wide sea. It occurred to him, for the first time, what it meant to be totally special to another being. Invaluable, even. Of course, it was not all perfect: he had hissed on a number of occasions when Georgie didn't get the message that he wanted time to himself, and her cutesy chat drove him mad. And even now, as he sat here on her lap, his belly full of marinated sardine, he still didn't purr but rather snored softly, one eye always *slightly* open … just in case.

'Get munching on that, boy. Evil captain never finishes his mains.' She cupped a bit of pancetta in her palm.

'He doesn't deserve Jamie Oliver's finest, but *you* do, my handsome Scruffs.' (The truth was that the captain preferred the call of double whisky over haute cuisine.)

The yacht's owner had been delayed due to 'an emergency meeting in Monte Carlo'. At least that's what Archie had overheard. The benefit of this was that Georgie was able to reset the master cabin. But despite remoulding the towel swans and cleaning out the dirt, no amount of wood polish removed the scratches from the bedposts and the gashes on the side of the mahogany ottoman – a gift, apparently, from an American business magnate whom the owner had met in Monaco.

So it was that the master cabin sat as a kind of ticking time bomb of Georgie's fate, ready to blow open her secret the moment the owner arrived.

The captain's watch fell during daytime hours, so Archie would need to be locked in the provisions store then – the only place the captain never deigned to enter. At other times, though, Archie was given the run of the decks with Georgie. The early morning watches were his favourite, when the little cat would take to strolling the moonlit foredeck, deciding on a furniture locker aft of the satellite dome as the ideal place to curl up, should the captain ever raise his ominous head above decks. Down in the provisions store, he quickly learned to identify the sounds that signalled his imminent rescue. One eye would open at the sound of Georgie's voice at the watch shift handover, then his ears would prick up at the distinctive *flip-flop* of her sandals. He would then raise his head as her hand touched the door handle at the end of the corridor. In time, he even learned to recognise the little flicker of the lights, before all of this, as Georgie clicked on the kettle in her cabin to fill her Thermos flask ahead of her shift.

Then he'd rise, arch his back, leap off his multipack box of washing-up liquid, and await Georgie's arrival at the door with her grip-sealed bag of scraps. Iberico hams, caviar, pork cutlet – they were always exceptional.

One thing he was thinking increasingly less about was the draw of home. Perhaps it was the air conditioning keeping him cool, or the fact that, in Georgie, he had found someone who could offer him more than his familiar East End streets could. Occasionally, when Georgie sang a familiar pop song which Archie recognised from the cafés of Whitechapel, he would be transported back to London for a moment on the looping notes. But the homesickness he felt in Rhodes was lessening, while the wretched aspects of London life – the scavenging, the uncertainty, the unfriendliness – continued to sit heavy.

The gullies of Spitalfields and pongy Thames foreshore . . . what wretched grot spots they are, really, when all's said and done, he'd think under the stroke of Georgie's hand as the sea whispered its refrain, which seemed to say: *thissss-iss-it, thissss-issss-it.* He'd round off his reverie with the thought: *I'll clap eyes on you again, London. But I ain't missing ya right now, I have to say.*

On his fourth morning, he awoke to an orange streak of sunlight catching the transparent globe of his eyeball. Unbeknownst to him, his tail had been tapping along to the beats of a tune Georgie was listening to on her phone. Over the side of the deck, the sea was awash with seaweed. It was nearing the end of Georgie's watch shift and he felt particularly groggy, having spent the hours of darkness careening up and down the deck, swiping moths overboard or gulping them down as snacks. He particularly enjoyed ambushing the ones that fluttered around the navigation lights at the bow. One had been so huge, and its wings had beaten so hard against his gullet, that he was forced to gag it up again. This had made Georgie and Jake giggle in their yellow life jackets back at the helm.

Groggily, Archie stretched. 'We should see Sicily soon, if the mist clears,' said Jake, emerging through the sliding doors with steaming flasks of coffee. Georgie pinched the navigation module's touch screen, making its map larger.

'We're not stopping there, are we?'

'Nope, just a fly-past. Ah, tune, George! I love me a bit of Muse!'

'Yup. And they're West Country boys, from down my way,' replied Georgie.

'Ah no way! You seen them live?'

'Yup. That's where I met idiot-boy Fin.'

'Is that Fin who . . .'

'Jake!' said Georgie. 'What's said at sea *stays* at sea. Offshore rules. Come on now.'

'Right, well since we *are* still at sea . . . ' he responded, stepping behind the wheel and sitting alongside her.

'Jake, I don't want to talk about him any more.'

Jake looked down at his coffee. 'Slipknot?' he offered, attempting to break the awkwardness.

'Oh God no, Jake. Nope, nope, nope. I hereby use my veto. No Slipknot. It's just rage coloured in.'

'They are absolutely *not* just rage coloured in,' said Jake. 'I swear to you, Georgie, by the time we get to Cape Verde, I'm going to have you converted to the Knot.'

Georgie giggled; this seemed to be an old joke between them. 'It's not going to happen. No way. But, by the time we get to the Caribbean, you *will* be a *Hamilton* convert.'

Jake grimaced. 'Musicals are living hell. How's the Very Important Puss?'

'He's fine. And you, Mr Jake, just haven't found *your* musical yet.'

The Caribbean? thought Archie, *For God's sake am I ever gonna . . . Wait. What's that?*

Archie lurched upwards. He had been half listening to the conversation, and wondering whether these two had ever seen *Sweeney Todd* of East End fame, when his ears caught wind of a peculiar sound.

'You see? Very Important Puss agrees,' said Georgie with a nod towards Archie. 'And puss's judgement is sound, we all know that.'

Shuddup, shuddup a moment, growled Archie, lifting his rear. As if impelled, he raced to the edge of the deck and stared out over the water. *Don't you hear that? That noise?*

'You heard something, Scruffs?' said Georgie.

Something, yes. There's something sounding out at sea, thought Archie, running forward along the edge of the deck. *There! There it is again! You must hear that?*

He craned his neck over the boat's side. The orange rays had gathered to a shimmering yellow that flashed over the water. Looming through the mist, closer than he expected, were the shores of Sicily in soft focus. Archie scanned the coastline.

Honestly, what in heaven's bells is that sound? Didn't you hear it?

'Silly Scruffs, you getting cabin fever?'

'Aren't we all,' said Jake, sipping his coffee.

The sound had triggered something primal in Archie. A deep, unknowable longing. Unthinkingly, he had ducked under the guard rail and begun toeing along the boat's sheer side, his paws slipping on the dew that had gathered overnight.

'Scruffs, what are you doing, you clown!' Georgie lunged forward, releasing the wheel, and flying towards the edge of the deck. Archie tottered forward away from her grasp.

I've just got to hear that sound again.

It was an uncanny sound; a song. A song that quenched a thirst he hadn't known he had. It lifted him in a strange euphoria, more potent than any catnip ever had. And it was going, drifting away. Maybe he could hear it again if he just kept very, very—

'Scruffs, here now!' shouted Georgie. 'Jake, Scruffs is right on the edge. He's gonna leap.'

'Chill, George, he's a cat,' said Jake.

Yeah, I know what I'm doing! Now keep schtum for a second will you? seethed Archie, his tail flicking to keep balance.

As they passed nearer the shore, features of the coastline began to creep through the mist. Archie's eyes scanned frantically. Among the bushes and concrete breakwaters of a marina, the shimmering outline of a gaggle of cats took shape.

It's them. It's the cry of those cats!

'Scruffs, please . . .' begged Georgie, finally braving a clasp about his belly.

Back off now! hissed Archie with breathtaking fierceness.

Georgie doubled back, hurt. Archie turned towards the deck and let out a huge cry at the cats on the shore.

There was something bewitching about the cats' cries. And it definitely *was* those cats on the breakwaters; he could just tell. He felt himself being pulled towards them as if by an invisible piece of nylon that *tug-tug-tugged* at his collar.

The mewing sound came back louder and clearer. *What a stonking tune! What a lush song!* Archie didn't recognise himself in the presence of the cries. He was overcome.

The cats' beautiful tones echoed in cadences around the bay. An otherworldly urge came over him. A carnal urge. An urge to be with those cats no matter what it took . . .

The yacht wasn't far from shore now. Archie looked down at the swilling water which had calmed with the nearness to land.

I could swim that, easy, he thought.

To his right the propellers churned mighty white froth. He walked forward to where the waters creased in silky strips from the bow. *Sod it, I'm doing it.*

He began bobbing his rear end up in preparation for a leap.

A grab on his haunches.

Put me down! hissed Archie.

'Scruffs, you'll die,' said Georgie glumly, her voice still hurt by his sudden desire to be rid of her. To be free. 'The currents here are strong. You'll be dragged out to sea. I'll let you off in Cape Verde, okay? I can't see you drown.'

Georgie lifted him by the scruff. *Fine, fine!*

'Give me five, Jake, just going to take Scruffs back to the store.'

'Shouldn't we just let him hop off here? He's clearly wanting to vibe with the other cats. He can swim ashore?'

'No, you psycho,' snapped Georgie. 'He's just being weird. He's our lucky mascot, he saved my bacon.'

'So you keep saying,' said Jake, frowning. 'What makes you think Very Important Puss is lucky? You going woo-woo?'

'I'm not going woo-woo. He's bringing us good luck, trust me.'

'You're not going to tell me you believe in dreamcatchers and all that?'

'No! It's just he ... I ... look, I'll tell you later. I'll save it for your mid-Atlantic breakdown. Just give us five, yeah? Go listen to Slipknot or whatever.'

Georgie ventured into the saloon, pulling closed the sliding door behind her with a thump, Archie wide-eyed in her arms.

'Listen, Scruffs . . .' she whispered, her breath warm against his fur. 'Just for a while I'm going to put you in my cabin, okay? There are some snacks in there. I'm sorry I can't have you leaping overboard to your death, you silly puss.'

I hear ya, okay, okay, it's fine, just stick me down now, thought Archie. His senses returned quickly when out of earshot of the cats' call, and he began to feel regret at hissing at Georgie. She'd looked out for him after all . . . her tickles and snacks were exceptional. Who was he to take aim at kindness? *I'm sorry.* His whiskers pulled back as he snuggled into the sweaty space around Georgie's armpits. *I don't know what came over me. I nearly swiped an' all. I'm sorry, okay? I'm sorry.*

'All right, okay, I know you're sorry.'

15

The Captain

One week later

I T IS AN ODD QUIRK, common to both humans and cats, that entry into a routine for meals, sleep and recreation makes time skip by. Almost without knowing it, the *Calypso Spirit* had sliced its bow through 2,000 nautical miles of balmy Mediterranean. Just past Morocco, the yacht, its crew and Archie, the little stray from Stepney Green, who so recently used to reside on a fly-tipped mattress, emerged into the wide Atlantic as the *Calypso Spirit* altered its bearing to face due south-west along the coast of Africa. They passed through squalls, the warm trade winds tossing waves over the deck; but it wasn't until the heat turned arid, and the decks took on a dusting of red sand blown in off the Sahara, that Archie realised he possibly wasn't heading home. Down, down, down they sailed, until they at least reached the tropical waters off the volcanic peninsula of Senegal.

One day, Archie ate a flying fish that torpedoed its way onto the deck in an accidental suicide, its mercury-silver skin flashing on the water-spattered deck. Unlike the fisherman's little boat which bounced over the waves, the *Calypso Spirit* lumbered, elephantine, through the ocean swell, nodded like a sage professor over its calms, or pounded like a raging bull across its stormy crests. Yet Archie never once felt seasick. Georgie herself had become ill in the squall just past Gibraltar, as had Jake, but Archie didn't feel a thing as he sat comfortably on the deck, inconvenienced only when the boat tilted so much that his body slid along the smooth plastic upper deck like a pancake from a spatula. Emboldened by the success of her feline smuggling, Georgie had upgraded Archie's on-board quarters to her own cabin, which shared a small corridor with Jake's. It was a vast improvement on the provisions store, and in its sun-cream-and-bubble-gum-scented privacy, Archie had pored over the pages of yachting magazines and novels, dozed soundly, and toileted on an open box of washing powder in the nearby laundry.

Alone with Georgie's books and trinkets, he began to build up a deeper picture of who she was. He even formed an impression of her mother from the small WhatsApp message previews that flashed up on her phone when she left it on the crumpled duvet:

Darling, worried about you. Can u message me when u can?? love mum x

And:

I think you should leave, darling. Don't like the thought of you bobbing about on a rust bucket on the Atlantic. You must be over him by now? mum x?

And:

Unc Jeff done back in, needs help on farm. Shall I
say yes for when ur back? baling and silage . . . easy
money . . . mum x

Occasionally, after a particularly good snooze, Archie would find himself thinking the fateful thought: *maybe this time.* Maybe he could stay with Georgie? She seemed to 'get' him, give or take. They could just sail the world. Certain things irked him occasionally about her, but that was just life was it not?

Maybe this one will stay.

He was just in the middle of one such reverie one morning when he awoke with a start.

What in the bells of St Botolph's was that?

He sprang onto his four paws. For a split second, he levitated mid-air before landing again and burrowing under the duvet. But the noise continued to burn his ears and seemed to shake the very air of the cabin.

An anchor dropping from the side of a boat is one of the most terrifying sounds on earth; a heinous clatter that rattles your very bones.

If some nutter pirate has taken over the boat, just let the end be quick okay, God? None of that drawn-out walking-the-plank palaver.

Out of nowhere, a muffled cry came from above. The captain.

'Anchor down. Engine astern!'

It was the first time he'd heard the captain's voice in a few days, thanks to Georgie strategically moving him from one place of privacy to another. The murmur of the engines tremored through the bedclothes as the great boat dragged its anchor along the seabed, eventually lurching to a stop like a dog at the end of its lead. Archie rose and wobbled on splayed-out paws.

Nasty noise, that. And I've travelled the Circle Line on that dodgy bit past Cannon Street.

Now the boat had become perfectly still for the first time since it had set off from the marina. Through the hatch above, Archie could hear a tapestry of new sounds, tinged with the sense of exoticism: foreign voices, peculiar-sounding birds, and the squeal of an ambulance or police car with an unusual siren. *I suppose this is land ahoy*, he thought raising his back into an arch and licking down his grey shire-horse ankles. *Better be decent grub here. And no more awful noises. Maybe I can see a few more gorgeous cats.*

This morning, Georgie had locked Archie in her cabin. Normally, she didn't, trusting Archie full well to keep his side of the bargain and not stray when she wasn't around. But today the door was closed, and for that reason alone Archie felt irked. He particularly hated it when he could hear the captain's voice and didn't have anywhere else to flee. Out of the room, the captain would be no match for his hiding abilities, particularly now he knew the floorplan of the *Calypso Spirit* well. But in a closed cabin, he was cornered. There was just the one door straight ahead ... and all the cupboard doors were reliably secured shut against the swell.

He lumbered down off the bed, examining the door handle with canny, pinched eyes. He had been locked in many rooms before, and escape was typically easier than most humans gave him credit for.

One, two, three ... hoooooyah! intoned Archie, leaping up the side of the door and looping his paws around the handle.

The latch released. He glided for a moment on the door's momentum, his paws still clasped round the handle. He let himself drop and trotted down the corridor to the saloon. There, on the table, all the crew members' passports were lined up in a popper-sealed folder, along with a sheet marked 'Cape Verde Customs Declaration'. Through the sliding door, he could see Jake looping a large rope around a cleat, his watch flashing a spear of sunlight into Archie's eyes.

He could smell the captain before he heard him. A miasma of whisky and sweat. Archie's tail spiked.

'What the hell, it's a bloody cat!'

Archie didn't know how he'd got there. As usual, he seemed to just materialise into view like a huge spectre. Now he stood at the navigation station, with only the large oval varnished table separating man and cat. It was the closest Archie had ever come to him and at this proximity, he was struck by his oddly long earlobes which wobbled when he moved.

Suddenly, he lunged at Archie, making a bid for the cat's tail.

Oi! Don't you THINK about it, mate! Archie shot back with a hiss, rising on his rear paws and boxing a clean swipe. Shocked at this, the captain tottered, arms flailing behind for support. Archie continued to stand his ground, his fur puffing him up to twice his size as his flashing gold eyes homed in on the man's neck, where a vein pulsed like a squirming earthworm.

You don't scare me a bit, ya mutton-headed muppet. Pack it in!

The man made an ursine grunt, swiping a clumsy fist at Archie. He'd clearly been on the drink.

BACK OFF!

The man's eyes turned to small chips of ice.

Actually, on second thoughts . . .

Archie doubled back, darting out of the sliding door onto the deck just as Georgie drew it aside to enter.

'Oi, bumpkin!' yelled the captain. 'There's a cat on board, an effing cat! It's probably got rabies, how the *hell* did it get on?'

A flurry of motion. Archie's vision blurred as he careened along the deck to his safe place – the sun lounger locker.

But the captain had seen his paws racing across the hatches above.

'Oi, Jake, it's up behind the locker. Get rid of the bastard.'

'Er, yes, Captain,' muttered Jake, glancing at Georgie.

Hmm this is all getting a bit pear-shaped, decided Archie, crouching low. It was the first time he'd set paw on the upper deck during the day in a good week, and the *Calypso Spirit*'s new position off the coast of Africa and the Sahara was highly apparent. Warm muggy air toasted the white PVC, and merely touching the chrome trim around the hatches felt like he'd placed his toe beans onto a halogen hob ring. Now his heart beat into his throat, and his tummy churned . . . not just with fear for himself, but also for Georgie.

I know his type, he thought. *Please don't get in his way. He'll clobber you one, he's been on the booze.*

'I can see its ears poking up. There, up by the locker!' the captain yelled.

He advanced with gargantuan strides, his footsteps reverberating. Archie raced forward, the boat getting narrower, narrower, narrower as he neared the bow. He was running out of room.

Oh jeez, jeez, jeez. Now I'm in for it.

A feline out of options will quite happily lunge into oblivion if it means the chance to escape an unmatchable threat. Archie had once been forced to jump off a pontoon into the Thames after diplomacy broke down between himself and a Rottweiler. The brown river water struck his chest with a *slap*; a sound Archie had never forgotten.

But this time, up at the front of the boat, staring down into the rainbow of the marina's oil-slicked waters, he froze. He didn't want to leave Georgie.

As the captain approached, Archie cowered, ears flat and eyes terrified – a kitten-like ball of fur.

Please don't. Don't hurt me.

The captain's huge hands lowered. Slow motion. A tug at the scruff. The little stray felt himself becoming weightless, his sinews bunching painfully around his shoulders.

Go on then. Just do it.

With a flick of his wrist, the captain lobbed Archie through the air. For a few split seconds it was almost beautiful – the aquamarine of the Atlantic spinning to puff-white clouds, as he twirled and twirled. Then a crack like shattering glass, and water engulfing his lungs.

The cloudy fructified green. Underwater. Fish darting. Squirming. Odd shapes. He saw the underside of the boat loom above with its eerie propellers. His lungs stung, gurgled as his paws beat and beat and beat, his four legs paddled as his vision turned bloody.

And then again, for the second time in as many weeks, the odd reality-stretching sensation, woozy and oddly euphoric, of a brain losing oxygen.

16

À la carte

ARCHIE'S HEAD BROKE THE SURFACE. He spluttered, his fur clinging to his face in gargoyle-like tendrils. The *Calypso Spirit* loomed like a great tower out of the water to his side.

But to his left, a marina wall, and ladders reaching down into the water.

He could see now that the yacht had been berthed stern-side to the shoreline. With gasps of air, Archie paddled towards the shore, his spine breaching the water's surface, and his grey hair sloshing about his sides. *C'mon boy, don't die.* Paws thrashing, he fought through the annihilation of the water until, at last, they caught the barnacle-noduled rung of the ladder. He scrabbled, limbs beating in all directions until finally he had a hold, and pulled himself up. *Humans can be mighty cruel. Why are they so cruel? God, I hope she's all right.* He padded along the marina wall leaving big watery paw prints on the hot concrete, which evaporated immediately. There he flopped, fur twisted and weedy, his chin hair in fronds, like a beard, eyes wide and gremlin-like. A soaked panting exhausted mass . . . all eye and bone.

Always underestimated, he thought. *Yet always here to fight another day.*

He coughed up a tongue of water, rose and shook his flanks until his fur puffed out in a salt-crystallised perm. Pivoting, he nibbled his rear leg free of a piece of weed.

Then, over the fissured yellow concrete, Archie heard a squeal. An argument had broken out aboard the *Calypso Spirit* and though his ear canals gurgled with water, he could still pick out bits of the furore which was accompanied by dull thuds.

'You're a tiny, *pathetic* man.'

Archie glimpsed Georgie in her white shirt behind the saloon windows. Her arms were flailing and her voice rasped with breathless rage. 'To do that to a defenceless animal. Seriously? Wanna make yourself feel big? Is that why you're a captain because you've got nothing to show where it counts?'

'Don't talk to your superior like that,' replied the captain, in a voice which surprised Archie in its slurred shakiness.

'You're a bully. You can take my P45 and shove it up your deeply average arse. I'm off. Toodle-oo.'

'Oi, don't leave, what are you doing?'

'Two days to find another chef before the transatlantic? Yeah, just thought of that now, huh? See you, moron.'

Ooft, savage! thought Archie. He tracked her as she strode down the gangplank onto the pontoon. A half-zipped-up suitcase spilled items as she went, carpeting the walkway with shorts, caps and trousers, but she didn't seem to care. She strode fiercely, her big eyes steadfast, and her right hand clutching her phone and passport.

'C'mon, Scruffs,' she said, passing by Archie and scooping him up in one arm, dragging her suitcase with the other. 'Let's find somewhere less depressing than this hellhole.'

* * *

Well that was brave of you, thought Archie. He squished his wet muzzle into Georgie's panting chest. His claws were hooked up over her shirt as she walked, his half-damp fur making him look like a sloth clinging around her neck. He was careful not to over-extend his claws, a balance he had perfected over the last week when sitting on Georgie's lap during the night watches, her soft presence gradually eroding the sharpness of his instincts.

They walked along the harbour breakwater, the wheels on Georgie's suitcase making a rhythmic *gerf-gerf-gerf* as they rolled over its concrete slabs. They dipped in and out of the shadows of other yachts – huge double-masted sailing vessels, their rigging draped in little flags, and enormous high-sided superyachts even bigger than the *Calypso Spirit*. Little dinghies bobbed, moored by a single rope and spattered with bird droppings. All the time, Georgie muttered, 'Bastard. Nasty, nasty bastard.' Archie could feel the tension in the bunched-up muscles around her shoulders. As they passed beyond the marina walls and onto the anonymity of a wide boulevard, Georgie's spasms of anger turned to the gentle vibration of a cry. She smoothed down Archie's damp, wiry fur.

'Scruffs, I'm so sorry,' she whimpered. 'I – I've no clue why people act like that. What's wrong with them?'

Oh don't fret, I've had much worse, trust me, intoned Archie.

She paused for a moment, cradling him closer in her arm. The smell of sun cream and raspberry lip balm wafted pleasantly. *Steady on, I ain't an Uber Eats backpack,* thought Archie, thinking back again to the time when he had, for real, accidentally been delivered to an address in Shoreditch along with a pungent assortment of matar paneer, lamb rogan josh, and butter chicken.

He felt joggled but safe; matted and claggy but warm inside; bewildered yet happy. As they crossed the boulevard, he took in the cinema of this new land: the high balconies of the apartment buildings that overlooked the harbour; the palm trees sprouting from the central reservation of the road; the singular way the lamp posts bowed out at their tops like monkeys scratching their armpits. All so luminous, all so strange.

Archie gazed up beyond Georgie's cheekbones to the sky which had cleared to a perfect blue, save a few wisps of cirrus-like fine brushed hair.

Thank the stars I met ya, Georgie, thought Archie, burying his head in her shoulder afresh, feeling another surge of affection. *The fisherman was great. But you, lady. You're the one.*

'Urgh, Scruffs, I've legit no clue what we do now, my little good-luck gremlin,' said Georgie, pulling a stray frond of hair back over her head. 'Like I've pretty much got zero cash ... '

They crossed another street, stepping between a column of idling cars and past a noisy market with T-shirts twisting from hooks like flags. Georgie paused to re-cram her suitcase beside a stall selling huge fish dangling from hooks – a great long tuna staring glassily and an octopus, its humongous suckered tentacles swaying Medusa-like in the wind. They were moving inland, but the trappings of the sea remained – ice-cream stalls, their fragrance of vanilla and pistachio and shops selling colourful African clothes.

Yup, I agree, we do kinda need a plan, don't me? thought Archie, catching Georgie's eyes at opportune moments when they lowered to meet his. *Surely, it's got to involve another boat?* It occurred to him, for the first time, that Georgie could be right – maybe he *was* a good luck charm at sea. If nothing else, the sea seemed to bring out the best in him – soft, good sides which, in his many years of straying, he had never witnessed in himself. And he seemed to bring out the good in others too – Georgie, the fisherman. But his mind never went beyond this to entertain the notion of any 'magic' at play.

Honestly, don't worry about me, thought Archie. *I'm tough as old boots. I'll kip anywhere. Tell you what, I can't help feeling we should find another boat, lady . . .*

A narrow street unfurled beckoningly, just behind one of the market stalls. Georgie ducked in, away from the din of traders and their swinging baskets of orange cayenne spice. A little way down, past the terracotta tiles of doorways, a café spread out dozily beneath the noon heat. The chirrup of music drifted out from inside, while on its terrace an A-frame board advertising *Coca-Cola* swayed. Georgie ducked in and took a seat, letting Archie assume a spot beneath the table. (That was one of the things he loved about Georgie – the fact he just *knew what to do* around her, and when he needed to do it.)

A waiter emerged, notepad in hand.

'Oh umm,' said Georgie awkwardly. 'Umm, errr . . . tapas, por favor.'

The waiter frowned.

'And um . . . una lecce for the um, gatto?'

'Português, Português,' replied the waiter in a surly manner.

'Oh eh um, Portuguese. Sorry, um . . .'

Caught out by her lack of language, Georgie pointed to something on the laminated menu that looked like a selection of fish. The waiter nodded, disappearing to the back of the café.

Shortly, the waiter returned with a huge platter of mixed seafood. Archie periscoped his head above the table edge.

Bloody hell, that's a lot of grub . . .

'I legit didn't order all this, Scruffs,' giggled Georgie quietly, tickling Archie behind the ears. The waiter laid down napkins, filled a glass of wine presumptuously and placed it alongside Georgie before retreating.

Well, guess we tuck in, lady? thought Archie, twitching his nose up at the seafood. He twisted his head and snapped off a king prawn, crunching it down shell and all.

'Ha, you don't hang about, do ya, Scruffs?' said Georgie.

Well I can't, ya see, thought Archie, through his little eating growls. *I never know* [chomp-chomp-chew] *where my next* [chomp-chomp-GULP] *set of grub is going to come from, see . . .*

'Well, bon appétit, Monsieur Scruffs,' said Georgie, picking at a langoustine shell and pulling out the contents of white meat, letting Archie lap some from her hand.

Mmm pretty damn langoustiney, that.

Out of nowhere, Georgie's phone vibrated.

'Hiya, Mum!'

Georgie's big eyes moved in concentration as she listened to her mum on the other end of the line.

A moped popped down the little side street. Georgie covered her free ear, frowning.

'Well *obviously* I remembered my passport, Mum. Seriously you're as bad as him, why does everyone think I'm dense?' she said. 'Okay, but I'm not my brother, Mum.' She sighed and took on a different tone. 'Yeah, relieved for sure … Oh Fin? Yeah, it's done the trick, not thought of him once … Yeah, kind of hyper, but relieved. But wait, Mum, you never guess what psycho Clive did, he …' She paused. 'Okay okay, yeah yeah sorry, just tell me the details then …'

Chatting voices. Somewhere far off a dog snarled. Georgie twisted her wrist and looked at her watch. Shock spread across her face, just as Archie folded his paw tips under themselves on her lap. *Pukka grub, that*, he thought. *And this lap is just the best. Like I'm no expert on laps, granted. But this one's pretty damn cosy.* He wriggled his rear haunches like a frog, and closed his eyes. Softly, Georgie's fingers tickled his nape … until suddenly, they stalled.

'What 2.15? … p.m.? UK time or Cape Verde time? Wow, okay.'

A pause. Through dozing eyes, Archie followed the path of a lizard tottering across a blue tiled doorstep, its little lungs pulsing as it darted in bursts. *Fair old life you must have lizard pal*, he contemplated dreamily.

And then it happened. In that moment, as the image of the lizard passed over his brain – such a banal unremarkable image – Archie felt a surge of happiness, more complete and dazzlingly pristine than he had ever known. Endorphins spilled like honey from squeezed muslin. *Life actually CAN be wonderful.* He knew in that moment that he would never forget being here, in this quiet side street, sitting under this café table with its plastic tablecloth, on the lap of his human.

For the rest of his life, the memory of this feeling would stay defiantly in his brain, often chanced upon, like an old love note stuffed in the back of a drawer of papers. He looked again for the lizard, intent on resummoning the euphoria (it had come and gone in seconds) as if the lizard itself had somehow conjured it. But it had scurried away. *Fair old life you must have, lizard pal*, he repeated, trying to forcedly rekindle the feeling. But already the brightness of the moment had subsided, like the white flare of a struck match settles to a yellow glow in an instant. He resettled his head on Georgie's side, drifting into delicious semi-consciousness as her chatter became indecipherable under the murmurs of passing voices and bikes.

'Yeah, no, I can get there, Mum. Yes, I've got a credit card.'

17

Departures

ARCHIE HEARD THE PHONE CLATTER onto the table. He didn't know how long he had been asleep. For a moment, he felt the customary knot of adrenal readiness in the pit of his belly, just like in London. But after two seconds, he detected the sweet, sun-creamy smell of Georgie and the knot eased into an extraordinary goofy happiness. He yawned, and poked his head above the lip of the table. Georgie was jabbing at her phone which was flat on the tablecloth alongside the half-finished seafood platter.

He didn't notice the melancholy in her eyes as she took in the beautiful disorder of the grey tufts behind his ears, leaning down to kiss the biscuity-smelling grey fur.

Rising, he placed his two forepaws on the table. Georgie rubbed his side, her knuckles rolling over its knotted matts.

'Finish off the clams, boy,' she said, moulding a scoop of crab pâté onto a biscuit. She sighed as Archie smacked his lips at the leftovers.

A special bond forms between two souls when they eat together, particularly if they are from differing species. And if the food being gobbled up is of exceptional quality and fear of judgement is at a minimum, it becomes all the more special. As he chowed messily at the clam, all Archie could think about was how, from now on, he was going to be a different cat; a mannered cat. He was going to go on the straight and narrow, let lie his past animosities and tread an adventurous path of well-meaning restraint, as befitted a human like Georgie. It all made perfect sense now; how other cats lived. *Of course* it did. All you need is good food, a sense of adventure, your health and (most importantly) a loving human and a cat *can* find nirvana.

It's damn straightforward, when you think about it, he mused.

Gone would be his scowling, his gunslinging swagger, his lashing out and his greasy, unpreened coat! He'd be a different cat; he'd be clean and have standards; he'd hunt just for sport and not for food. He'd snooze and rest languidly for days on end on clean linen ...

The Cape Verde streets were growing busy now. Tourists paused at the mouth of the little side street, eyeing down its length at the café with hungry curiosity.

Archie's ear twizzled. A peculiar sniffle from Georgie.

He didn't look up. His paws were still folded under him on her lap – a grey sphynx, with oversized paws; the breeze blowing the stray hairs sprouting inside his ears. As he grinned a Cheshire smile, his mind caught itself in the intoxicating updraft generated by new love. *Trekking would be flipping brill with Georgie,* he thought. *Cleaning a room out? Proper heaven with Georgie! Oh my God, imagine what a laugh playing string-chase would be ... with Georgie!*

He still hadn't seen Georgie's eyes.

Eventually, she lifted her phone and thumbed over its constellation of apps. She found her way to Google, and tapped in 'Cape Verde departures', the little audio *click click clicks* of the keyboard making Archie slow-blink.

A chatter of voices. A little girl with braided hair cartwheeled across the street's mouth.

Maybe we could stay here for a bit, thought Archie. *There's no rush. She seems to have money, she has nowhere to be.*

He rolled over and hooked his paws in the air.

The waiter came over and Georgie paid, lifting Archie gently to the ground. Archie trotted alongside her like an obedient dog, weaving in and out of people's legs as they reached the main street.

Steady on, slow down! blimey.

Occasionally, Georgie would stop and make a strange sniffle. But for Archie, it simply didn't register. Now and again, his trot would turn to a gallop for a couple of seconds as the throng of crowds became dense in the market square. Once, he lost sight of Georgie behind a woman dragging market wares tethered to a cart. But he found her again as her gold sandals and white shorts cut ahead through the crowds.

Eventually, she came to a stop, crouching down at a doorway. A new market was just being set up and women carried rainbow-coloured scarfs in wicker baskets atop their heads, hauling them down onto the stalls ready to entice the afternoon crowd. Beyond, taxis idled in a heat-shimmering fug of their own fumes.

Flip, it's noisy here. Wanna head inland? I'm a dab hand at surviving in heat, it's fine.

'Scruffs, stop meowing, hang on. I don't know . . . I, um . . .'
There's loads to see and do. I'm well up for a dip. Do you wanna swim?

'Scruffs, please, chill. Stop meowing like that. I—uhh, I dunno, Scruffs.'

What?

'You'd hate a rehoming shelter.'

Rehoming shelter? Behave! Don't bring that up. Why did you bring that up?

'Scruffs, don't climb up on me, boy,' said Georgie, her huskiness thickening as often it did in moments of stress.

Bet there are some bangin' beaches up . . . What's up?

And for the first time, Archie saw the heavy tears gathering in Georgie's eyes.

At first, he felt confusion – a response which prompted him to peer calmly but enquiringly at her face, his ears pulled up into sharp curious triangles. Georgie covered her face with her hands, holding back the sniffles. His next thought was concern. *Is she ill? Can't be me, I didn't even scratch . . .*

But it was when he went to nuzzle her and felt a peculiar reluctance there that he started to worry. To panic.

'I'm sorry, Scruffs, I've got to go. Please don't hate me.'

A shudder tore at Archie's belly as if a great tectonic plate had shifted there, moving everything that rested upon it – the mountain ranges of trauma, every glowing city of past desire and need, right down to the tiny incidental kerb-side weeds that occupied the B roads of his neural pathways. He sat motionless in the aftershock.

'Scruffs, come in here, come over here . . .'

She lifted him up.

Be gentle, belly's full, he thought with strange automation.

A cat sauntered past, stopping at a stall to lap the yolk of a broken egg. Archie didn't notice it, didn't even smell its approach.

'I'll never forget you, Scruffs.'

You can't go.

'I'm not from here, Scruffs . . .'

But you're a traveller, like me. You're meant to be roaming. That's what you do, can't you see that?

'I can't stay here, Scruffs. I want to go home. To stay put in one place.' Georgie's weeping became louder and turned to ugly gurgling sobs. Archie raised his doe eyes to hers, padding his big kindly paws against her belly.

'No, Scruffs, no. I just . . .'

Georgie moved him gently to the ground. Suddenly, Archie felt his head surge with heat as if his heart was squeezing all his blood there, leaving the rest of his body cold and numb. He watched aghast as Georgie thumbed the release of her suitcase handle, lifting it up until it clicked, her eyes fixed on his little form on the ground in front of her.

'I'll always remember you, puss, puss.'

Then she pulled herself away with surprising swiftness. She turned back three times in total, each time becoming smaller and smaller in Archie's field of view, as though drifting off on unstoppable waters. On the second time she caught him mid mew. At one point, Archie went to rise before sitting down again.

And then he lost sight of her amid the welter of legs and wheels on that hot Atlantic island of Cape Verde.

18

The Mistral Cup

HE DIDN'T KNOW HOW, but he found his way back down to the harbour. Something inside him just needed to see the ocean, and it was the only place where there was any let-up from the heat. The breeze swept off the Atlantic as he moped and sat; rose, moped and sat again in the litter-strewn space behind the marina breakwaters, the birds jousting over scraps. Neck bowed, as if about to gag, Archie padded over the concrete, the squawks of gulls grating in his ears.

Numb. Totally and utterly numb.

One thought kept looping back. Georgie's body: her chest rising and falling, her tendons, and all the thoughts that made her who she was. It filled him with an immense sadness – the thought that these things still existed but he wouldn't be around them any more. *Why?* He mewed long and hard, and fell to pacing the wide hot pavement again, up and down like a caged lion, not knowing where to place himself, or where to go. Gusts of wind flaked off bits of conversation from the boats in the marina, or cries from the parasol-lined beach. None of them engaged his mind. Reaching the edge of the marina wall, he gazed down at the seams of light piercing the depths like yellow ribbons.

So there we go, he thought finally. *On my tod again. Why do people always leave?*

His brain shuffled through theories and their reflexive rebuttals. It wasn't like he thought Georgie and the fisherman didn't care; he knew they did to some degree. But what was it about *him* that meant they didn't care *that tiny bit more* to make the effort to stay? Fight that little bit harder? Was it his lack of silky, shampoo-ad fluff? His insatiable appetite for fresh seafood? Or (as was most likely the case) his cantankerous nature – that thing deeply woven into him whose thread he couldn't fully tear out, no matter how hard he tried. That was it. When it came down to it, they just didn't want him, and his nature, *enough*.

I know I'm not perfect, but who is?

The loss of Mrs Colwell was bad, but had drifted out of his mind within a day. The fisherman was considerably worse. But at least those were borne of circumstance. This felt different. A juggernaut of feeling. Each time, he'd made himself that little bit more vulnerable – his innermost tenderest sides unfurling, like the horns of a snail, only to be crunched under foot. It wasn't worth it. If this was the cost of letting people in, he'd rather not.

And then there was the sea. What force did he have over it? Or did it hold some force over him? Or both?

He sank to the ground in a wretched sprawl, his whiskers lank, trying to separate the sticky notions that warred in his head.

It is me. I did have a go at both of them, hissing a few times. Why should she have to put up with you, Archie, you spiky mess. Useless ball of fat.

He wound back through the faces of every human who had come close to accepting him: Georgie, the fisherman (where was *he* now?), the shopkeeper at the Asian store on Mile End Road who gave him a bed behind his counter before a man from Environmental Health insisted he moved on (that was only this year, come to think of it); the local librarian who let him snooze on the photocopiers, before a pen-pusher from Tower Hamlets council argued that cat hair would ruin the duplex functionality (to be fair, it had). All of them transient.

In a breathless panic, he suddenly found himself wanting to 'speak' like a human . . . to *become* human; to develop vocal cords and cry out his story: 'I am Archie of Stepney Green. I'm a stray and I'm tired and dying of pain. Help me.'

He paused. Unknowingly, he found he had walked quite some distance. He was now on the outer side of the marina wall, where the two great breakwater arms came within touching distance, save for a narrow gap of ruffled water – the threshold of the mighty Atlantic. To the side came a faint squeaking where moored boats rubbed against their fenders.

A crackling voice drifted through the air, muffled by layers of static. A radio. Archie wouldn't have understood the news bulletin even if he could understand the language. A little way along the breakwater, a street vendor sat behind a wheeled cart selling beachwear. Out of the corner of his eye, Archie saw him tweak the knob on a radio cable-tied to a parasol pole. A flock of multicoloured hats and trinkets fluttered in the wind, their beads tinkling merrily. The vendor straightened as two tourists approached. Moments before, his eyes had furrowed – turned towards the radio as if something of unexpected interest was being announced.

Why did I get onto that effing plane? If I'd known it'd open the floodgate to all these . . . feelings.

Just as his ears settled on the warble of the street vendor's radio, there came from nearby the rustle of fabric being pulled along a surface. His ears locked on to new noise, shutting out the rival sound of the news bulletin, at the very moment the vendor leaned in towards his English-speaking customers and translated the spiel from the radio:

'A boat . . . a big boat with rich man! It sank! It says here on radio. Superyacht, called *Calypso Spirit*.'

But by now Archie had been drawn irrevocably towards the rustle coming from nearby. Typically, a rustle meant food of some sort. He came to rest alongside a little bollard and rubbed his flank along its rough, notched surface – a pleasant reminder that he still had feeling.

Daft runt, thinking you could play 'appy families with a human.

His fur had now dried into scruffy peaks, sprinkled with salt crystals. Peering down, he discovered the rustling was coming from a sail bag being carefully packed on a boat deck. The boat's mast, which seemed unfathomably tall compared to the others in the marina, rocked in and out of the sun, casting an alternating bar of shadow across Archie's face, like a pendulum. It was a slender, narrow boat and sat low in the water. It reminded him of the kind of important sailing boat that sometimes prompted Tower Bridge to open its famous arms, much to the delight of camera-clutching tourists. Long mooring lines ran from the dock's edge down to its cleats. It gave off an odour of hot polyester and oil.

From inside there came the *chink* of things being moved around. Whoever was aboard was moving quickly, and the boat was small enough that their weight was making it heel noticeably in the water.

And perhaps it was a clarion call from the ocean; perhaps it was the sudden uplifting breeze or the intriguing nature of this little boat, with its many dangling ropes, but Archie decided he needed to board it.

Gotta get back in the game, Arch ol' boy. You can't just give up. I just know the sea has the answer.

He walked along the wall, surveying the boat carefully. If he was going to leap aboard, this time he wanted to see what he was getting into. At the helm, a spherical compass gleamed in the sun. Ropes lay everywhere: long ropes, ropes through cleats, huge fat ropes round silver winches. Along its side ran a huge sponsorship label for an insurance company, and at the stern two dagger-like rudders disappeared down into the grey-green water like shark fins. Something about the boat seemed out of place – it was somehow too small and playful to be just a breakwater away from the treacherous Atlantic. It seemed to goad the water: 'Atlantic, eh? Come on then, give me your worst!' In this way, it reminded Archie of himself.

A cloud veiled the sun as a gust sent the boats into a bobbing frenzy. Without warning, a spry, muscular woman sprang up from the boat's interior.

'Arbour master! When will ze passport office reopen, please?'

She was lean, almost wiry of form, dressed in a pink T-shirt and khaki shorts, and clamped a bundle of waterproof jackets and a fluorescent yellow life jacket under a tanned arm. Archie stared, his tail tip twitching.

'Excuse me, ze Mistral Cup race is starting soon, we need ze . . . emigration stamps, please?'

She dropped her gear onto the deck with a short-tempered *flomp*. Grimacing, she held the radio to her ear, her small eyes pinching uncomfortably in the glare from the white fibreglass. She lifted a Velcro flap on the pocket of a foul-weather coat which lay on the deck, extracting a pair of sunglasses which she placed over her head before applying sun cream about her neck and face. Archie watched closely. The sunglasses gave her an edgy, sporty look, which brought her slightly strange pinched features and lean stature into their own, and made them make sense. She was the type of human who, in Archie's experience, was accomplished – agile in body and brain, like the very best of Uber Eats cyclists. Still clutching the radio to her ear, she took a leap from the boat's companionway into its cockpit, stopping to yank a rope tighter through its cleat.

'Please name your vessel,' the radio warbled in her hand.

She lifted it to her mouth and spoke clearly and deliberately in her thick French accent.

'*Zephyrus, Zephyrus*, sir. We are ready to depart for ze Mistral Cup.'

'Roger. Can confirm passport ready for collection.'

'Mon Dieu. Fin-al-e-*ment!*' said the woman to herself, flinging the radio onto the seat and coiling a rope over her shoulder. Her skin was bronzed and matte in the kind of way that shows up imperfections which, in her case, took the form of several pink scars on her hands. She leaped, gazelle-like, up to the boat's bow.

That's French, non? thought Archie. *She's come a long way. And by herself, as well. Impressive.* A thought of Georgie bubbled up in his brain, but he batted it away.

The woman picked up a folder and raised her legs one at a time over the boat's side rail, before jumping up onto the marina wall with an almost feline elasticity.

All of a sudden, the two met eyes.

'Oooh! Salut, mon beau minou!'

Archie started, mildly taken aback by the sailor's tone, which became suddenly soft and almost sing-song in his presence. She lifted off her sunglasses and crouched.

'Ici minou minou ... Are you boy or girl?'

She raised Archie's tail. 'Ah, un garçon.'

Well that was humiliating. Archie winced and narrowed his eyes, promptly whipping his tail back around his body. The woman straightened, still looking at him, and cocked her head to the side with a little chuckle. Then she turned, her body moving slightly before her head, and strode along the breakwater wall. Archie watched her, and to his surprise, she turned back, chuckled, and continued her walk.

In the stillness, Archie looked at the unoccupied boat.

Well, there's no point just kicking about here feeling grim, he thought, gazing inland at the palm-tree-laden boulevard. *It's still too ruddy hot for this coat of mine. And France is closer to home than here. If I can get to France, I can get to the Eurostar, and then London.* With a wrench he spied the market stall where Georgie had left him. It was getting packed away. *Too much pain. I'm jumping ship and buggering off north.* He edged his forepaws down the weed-slicked marina wall, pivoted off a fender, and leaped aboard, landing crisply on all four paws.

The boat's deck was rough underpaw with non-slip coating. Carefully, Archie do-si-do'd over a winch, pulling himself up upon the boat's fibreglass cabin roof. *Let's give this gaff the once-over.* He found himself immediately less glum being aboard a boat again. It was an indescribable thrill, hard for a cat to quantify – the smells, the bob, the *chup-chup-chup* of the water kissing the hull; the co-mingling of style and functionality. Unlike on board the *Calypso Spirit* (whose recent sinking Archie still had no idea about) everything looked muscle-driven and manual. This boat had no side rails to speak of, just two very thin wires which ran the length of its entire edge. Gracefully, Archie trod over the lattice of ropes, each at differing degrees of tension, and coloured, like trainer laces. He sniffed each in turn. It pleased him to follow them with his eye to see where they disappeared, a pastime not unlike following the path of a fleeing mouse. Arriving at the entrance to the cabin, he peered down. A tiny, marvellous universe spread out before his eyes. Everything in the boat's cabin was miniature but mighty: chaotic but perfectly ordered. There were no plush cushions, or veneer tables. No home cinemas or champagne on ice. Instead, his eyes flicked from gas cylinder to hob kettle; from pots hanging on hooks to technical schematic diagrams, fuse boards, and a bank of blinking lights.

Crikey, I love it! It's like the control room at Liverpool Street Station, thought Archie. Everything was functional, except for a little photograph of a group of humans and a series of hand-written letters. Pinned above the letters was a quote which caught Archie's attention: 'The sea breaks a man, and then shows him who he is' – *Anon.*

Archie edged reverentially down the ladder into the cabin, letting his polydactyl toes splay wide on the narrow rungs, tail upright for balance. Despite being a thinking (and, upon recent discovery, feeling) cat, Archie was still feline, and, as such, had the non-human advantage of having moods that were easily dissolved by a) food, or b) a new environment. Unlike a house cat, however, Archie's curiosity was hard-wired to understand how practical elements could lend him ideas for survival, not just comfort. Where a house cat might have seen dangling strings for idle play, Archie's eyes scoured for the nooks, dips and crevices that could be home to mice, warm pipes or condensation he could lap.

Hmm, no chance of a comfortable kip spot here, is there, he thought. *Where d'you put your trotters up on a boat like this?*

Then he spotted something: a little recess where towels had been piled like lasagne sheets. He tiptoed over, paws nimbly negotiating the uneven floor; neck swivelling like an owl's as he took it all in. He pushed his way into the small recess and sandwiched himself between the bulked-up towels. It was tolerable, if not highly comfortable. A small vent blew air across his whiskers, making their tips jiggle. *Ain't tickety-boo, but I could make this work,* he thought.

He tucked his paws under him and started to doze. He was just starting to drift off when his ears pricked. Footsteps fast and frantic.

'Allez, c'est parti!'

The sailor jumped the last few ladder rungs playfully. She slid her sunglasses up onto her head and bent over a little desk, clicking things on a computer screen. Archie heard her breaths – long and calm, not like she had just sprinted down the marina. A body trained for endurance.

I gotta say, you give me confidence, madame, he thought. Unbeknownst to the sailor, his head stuck out from his lasagne towel bed like a little cat-snail.

A page flicked up on one of the computer screens. Archie's eyes narrowed:

Mistral Cup Competitor Portal

Category: <40' vessels, single hull

Competing Vessel: *Zephyrus*

Skipper: Hélène Garnault

19

Hélène

THERE WERE TIMES WHEN ARCHIE would fall asleep so quickly it was as if a circuit breaker had been flipped in his brain. Rather than gradually drift, there he would be – sitting quietly mid sphynx pose, when suddenly *plonk,* his head would drop into his paws.

He didn't know how long he'd slept, but was awoken with a start – by the *click-click-click* of a winch up on deck.

As he'd discovered in the Airbus's undercarriage, he could sleep through all kinds of motion chaos if he was exhausted, well fed and/or cold enough. The seafood platter he and Georgie had shared had given his tummy a good workout and the heat had had its usual soporific effect (not to mention the emotional exhaustion caused by an afternoon of existential rumination).

Only a gentle sway suggested to Archie that the *Zephyrus* was, in fact, sailing. Now and again he heard, too, a gurgle of water against the hull, like bath water being sloshed, and the restless *snap* of a sail half-filled with air. Packed in his bed of towels, he must have wriggled during his sleep as he was now fully ensconced, his head tucked back, and only a single paw protruding out of the cocoon. Nevertheless, he awoke dry of mouth, his tongue like sandpaper as he tried to wash his paws.

Eventually, he wriggled himself out of his nest. *Now what's the game plan, Archie ol' boy? Reveal yourself right away, or keep on the down low?* He knew the perils of surprising a human and how it *could* bring out their true colours – and 'true colours' in a human could encompass anything, from a sudden shriek to a sudden kick. None were pleasant, but some were more dangerous than others. He padded silently over the cluttered floor. It was only then he realised it was dark outside, as the light was dim coming through a portlight above the computer screen. A delicious vinegary scent emanated from somewhere over by the navigation station which he discovered, upon closer inspection, was a bag of starchy snacks. He snatched one from the open bag as the light from the navigation monitors bathed his fur momentarily in a wan glow.

'MERDE!'

Archie sprang in a tangle of paws. Hélène's cry had come from up on deck.

Has she seen me? Flipping heck, I don't like her anger . . .

He scuttled under the table and stared up through the portlight.

Nothing.

Blimey, that got me that one did.

The extent of his shock brought home how *quiet* it was at sea without an engine. Compared to the roar of the *Calypso Spirit* or the insistent *phut-phut-phut* of the fisherman's little boat, this was silent. All sounds were elemental – a slosh of water, the crack of a sail – and any sound that broke from this natural orchestra came as a terrific shock.

'Argh! Bordel de merde!'

Okay, something's definitely going wrong up there, thought Archie trying not to tense his claws at the outcries.

Footsteps overhead. Suddenly Hélène was tapping down the ladder, the *crssh–crssh* of her Gore-Tex coat deafening against the silence. Archie scrambled under the table, convinced he had been seen. But no: instead Hélène sat purposefully in front of the bank of computers, clicking the mouse frustratedly. From under the table, Archie could just make out the underside of her jaw, clenched in concentration.

What on earth is up with her? . . . wondered Archie. Hélène rolled the mouse wheel, zooming into a map of the Atlantic Ocean. Here and there little dots were positioned, with pop-ups offering meteorological jargon. *Ahhh right yes, so she's definitely in a race,* concluded Archie, noticing Hélène's particular interest in the dot labelled '*Zephyrus*'.

'La dernière!' barked Helene. 'Je suis la dernière!'

She traced a dotted line with the cursor which clearly marked the progress of the *Zephyrus*. Its position against the competing boats appeared to have started well, but had quickly run into trouble. She appeared to be nearing an area of sea called 'the doldrums'.

Flipping heck, we're not meant to be passing over all that sea, are we? All of that humongous blue in this little tub? Archie's breathing stalled for a moment in panic. Again the mouse *crkk–crrk*'d as Hélène rolled its zoom wheel in and out, the 'out' revealing just how huge the Atlantic Ocean was, not only top to bottom, but left to right. Stricken, Hélène dropped her hand onto the countertop with a thud and rubbed her forehead with a rugged hand, which Archie could now see was pocked with blisters, just like the ones he got on his back in winter. Her breath became ragged in what Archie thought was a sob, but was in fact a moan – the sort of unpleasant guttural sound humans only make when they're sure no one else is around.

She needs a friend, I reckon, thought Archie. *Now's as good a time as any to introduce myself. I'm away from the water . . . better now than never. Surprise, surprise, madame!*

'Mroaw?'

'BORDEL!'

Hélène lurched extending her hand to the lip of the countertop. Silence. Archie suddenly realised that with her human eyes, she probably couldn't make out his presence in the gloom. A rustle as she un-Velcroed a flap on her jacket and extracted a torch.

'C'est quoi, ça?!' she cried, rising to her feet.

As the light flickered across Archie's face, the little cat blinked and mewed sheepishly.

Yeah, hello. Only me. Little Archie of Stepney Green . . . I'm trying to get home to London, I am. And you being French, I was hoping you could get me part way?

He rose, feeling a bit silly and circled slowly around Hélène's ankles, tail high. *Could at least say 'hello', hey? Takes a lot for me to behave courteous, y'know.*

Hélène chattered some rapid-fire French words, still aghast. Suddenly something seemed to click, and she switched on an overhead light.

'Ahhhhh! Le petit chat! Tu es le petit chat du port du Cap-Vert!'

Better! prrrp'd Archie, raising his head into the path of her stroking hand.

He sniffed Hélène's coat. As usual, Archie could tell a lot from just one sniff of a human's clothing and the bouquet of odours on Hélène's jacket cuff spoke volumes. *You've had an energy bar, madame. And a gingernut within the last hour,* thought Archie. *And are those traces of . . . Dior J'adore?* (Archie knew the leading perfume brands well, not to mention their carefully diluted knock-offs. More than once he'd borne witness to a gang raiding a pharmacy for bottles of Paco Rabanne and Chanel only for them to fling them into undergrowth when the police rounded on their tails.)

Hélène beamed. Archie felt immediately warm at being in the presence of a smiling human again. Thoughtfully, she tickled her fingers around the perimeter of his string collar where the skin had grown irritated. Eventually, she rose, cooing more unintelligible (but seemingly French) words before opening a small fridge and extracting some meticulously stacked and labelled cartons.

Oh God no, not hungry, madame, thought Archie. *Thirsty, more like. Thirsty. ADAM'S ALE. Hello? No, no, no. I said no grub. Oh hang about, that smells banging – what's that?*

As she took out one of the cartons, a worried look crossed her face. She felt the carton top with the back of her hand.

'Zut, le frigo ne marche pas.'

Ah lovely jubbly, it's liver pâté! Man, I love this stuff. Give it to me. 'Ello, madame? GIVE IT TO ME.

She scooped a bit with her finger and tasted it, before lowering it absent-mindedly for Archie to lick off her finger. She then took a flask and splashed a little water in its lid for Archie to lap at. It was dawn now, and the sun was strengthening through the portlights while the gentle soundtrack of the Atlantic slurped moodily about the hull. Hélène grinned at Archie in surprised delight between moments when she broke away and looked gloomily at the monitor. As she moved her head, two toggles dangled from her jacket.

Oi, oi, OI! Let's be havin' you, RODENT!

'Ah, non, non monsieur!' laughed Hélène.

Oi! let me 'ave it, you meanie! You don't know what I've been through. No, don't want tickles. No, I said I DON'T want tickles. Didn't you hear? OH DO YOU WANT SUM?

Archie's paw had spliced the air with its customary effectiveness. Hélène teetered backwards, a curse flying from her lips in her mother tongue. Archie zipped into his towel bed, eyes furious; tail snapping in angry curls.

Damn her. OBVIOUSLY I was done with stroking. She knew that! If she wants some, then she can TAKE ME ON! I dare you, lady!

The rush of anger. It made Archie feel alive, that's for sure. He remembered now how addictive it was; how it would give meaning and energy to his life in London. His brain coursed with cortisol and adrenaline – the cocktail that had fuelled so many cat-on-cat battles in London. He had just seen red. And Hélène, not being Georgie, he had reverted to war mode. The lash-out had brought him a strange yet familiar comfort, though this curdled quickly to shame. He was back, for a moment, in the world he knew – but somehow, as a changed cat.

Archie regarded Hélène intrigued. She was moving about with swift, survivalist efficiency. With practised ease, she opened a first aid box strapped to the boat's side, taking from it a plaster, before dabbing some cream onto the bleeding punctures on her wrist. Having applied this with precision, she took the cellophane from the plaster, scrunched it, and dropped it in a little caddy marked '*Recyclage*'.

That was bang out of order, he thought. *You wretched ball of fat. No bleedin' wonder no one can stand you.* His mind turned to the Atlantic, stretching down for miles and miles beneath the fibreglass under him: the grim-faced fish swimming in pitch black, like the ones he'd see on the Billingsgate ice trays. *You wanna watch it, Archie,* he thought. *End up over-board here and it's curtains, mate. Best make up . . .*

He re-emerged from the towel nook and nonchalantly began prowling around the cabin, sniffing bits of equipment. He caught Hélène's eyes, which looked hurt. She sucked between her teeth, rubbing the plaster.

Look, I'm sorry, madame.

'Tu es une sale bestiole, tu sais?' she said with a glare.

He hardly needed a translation. Nasty creature, he was.

I am. But I'm trying. I'm trying, I really am.

20

As If From Nowhere

Four days later

G*OTCHA!*
Archie swiped the fish from the water. Its body, metallically silver, looked as if it'd been dipped in chrome. He had hooked it with a single claw, right through its dorsal fin. The water responded in great O's, radiating out over the hot blue doldrums. It was flat, calm as far as the eye could see.

Archie was perched on the bottom rung of a small ladder, hooked over the *Zephyrus*'s stern. It was a fine fishing spot, bringing him to within whisker-touching distance of the sea. Gazing into the depths, his thread-thin pupils traced fingers of sunlight, down and down, as they flickered their own aurora borealis into the surface. It was at the point they vanished that the fish gathered in glittering shoals, and today, in these flickers, he timed the perfect swipe. Lunch, for both him and Hélène.

In just four days he had changed considerably – his coat had now thinned into sparse wisps of fur. His face and flanks had grown narrow, almost wizened, and when he walked, his eyes pinched in an almost permanent squint. His tail was no longer plumy, its vertebrae fully visible, and a downward curve had formed in his spine, as if it was literally being pressed by the high pressure. Despite this, he was in no pain. He had, in line with his exceptional talent in the area, adapted.

Clutching the fish in his jaws, he climbed the ladder back onto the *Zephyrus*'s deck. This was the first time he'd ventured fully out on deck since the boat's departure from Cape Verde. The sun had made it simply impossible. Below was hot, but it was better than the direct sunlight. He passed the days with Hélène, lounging in a sort of numb lassitude, growing ever hungrier as the failure of the fridge led to stocks of dried food becoming quickly exhausted. Still they had no wind, leaving the racing boat standing on the glassy water. Fortunately, he and Hélène had become attuned. Something about the instinct of survival had brought them together, with cat and woman quietly learning from each other's resourcefulness: Hélène learned from Archie's method of spot-reducing dirt, rather than opting for full body clean, while Archie took note of Hélène's excruciating care around the consumption of water. It wasn't long before Archie became aware of the gravity of their situation. *It's possible we will not make it through this, you know,* he'd think to himself, panting next to a fan alongside Hélène, who had taken to staring for minutes on end at the same spot on the floor.

Archie was a good examiner of human mannerisms, and he studied Hélène's with particular fascination as the days went on. Her eating became a particular point of interest.

Food aboard the *Calypso Spirit* had been a Bacchic frenzy of flavours and fanciness; aboard the *Zephyrus* it was one thing plain and simple – fuel. Three times a day, at perfect intervals according to a small digital clock, Hélène would extract a Tupperware box from a cool box trailing in the water, where the temperature was coolest. She would then fry the food, or boil it, eyeing the water line in the saucepan with scientific precision. Eating would happen in small bird-like pecks, methodical and slow, with even spilled crumbs dabbed up with her thumb and passed into her mouth. Then, Archie: just before she reached the bottom, she'd pass the remainder to the cat with a tickle along his scabby back, and a quiet whisper of *'Voilà'*.

Cheers, madame, Archie would retort with a small 'prrp'. Now that pâté was well and truly off, the food, to Archie at least, tasted horrendous. But it did the job. It kept them going.

Watching poor Hélène as the days ticked by was like watching a breakdown play out in silence. Hélène's features, Archie had come to realise, resembled a beast's – not in the way they were set, but in the constant, restless hunger that stalked behind them. Her eyes had turned hollow and her skin had taken on a sallow hue which made her look almost waxen. In her eyes, Archie could see both fear and the chemical reflexive reaction to fear – panic. Sometimes, seemingly deep in thought, she would hurl something suddenly from the navigation desk across the cabin, before carrying herself up to the deck where she'd slosh sea water over her face and stare over the shimmering water, as if her brain itself was trying to pick up a radio signal from a faraway land. Other times she'd fix Archie with a queer, almost uncanny look that made him reel. Hélène was changing. She was becoming less human.

But then, at other times, she'd surprise him. One afternoon, finding a rush of energy from somewhere, she beamed and chatted away almost manically at Archie in French, her face and voice morphing between emotions, as if sharing some deep, never-before-shared secret. At moments like this, Archie felt a strange primal connection with her, even though he couldn't understand her language; and he knew she felt the same towards him.

Suspicion, however, had crept back into Archie's belly. The trust he'd placed in Georgie, before her untimely departure, had been thwarted, reawakening the old stray tendencies of apprehension and hypervigilance. *You just never bloody know,* he'd think, peering sideways at Hélène through his lizard eyes. *Could you be a traitor?* He knew how isolation could affect humans; equally he knew how mechanical failure (which now included a rapidly exhausting battery) could bring stress and worry. However, Hélène had clearly trained for these things: she quickly located, for instance, an emergency solar panel and a U-shaped instrument she used to look at the stars in an attempt to navigate. But the hunger? Could she deal with the hunger on top of everything else?

And so it was, on the morning of the fourth day, that Archie made a decision. He was going to go fishing. No matter what it took, no matter how much he burned under the beating heat, he was going to get out on deck and pit his predatory wits against the elements in search of a proper meal for himself and his skipper. It was time to brave the open deck.

This is not how I die, he had thought as he pawed up the ladder from the cabin and out onto the deck, flinching as the sun hit him.

Now, the little tuna had become still. Archie sniffed it, mesmerised by its metallic sheen. He took it in his mouth, feeling a buoyancy of spirit as he carried it to the centre of the deck. *Hope it ain't poisonous.* Hélène was at the bow attempting to attach a new sail to the rigging, which flapped limply.

'Mroaw!!!'

The mew crackled in his dry throat.

Hélène's jaw dropped. 'Mon Dieu! Bravo, minou! Tu es génial!'

Too bleedin' right I'm a genius, thought Archie. *Someone's gotta save us out here, or we're both gonna cop it.*

Lowering, she crouched in front of Archie, beaming, as if he had laid a golden ingot at her foot. Archie gazed through sunken eyes and let his stringy coat get smoothed down by Hélène's hand. *Apart from anything else, this here fishy is a peace offering, madame,* thought Archie. *I didn't mean to lash out, the other day. If we're gonna get through this, it's gonna be together.*

'Mon brave minou,' breathed Hélène.

Enough, gawping, get it on the hob. That's a fine poisson there, and they don't just sacrifice themselves. I'm used to nicking tiddlers from the beaks of . . . Oh 'ello what's this . . . ?

A jolt.

Still squatting, Hélène put her hand out to steady herself. The pair looked around. The boat seemed to flinch and skitter. Disbelieving, Hélène squinted upwards. A gust had billowed out the sail like a polythene bag caught on a fence. The sailor leaped up and raced to the bow, turning back to take in the mast in full, her eyes pinched against the sun.

'C'est le vent!' she whispered. 'Un souffle de vent!'

A smile broke over her face. All around them, little patches of roughness zigzagged over the water's surface as if a spirit was gliding over it. Now the great sail tugged making the whole frame of the boat tilt. Ropes became taut. Things hummed. The sound of splashing broke the stultifying, long-brewed silence. Archie steadied himself on his polydactyl paws.

'Incroyable,' said Hélène, almost reverently.

With the boat having come to life, Hélène danced and punched the air, offering prayers to an unknown god. Archie weaved through her ankles, tail aloft, his pelt relishing the wind against his sweat. He nuzzled into Hélène's leg and pressed his dry little nose into her knee. She scooped him up. He offered no resistance. Beneath them the boat darted like a stung colt, leaping over the waves with abandon. They couldn't communicate it to each other, but it was the most exhilarating moment of both their lives.

And to think I only walked out on the deck to go fishing! thought Archie. *Don't forget the* poisson, *miss!*

Hélène carried him back to the stern to take the wheel. Either side, the hull cut through the water, sending spray overboard in glittering rainbow arcs. After a while, Hélène headed below deck, the autopilot holding the wheel. She twisted on the gas and sparked up the hob. Soon the smell of fried fish and lemon was wafting out over the cabin.

The pair ate ravenously, Hélène picking up the fish and gnawing its bones while Archie chowed between high-pitched growls. A near immediate change came over Hélène at the consumption of proper food, and her pinched features seemed to recede and soften. She tickled Archie along his neck and back, until his spindly tail lifted into the sun. And something sparked in Archie's chest never before felt – some quick energy, like a flash of lightening, the primitive herald to something far more epic.

21

The Ship's Cat

THE SPRAY-RIDDEN, WINDSWEPT DAYS ROLLED into one. Routine took hold and Archie's fishing skills, in quieter moments, ensured a fair supply of food off the stern. Four days raced by in which both cat and human began to feel more robust of mind and spirit with each passing day. The *Zephyrus*'s passage across the ocean continued with the same heaven-sent spriteliness, Hélène still tracking their course by the stars, until one morning, Archie was awoken by something peculiar.

Of course, Archie was often rudely awoken, most commonly by unpleasant noises. Typically, the disruption came in the form of a motorbike revving, the deafening skirl of a drill digging up a bit of pavement, or sirens from a police chase on the Commercial Road. Very occasionally it was semi-pleasant – the frames being erected for Whitechapel market, if he happened to be up that way, or the off-key first strums of a busker on Bethnal Green Road. These were indicators of a possible breakfast to come, if he played things right. The worst awakening he could recall was when a sleeping bag he was curled up in suddenly began moving – with him in it. Opening his eyes, he saw to his horror he was about to be slung into the hydraulic jaws of a bin lorry. Even here at sea, now that the *Zephyrus* was carried by fair winds, he'd often raise an irritated eyelid at the *click-click-click* of a winch as Hélène sheeted in the sail, or adjusted the tension on the boom.

It was unusual, however, for Archie to be awoken by a *smell*. Perhaps he'd just never had the opportunity to be awoken by odours, or they weren't strong enough to rouse him. But suffice to say this morning, as he lay sprawled and snoozing on the deck, it was a smell that lifted Archie from his slumber.

And with a *jolt*.

He had been sleeping on one of the towels up on the deck which Hélène had laid there, rightly assuming he found them comforting. Perhaps because of a change in latitude, the weather had turned more cyclical, with squalls washing over the deck after stultifying, humid mornings. They offered a fine chance for a refreshing shower. This morning, however, the air felt pure and unladen; for Archie, positioned just forward of the cabin ladder, but far enough back to avoid the biggest splashes over the bow, it was just about perfect.

I know that smell. Damn right, I KNOW THAT SMELL.

He lifted his chin, pupils narrowing as he looked overboard.

Belly-crawling, he slithered along the deck to peer down the portlight to see if Hélène was cooking anything. Nothing. He knew she wouldn't be, not just because he hadn't caught a fish today but because this smell was distinctly *not* a fishy smell. Or a boat smell, come to that.

He raised his head towards the sky and gave two sharp intakes of breath, his nostrils flaring.

Is it . . . leaves?

It was an intoxicating earthy smell. After days at sea, the wonderful novelty of the scent engrossed him like a drug. Memories illuminated – of grassy London squares, their pavement slabs glistening with recent rain . . . the drizzle-patted tulip beds of Victoria Park, alive with worms. The smell took him home; it was the closest he had ever come to time travel.

And it was all the work of his nose.

Well blow me sideways, if that ain't the pong of land.

He rose and prowled the boat's perimeter, stopping inter-mittently to stare, with twitching tail, at the horizon as if a mouse might skitter along its sharp line of sky and sea any second. Finally he sat, tail swishing over the shiny deck, perplexed.

'Bonjour, mon beau,' said Hélène. She had a single hand on the wheel and was chewing a gingernut biscuit. Archie greeted her with a shut-eyed 'meow' followed by a cheerful *prrp*. He ambled over to meet her hand. *Fine day, eh. Do you smell that whiff too?*

A tropical sun was sending orange glitter over the ocean, like sparks from struck flint. The wind whistled through the rigging and carried the little boat in splashing nods through the water. *You been handling earth, miss?* enquired Archie, with a snaffle at Hélène's hand. The hand gave way to tickling fingers, but no clues. Hélène clearly hadn't picked up on the smell and continued to nibble at her biscuit, while holding the wheel steady with her foot. She cupped one hand to catch the crumbs, promptly eating them off her palm before washing them down with a sip of water, attained from an ingenious sheet and bucket device she'd crafted to collect rainwater. For the last two days, the boat had remained without power but the winds were fair. The gas stove allowed for home-cooked, if spartan, meals and somehow, as if by magic, the winds lulled just long enough in the early evening for Archie to fish over the stern, never failing to guddle a handsome catch. Hélène was sailing by the stars in the style of mariners of old, her joy at being fed and on the move clearly outstripping any malaise about her prospects in the race.

With docile contentment, Archie plonked down on the ship's bow, his forepaws overhanging either side of the boat's nose.

He missed the first blink. His eyelids had shut moment-arily with the sibilance of waves. But the next flash he clocked immediately – its pinprick of light a microscopic trigger on his retina. He jerked his neck upwards caught between wonder and disbelief.

Oh 'ello! That was a thing, wasn't it? A flash? What was that?

His fixed his gaze on the horizon, breath held.

Yes! There it is again! This time, the light sent a radial band sparkling over the water'. *Oi oi! Something's out there. Come and have a butcher's at this. There's a light out there.* He turned to look at Hélène, who was running the nub end of a spoon under her nails, her foot still resting on the bottom of the wheel. Archie mewled and circled on the spot.

'Que se passe-t-il, monsieur chat?'

Look at that, lady!

Another sweeping glimmer over the sea.

Hélène stood on the deck to the side of the helm and raised her slender neck overboard. 'Une baleine?'

Well I don't know what it is, but there's something out there.

A *scrunch* as Hélène pulled the flap on a Velcro pocket and extracted a set of binoculars. She raised them to her eyes, her lips becoming taut and white.

'Ha!' she barked suddenly, causing Archie to leap. 'Terre en vue!'

Oooft chill out, calm down. What's that you're saying?

'Monsieur le chat, on est arrivés! Land ahoy, boy!'

* * *

The ensuing hour felt long and stretched. With each minute, the glimmer on the horizon grew stronger, eventually giving way to a faint strip of land. With no technology, little food and after days adrift, the tiny *Zephyrus*, one Frenchwoman, and Archie, the stray cat from Stepney Green, had found their way to land. Hélène leaped and ran, splashing water into her face, and busying herself with preparations for landfall. Ropes appeared from lockers, sails were lowered and the little translucent popper folder containing her passport Archie had seen her with in Cape Verde emerged from a drawer by the navigation station.

I knew there was something out there, thought Archie as the striped silhouette of the lighthouse took shape against a jagged mountain. Now great hills rose in dagger-like spears of green, their tips puncturing a membrane of cloud. Closer by, the sea hurled itself against jutting headlands, crashing in high columns of spray. A coastline was forming – impossible after so many waterlogged days; and yet stubbornly real.

The smell of earth started to be overshadowed by other aromas as the land loomed proudly higher and higher in their midst. Archie's twitching nostrils picked up a new bouquet – of coconut, sandalwood and sizzling spice.

Waaaaait a minute. Is this really France?

As the boat edged closer, the features of the shoreline took shape. Eventually, he could pick out the waxy fronds of palm trees.

Oh flipping Nora, where have I wound up now? I thought it was still too warm . . .

A restaurant panned into view, with a wooden roof and a flashing pink neon sign, a knot of moored boats, and all along the coastline, a white beach stretched in a curve, soft-focused by a mist of sea spray. Behind him, Hélène whooped and squealed in a contagious display of wonder. Archie, too, couldn't help but be taken in by the vibrant ludicrous beauty. And then came the food smells – oh the food smells! As they neared the beach restaurant, the aroma of grilled lobster tumbled on the air; fried saltfish, jerk spice chicken and even the molasses-rich whiff of rum. They made him mew involuntarily with hunger. Hélène's joy was enough to overshadow his shock, but those smells – they were like a spark to a touchpaper, reinvigorating his appetite afresh after days of scarcity: the prospect of an *actual* meal . . . mouthwatering cuisine in all its saucy glory.

Oh well, here I am then. Who'd have thought it? That Archie, the stray with hardly a stale bit of kibble to rub between his paws would wind up here, via a superyacht, a Turkish fishing boat and an Airbus undercarriage. Land of tropical wonder.

Moments later, Archie spotted an inflatable boat racing towards them at full speed. He didn't hear the yells coming from its crew at first but leaped in fright at a *pop!* that rang out from the shore. Across the water, a thread of orange smoke rose into the air. As the boat neared, its hiss in the water mingled with the squawks of birds which had come out to greet the *Zephyrus*, and disguised the voices of its crew. Its whooping cheering crew. Soon, the little boat swooped up alongside the *Zephyrus* in a flurry of spray. Archie curved his spine, reversing back from the edge of the boat with a growl. *Oi, get out of it! What d'you lot want with us, eh?* At the boat's wheel was a woman in a bright white T-shirt. Accompanying her was a man in a shirt with pineapples on it, a large camera hanging from his neck by a strap. Both were yelling and chattering excitably.

But it wasn't the pineapple shirt or the cries which most engaged Archie's attention. It was something else about the man – not his beefy face, nor the odd tattoo on his ankle, half lost under a sprouting of hairs. What Archie couldn't stop looking at was his teeth. The pineapple-shirted man's teeth were needle-like, and angled slightly backwards into his mouth, like a shark's. Instinctively, Archie found himself lowering behind a winch, ears twisted back, hiding himself from those teeth as if they might gnash right out of the man's mouth at his throat.

Suddenly, shark-toothed man looped his arm around a cleat and pulled himself and his boat in against the *Zephyrus*, placing his elbows on the deck. He raised the camera around his neck and clicked the shutter brazenly. The woman driving the boat grinned through thin gash-like lips.

'Coooongratulations, *Zephyrus!*' she cried, in an American accent. The man followed suit. '*Zephyrus*, you aced it, man!' He clicked his camera again, checking the screen at the back. Then he reached into the pocket of his shorts and extracted a smartphone which he extended at the end of his meaty arm in Hélène's direction.

'You've just smashed the world record for the fastest westerly run in an under-40-footer.'

'You made history, Hélène! Want to say a word to *Yachting Matters*?' chimed in the woman.

The shark-toothed man grimaced back at his colleague. 'How does it feel to be queen of the seas?' he enquired.

'If you could bottle this feeling,' said the woman, 'what French wine would it be, Hélène?'

'You gonna be living it up tonight, Hélène?' piped up the man.

Now the woman also produced a phone, but held it away from her in a selfie pose with the *Zephyrus* in the background and two fingers up in a peace sign.

Hélène, who had been sitting at the wheel of the *Zephyrus*, gawped silently.

'Yo, skipper, we thought you'd foundered, Hélène! What happened out there? You lose your GPS or something?'

'You went from vanishing to winning, Hélène! How does someone do that?'

'Did you lose power, Hélène?'

'A Frenchy winning the Mistral! It's so fitting, Hélène. Are you gonna call your husband . . . ?'

'Or your wife, Hélène? What will your wife think of this?'

'Did you have to drink your own pee, Hélène?'

Hélène stared from the helm. Her slender mouth parted and closed in a vain attempt to speak; to find the right language to describe wondrous events of the previous days. Archie could see the animal within her; the animal she had been forced to embody, poking its head up through her soul; the animal that brought her closer to his feline mind. She had become suspicious and scowling. Slowly, she rose as the couple on the inflatable boat fell silent in a mixture of awe and froth-mouthed expectation.

In an accent thick enough to slice, she said, 'I ask please that you leave us alone. I speak later. I have not even crossed the line.' She waved her hands in a *shoo* motion. 'Allez-vous en, s'il vous plaît.'

Damn right, allez-vous-bloody-ON, you pair of muppets, hissed Archie, leaping from behind the winch and swiping at the fat-armed shark-toothed man. *Sling your hook!*

'Sunnuva!'

The man recoiled, treading stupidly about the bobbing dinghy. 'It's a … it's a damn *cat*. Hélène, what's with the goddamn cat?'

'Whoa, you have a stowaway cat, Hélène?' shouted the woman at the wheel.

The man rose again, looping his meaty arm around the *Zephyrus*'s stanchion. *A definite wrong 'un,* thought Archie. *Sometimes you just know.* He crept forward once more and launched a full-out viper whipping attack on the man's knuckles, leaving a three-claw gash on the back of his hand. *Leave – her – effing – ALONE, you muppet.*

'Sunnuva gun.' The man yanked his arm back. Blood plopped down onto the boat's rubber bladder. 'Goddamn, Jen, that sunnuva-gun cat's a maniac!'

'How does it feel to be a record holder, Mr Kitty?' asked the driver woman, ludicrously.

Do us a favour, scowled Archie. *We've 'ad our share of grief. Go sling your hooks!*

Another little boat whirled up alongside the first.

'Oi, we have an exclusive, you clown, back off now,' said the woman in the first dinghy.

The driver of the second dinghy didn't respond. He was a journalist of Caribbean origin, again with a camera round his neck, and had a stubbly beard and a coloured rag tied up in his hair holding back a flurry of braided locks.

'Hold on there!' he said in a thick Caribbean accent. He outstretched a finger towards Archie, a grin on his face. It was a genuine smile, unlike the inane gawps of the journalists on the other dinghy. Something about the man gave Archie a safe, warm feeling.

'Nah man, no way!' said the man, still pointing. 'You the Ship's Cat!'

The journalists on the first dinghy gave a bewildered glance.

'Dude, *what?*' said the shark-toothed man.

'He's the Ship's Cat! He's a magic cat, that one. My friend in Europe wrote an article about him.'

PART TWO

NOSTOS

(νόστος): 'HOMECOMING'

22

The Scoop

ARCHIE LICKED THE FIZZY REMNANTS of rum and Coke from his toe beans, feeling woozy. *'Magic cat,'* he intoned. *Do me a favour. I'm about as magic as Peckham pigeon.*

From his ridge-top position, thirty feet above sea level, he watched as a purple sunset exploded over the peaks of Antigua. Several miles over the sea another island – a volcano – smouldered, a wisp of smoke bubbling from its peak. With his back to the view, Archie crouched under a bench next to a straw-roofed bar where revellers gathered for drinks. A steel drum clanged a reggae beat while a Caribbean conductor whirled a glowstick to keep time. The sound of these drums wasn't unfamiliar to Archie, who'd heard their cheery sound waft up from Hackney Marshes on summer nights. But hearing them here and now, his legs aching deliciously from being stretched, and his nose sniffing out bits of dropped jerk chicken, felt indescribably magical.

Guess I ain't getting home any time soon, am I . . . he thought resignedly.

The last few hours had been a whirlwind, but that was not what occupied his mind most. He couldn't stop thinking about the words of the journalist – the man of Caribbean origin. When the *Zephyrus* eventually dropped anchor, he and Hélène had disembarked into a media frenzy: people, cameras, champagne and race staff, their clothes emblazoned with the logos of sponsors, all lined the beach next to the harbour. Everyone had clamoured to speak to Hélène, meaning she and Archie quickly became separated. Only now, having found his way up the hillside, was Archie beginning to ruminate on the ocean passage . . . the strangeness of it. But more than this, there was the strangeness of the *other* boat journeys . . . all odd in different ways. Two parts of his brain began to war: the first and strongest part was his cynical mindset, forged through years of straying. And that ran as follows: *there's nothing out there. Nothing. You're born, you live your life, you die. And that's that. Everything else is cobbles.*

But this brick-wall rationality was cutting head on into another, newer force: the force of cumulative recent experience. Had it really been the case that this little boat had drifted into a windless sea, lost all electrical power, suffered multiple system failures, only for its near-famished cat-and-human crew to be blown to the Caribbean in an unforeseen transatlantic record? It seemed unconscionable. That was three boats now; three boats he'd sailed on enjoying – dare he think it – good fortune, despite adverse circumstance. The fisherman's boat had survived the storm, the *Zephyrus* had broken a racing record, and the *Calypso Spirit* had suddenly developed a taste for petrol.

Bloody hocus-pocus, he thought, rinsing his face with a damp paw. *Don't go there Archie. Don't believe it. Might as well believe there are fairies dancing at the end of the garden.*

And then it hit him: *It's whenever I prowl the decks.*

Yes, that was it. That was *literally* when the change came. All three boats were ill-fated *until* he stepped out on the decks, at which point their fates miraculously, inexplicably, changed.

He ventured over towards the dance floor, heavy under the glare of the epiphany and its attendant knotty notions. How could it be possible? He was a cat who'd lived his entire life believing, in every sense possible, he was entirely *un*special. Perched on the edge of the dance floor, he watched the blur of legs and limbs as they whirled to the beat of the steel drums. He wanted to find the man on the boat – the one who had called him a magic cat. The comment continued to spin in his head as he traipsed beyond the dancers and up a cactus-lined path, pulled by the smells of a fragrant tropical evening. Here he flumped down next to a sign that read *Shirley Heights*. Under it was a series of arrows pointing to locations from all over the world. His eye fell to the second one down: 'London (4,071 miles).'

Good job you're doing in getting home, pal.

A particular bugbear of Archie's was the humans' obsession with folklore and the witchy power of cats. It was the same tail-flicking irritation he'd feel when hearing the street evangelists cry 'love thy neighbour!', knowing full well they'd return home to cosy beds while other humans slept under bridges. Why was it, then, that the Caribbean man's comment kept returning to him? On some level, he realised – terrifyingly – it must all be true. This stuff didn't just happen ... it *had* happened. There was something 'magic' going on.

A saline breeze whipped into the clearing. For the first time in weeks, he felt a little cold and took to curling in his polydactyl claws. *Urgh, what's going on. Can't a cat just be a cat?* A foot stamped beside him, narrowly missing his tail. The noise of the steel drums began to stretch, taunting his ears. *Blimey, the rum out here's blow-yer-paws-off strong. I feel pissed as a cricket.*

A glass smashed. A shriek of laughter. A coconutty odour from spilled white fluid. His belly churned its meaty contents. He felt a pressure at the back of his throat.

Ah gawd, not again . . .

He retched and, for a second time on his odyssey, puked spectacularly.

He edged back from the vomit with a growl.

Honestly, Archie mate, pull yourself together. Messing around on boats . . . getting pissed in the Caribbean? You could always handle your food and drink. What's become of you?

With Hélène still consumed by a frenzy of story-hungry humans, he was very much alone once again and struggled to know where to put himself. But while this separation was hard, it didn't floor him like the departure of Georgie. The *shock* of that had come from the fact he thought they would be together indefinitely. He and Hélène were different – he and Hélène were two animals on an ark, destined to part ways when they arrived at their destination.

Eventually, his paws took him back down to the cove where the palm trees waved their waxy leaves in the gloom. Yachts bobbed in clusters. Some looked cosy, while others sat dark and still, shouldering off the wild Atlantic – the endless Atlantic which, if you followed it right, would flow right up around the hump of Kent, past Southend and

Thurrock; past Canvey, Tilbury and Gravesend, until eventually it lapped on the storm grilles of East London.

Down the hillside, the dancers began peeling away, staggering arm in arm to their beds.

Everyone's a couple, thought Archie, eyeing them glumly.

Suddenly, he heard Hélène's name mentioned. Off to his side was a media tent connected to the race, buzzing with activity. Archie promptly sidled over, soon finding his ears swivelling at another notable mention – 'the cat'.

'Ello. If it's me they're chatting about, I wanna hear what they have to say.

Carefully he lowered his neck to the ground. A zip, that linked two of the tent's plastic panels, had parted slightly. The voices were intent, and marked by an unpleasant, conspiratorial glee. Wafting through the gap was an odour of stale human sweat.

'It's the cat that's the scoop, man,' muttered a voice.

Shark-tooth geezer! Archie flinched, immediately recognising the distinctive American accent of the journalist he'd confronted on the dinghy. The second was higher and nasal, and seemed to speak between breaths. As on the boat, he found himself cowering at the mere sound of shark-toothed man's voice, which seemed to hang oppressively in the air.

'I know, I know,' replied the nasal voice. 'And it's the same one they're talking about in Europe, with that collar. We're *made*, right? You did see that collar, yeah?'

'I mean, I think so.'

'Did you or didn't you?'

'Argh, I can't be sure,' replied the shark-toothed man, frustrated. 'Yes, I *think* I did. Like, eighty per cent.'

'Wow.'

'Exactly. That's our story right there, Kev. We get the cat, we syndicate, and *boom*.'

'How many impressions did you say that story has online?' replied the nasal voice.

'About seventeen mil. Hey look here.' Archie held his breath as the shark-toothed man's voice became muffled with capering glee. 'This story is all over in Europe. It made the red tops in Turkey. And look – this is what the Greeks ran …'

'Damn, is that … ?'

'Yup, that's the *front page* of their national.'

A snigger.

'It's the same damn *cat*, Kev, I'm telling ya.'

'No, man it totally is. Like, totally. Have you heard about the reward that's going for it too?'

'You're kidding me!'

A knot formed in Archie's stomach. The sort of knot he felt when he knew a big dog had his scent and was slathering for a scrap.

'Nope … look here,' replied the nasal voice. 'And see the collar, there's that whatchacallit … Arabic thing … Keeps the evil off you, or whatever crap that lot believe in. See it?'

A pause as the two men evidently looked at their respective phones.

'So it looks like the *LA Times* has covered it, CBS News and … ' The shark-toothed man paused. A few dull taps against his phone screen. 'Look at this, Kev – a campaign called Find the Ship's Cat – twenty-four *million* views!'

'W-w-wait, go back, go back? Who put up the reward? Hey, don't we know that guy? Ain't he the captain of that superyacht that sank the other week?'

'Off Cape Verde? *Calypso Spirit?*' Clearly finding this line of conversation uninteresting, shark-toothed man returned to excitable outbursts about the viral fame. 'Forty *million* views, Kev! Make a film of the Ship's Cat.'

'No way.'

A crunch as a phone hit a table and the creak of a chair. The pong wafted strongly as Archie caught a glimpse of the pineapple shirt at the parting of the tent panels – the *same* pineapple shirt.

The *click-click* of finger bones being cracked.

'So, LA Press want to interview Hélène Garnault but she's being an ass, you know what the French are like. The cat's a stray, so if we get it, it's ours, man. Remember grumpy cat? That little scooshed-up-face asshole? Its owner is worth *a hundred million dollars*. All the IP from merch and licensing. That's what a famous cat is worth in these crazy-ass times of social media.'

There was a silence. The fur along Archie's ears shook in the wind. He felt a sneeze prickle in his nose. He forced it back.

'So where is it?' came the voice of the nasal man.

'It's on the island somewhere. It ran off when Garnault docked this morning.'

'It'll go to where there's food. Back of the restaurants over on Falmouth Harbour?'

'Yeah, probably.'

'We gotta set a trap. It's a stray – a fearless bastard. It's used to scavenging.'

'You reckon, just a stray male? A moggy?'

'Yeah.'

'Hmm …'

Archie rose, the hairs at the root of his tail brushed up in anger.

They don't know who they're dealing with! thought Archie. *Just let 'em try. There ain't nothing that can out-guile this cat. Not Archie of Stepney Green.*

23

Rumbling

*B*UGGGGGGGERRRR!

The drop wasn't far, only a couple of feet; but he knew immediately – he had been trapped.

In the gloom, Archie thrashed like a wild thing, kicking and hissing. His voice turned to a single guttural growl. *Get me outttta here!* Blood thrummed through his veins and around his ear canals in deafening pulses; his yellow teeth bared to an invisible belligerent. He could feel his pelt clamp round his body like a suction-sealed bag, tightening around limb, paw and ear. Frantically, he managed to hook a paw outside the cage and curl a claw back on the bolted door. He jangled at it intensely but to no avail. Instead, a sharp piece of wire from the homemade cage cut into his paw pad. He didn't even feel the pain. His mind was dead to it. All he felt was fear, red and hot, and the skirl of language: *what-do-I-do-what-do-I-do?*

How had he come to this? Well, last night he had found himself on a quiet beach and drifted off to the gentle slosh of the sea. *I can see why the Shoreditch hipsters like it out here,* he had thought. He had, of course, thought back to the overheard conversation and kept his wits about him. But then again, he'd overheard many threats in his time but very few frightened him. Poison, tranquilliser darts, cages with treadles that sent a metal door clanging down – he'd seen them all. *You'd have to wake up preeeeetty early in the morn to outwit Archie of Stepney Green.*

It all started when he awoke on the beach to the drone of a vacuum cleaner. It was coming from a little makeshift beach shack off to his side; an auditory assault on the perfection of his surroundings. *Wonder where Hélène is,* he had mused, remembering the easy safeness he felt in her company. Distracted by this little reverie he had risen on his legs, passed a tongue-dampened paw over his face, and mooched along the sands between scuttling orange crabs.

And then, the wondrous scent. So intoxicating. It had stopped him in his tracks, literally, with a sand-lined forepaw hovering mid-air. There was a smell of leftover meat coming from the beach shack's bins, but that wasn't it . . . this smell was different; and he knew it well – the unmistakable pheromoney smell of a she-cat on heat.

Oo, hello! Single cat, reveal yourself!

Automatically, he had uttered his famous guttural mating cry – a courtship cry that had awoken many a Stepney Green resident at 4 a.m. To a she-cat, it wasn't the most attractive cry of the East London strays, but it was well-known, and conveyed all it needed to about the proximity of his hungry loins. The smell of the she-cat rose, pulling him irrevocably towards a shaded patch of jungle floor up the beach.

Come on, let's 'ave it, he mewled, stalking panther-like among the litter of coconut shells and driftwood. He sniffed the ground eagerly, eyes huge.

And there he had plummeted, his nose having led him slap-bang over a trap where browning palm leaves had been laid over a caged hole. Hook, line and sinker ... snared by carnality.

A cat can only thrash for so long before it exhausts itself. Now, after several minutes of flailing about, he fell still. His corrugated nose smoothed out. There were many unpleasant things which Archie had encountered which would knock the average house cat for six: sleeping rough for nights on end, a night without food, being locked in sheds. He could handle it all with calm resolve; but being trapped underground, *successfully* trapped by malice and guile, that never lost its terror.

Bewildered and shaking, he slowly forced himself to regain some composure. He sniffed the cage's makeshift mesh to try and build a backstory through scent. Was there a trace of human sweat there? Poison? Food? But he could only smell three things: the metal of the cage, the putrid odour of rotting leaves, and the unmissable odour of a she-cat on heat which had been daubed all over the cage and leaves.

A bloody honey trap, the bastards! They've bloody honey-trapped me!

He mewed long and hard, each cry sending his thin fur spiking and falling, like dragon hide. Looking upwards, he could make out a tiny patch of blue sky amid the criss-cross of decaying leaves and driftwood that had been carefully scattered to conceal the trap's entrance. Shaking with adrenaline, and hearing nothing but the wash of sea up the beach, he fell to plotting. But his mind wouldn't let him. Instead it filled with something else – faces. All of a sudden, a slideshow was panning in his brain of all the sailors he'd encountered. Georgie's big eyes; the fisherman's bushy moustache and oil-stained shirt; Hélène's lithe body and piquant, intelligent face. Each image panned over his mind as the cage became hotter.

As the sailors flickered through his brain, their features pulled in expressions of concern as if seeing him through time and space, an odd feeling gathered in his chest. A sort of resonant rumbling. It was a pleasant yet strange feeling – something he'd never before experienced – and was matched by a fluttering that tickled behind his nose. Intrigued, he pulled his mind back to the faces of the sailors and found that the sound grew louder whenever he fell to reminiscence. Memory was driving emotion, which in turn fuelled this new silky motor in his chest.

He didn't realise it, but for the first time in his life, Archie was purring.

What in the hell's bells is going on now?

It took him a moment to realise that what he was experiencing was the vicarious feelings of others, imagined, and living *through* him. When he flinched in pain, it was Georgie's tear-strewn eyes that salved his hurt; when he licked his bloodied paw, it was the fisherman's moustached mouth that curved in soft concern; and when he gazed hopelessly around the dark cage, it was Hélène's bony fingers he felt behind his ear. Their imagined emotions were a magnifying glass, concentrating a golden dot of sunlight upon his heart.

Eventually, the purring drew his entire body into an unexpected calm.

Some minutes passed as the purr lapped its calming waves through chest and soul. The heat rose to a stupefying fug, making his mouth run dry. After some time, the purr became ragged, faltering. He gasped through the foetid air with increasing effort as his mind began to crack up like a hammer-hit pane. Thoughts dissolved into shapes, geometric patterns and weird blobs of light. He tried to push them aside but they always rolled back to the centre stage of his brain, like a marble rolls to the middle of a bowl. He tried to summon good thoughts – the lovely smell of damp London soil after rain, delicious meals … the faces of the sailors, but the shapes shouldered past. His thoughts had turned bullying.

He passed perhaps an hour in this state; maybe longer. In all that time, the purr juddered through his body, both expending energy and yet somehow supplying it; taking and giving; keeping him alive. As the midday sun reached its zenith over the tropical beach, the serpent-hiss of sea began to wrap itself around him. Occasionally, he uttered a pathetic mew. Dampness grew under him. Urine? Blood? The sea? He didn't know.

This is it, he thought, deaf to the footsteps that came closer, closer, closer.

The cage shook. His eyes parted a millimetre. Through the cage's mesh, he spied two fingers.

<h1 style="text-align:center">24</h1>

<h1 style="text-align:center">'Rise 'n' shine,
Whiskers'</h1>

'I THOUGHT WE'D KILLED IT, DUDE.'

Two voices chittered in nervous spurts.

'You fed it?'

'Nah, it's too dehydrated. Look . . .'

Light behind Archie's eyelids. A faint smell of cologne.

'Hey, pass that bottle. No, no, that one – by the closet.'

The crackle of a plastic bottle being squeezed.

'Hey! Rise 'n' shine, Whiskers!'

'Mick, what if it has one of those GPS chip things? Our every move is gonna get tracked.'

'It ain't got no GPS tag, Kev, look at the moron. It's a stray . . . basically skin and bone. It's been halfway round the world and no sunnuva's caught up with it, so that's good enough for me.'

'Okay, if you're sure . . .'

'Course I'm sure. It's a funky-haired stray that's travelled boat to boat, dug through the trash in the ports, and now they say it's bewitched or whatever. That's why the scoop's so damn big. Here, this ought to get it going ...'

A cold skim of water across the face.

Head bowed, the little stray gradually parted his eyelids. The flecked fibres of a carpet swam into view. They were pushing up through the metal base of the cage – the cage he'd fallen into – what – a day ago? An hour ago? He couldn't tell.

Accosted olfactory receptors: the stench of human sweat and polyester. Mixed with this, the whiff of air freshener – the commercial type used in hotels where there's a lingering drain problem. The water that splashed into his face had a hint of human saliva in it, with undercurrents of gingivitis. All this swirled and competed as Archie's brain flickered back to life with each lap from the white hotel mug at his paws. A podgy man moved closer, refilled it. Written around the mug, in italic writing, were the words '*Athena of the Seas. Luxury, afloat*'.

'It's definitely the one, Mick. Look, the collar – the Muslim eye thing.'

A piece of ham sandwich appeared, which Archie nibbled at, the butter getting trapped in a bit of his scraggly chin hair. He lifted his head letting his eyes travel above the mug to a pair of curtains patterned in blue and orange blocks; then up further to a brass-edged porthole window, a wall-mounted smoke alarm, a spotlight ... up, up, up until eventually it met the face of his captor – pineapple-shirted man from the dinghy, his teeth more shark-like than ever. His beefy features pulled into a malicious grin.

'Well hello, Whiskers!'

'So now what do we do?' came the nasal voice off to the side.

Archie swivelled his head. In the shadows sat another man, leaning against the cabin wall, his arms looped over his bent legs. Just by looking at him and spying the blotches on his shirt's armpits, powdery like a salt mine, Archie knew he must be the man that the shark-toothed guy had been conspiring with in the tent last night. Archie assessed his eyes, which were starey and refused to blink. He was skinny, and something about his black clothes and gaunt features was eerie and bat-like, as if he would've been better suited to hanging upside down in a bell tower but had instead found himself in the grips of a morally bankrupt media career.

He don't 'arf give me the spooks that feller, thought Archie. The cat knew gangster dynamics well in both humans and felines, and he clocked, in an instant, that the bat-like man, while being full of it to begin with, was a coward and now getting cold feet. He had the jumpiness of an unseasoned criminal in too deep.

'We'll smuggle it off at Boston,' said Mick, scratching off flakes of skin up his arm. 'We'll get some professional shots, take the scoop to the *NYT* and *Wash Post*, saying we got the magic crazy-ass Ship's Cat they're talking about in Europe … the one that's the viral sensation …'

'Argh, I dunno, Mick,' responded bat-man Kev, yanking in his bony shins. 'You think it'll be enough?'

'Sure. We're talking twenty k *easy* for an exclusive on a story like this.' Mick's voice took on a wispy sibilance when he spoke at speed through his needle-like teeth.

'Twenty thousand dollars? For a story about a cat?' replied Kev.

'Easy. Trust me, dude. I've been in this game a loooong time.'

'I dunno, Mick, it's just a cat. And you know what people are like about animal welfare, we'll be toast.'

'Hey, Kev … *Kev*, look at me. Grumpy Cat …'

'Yeah, I know I know, a million dollars,' said Kev weakly.

'*Ten million*, buddy. And it's not the only one. There're tons out there. You heard of "Pomster", that Pomeranian thing? They dress it up in goofy clothes and publish books about it. Guiness World Record holder. Its Christmas Annual was a *New York Times* bestseller three weeks in a row. They're signing it to a *merch line*, man.'

'A dog can't hold all that money, Mick.'

'Well *of course not*, doofus, it's all locked up in the accounts of its registered owners, while they splash about their pools in their mansions in the Pacific Palisades.'

'Do you really think we could get money for this thing?' said Kev.

'Come on, Kev man, wake up!,' said Mick with a snap of the fingers. 'This little runt has twenty million reads across six Reddit threads. It's clickbait gold. In fact, those sons of bitches are *already* making money from it, so why shouldn't we, huh? And to top it all, some Asians or Arabs do *literally* think it brings good luck to ships. What we have here, Kev, is a kitty goldmine.'

I'd like to see you try, you muppet, thought Archie. The water and food was starting to stoke the furnace of his anger.

'I mean just look at it, it's got this goofy fur, it's got that crazy-ass collar and weird fluffy ankles. It's photo clickbait, before you even get into its story.'

Go on, you plonkers, you natter away, thought Archie, his ear subtly swivelling to catch each bit of conversation. He eyed Kev's bat-like features calculatingly. *You're the weak point, mate*, he thought. He gave his fur a lick, nibbling at the crusted blood on his paw. Now his veins were twingeing with the prickle of adrenaline, his legs aching to be flexed. *You know what, if they want some, they can 'ave some!*

But he knew better than to let them know as much. He kept his movements slow, deceptively weak, his blinks sluggish and laboured. *Keep it cool, Archie mate . . . Bide your time.*

'What if it needs the bathroom, Mick?' piped up Kev.

'So it can go piss in the shower.'

I got standards, ya know, grumbled Archie inwardly, feigning an exaggeratedly weak plod over to sniff the edge of the bedside table. He rubbed his cheek against it. *Just keep being cat, Archie boy. Just keep being cat.*

'C'mon now, Kev, let's go get them dice dancing, man!' cried Mick with a gestural shake of his palms.

Mick plonked his behind on a chair and began pulling on a pair of trainers over dirty white socks. As he scratched his fat ankle, Archie noticed afresh the tattoo nestled in its copse of hair. 'Stack me up, baby!' he yelled, 'cause daddy's gettin' kitty money and wants a new yacht!'

'There's a casino aboard?' muttered Kev, lifting himself out of his crumpled weedy pose.

'Course there is, man,' replied Mick. 'We're on the *Athena of the Seas*. It's "luxury afloat"– a goddam city on water. There's everything aboard. Let's go. See ya, Whiskers!' Mick picked up the keycard and flicked it over Archie's ears. He sniggered, his mouth pulling into a nasty capering grin.

Oh, just you effing well wait, you berk, seethed Archie, locking his glassy yellow eyes on Mick's.

'It's getting more alive by the minute, look! C'mon, man, let's go. The B Deck casino opens at eight and Mr Mick Dibbuck is feeling *flush*, baby!'

Yeah, yeah, yeah, berky-McBerk-face, thought Archie, plodding a few theatrically frail steps back to the cage.

Mick grabbed his wallet from the side table as Kev slicked back his hair with a hand in front of a mirror. A seasoned feline escapologist, Archie needed only the narrowest window of opportunity, and he knew this would come from Kev. As Mick dawdled to find his phone, Kev flicked off the lights, plunging the cabin into darkness at the same moment he opened the door.

Perfect, so long, muppets!

Archie zipped through the gap, racing down the corridor. It was a few seconds before either of the men noticed.

'What the *hell?*' screamed Mick.

'What, man, what? Keep your voice down.'

'The damn cat, Kev! You let it get out. There, look!'

Archie galloped like a tiger. It felt wonderful. Underneath his paws, the plush carpet sprung like Serengeti grass. As he ran, he realised he had a slight limp but nothing that would affect his dexterity. He had a rule when fleeing within buildings: a rule he referred to as *the old two-lefts-one-right-double-down ploy.* Experience told him that the best escapes in a large building were made by taking two left turns, one right, and then descending a flight of stairs. It never failed to outwit pursuing humans and had worked a treat in Docklands office blocks, shopping centres and – most famously – at an Ibis Hotel in West Ham after an exchange with a group of football fans turned *a bit pear-shaped.* Humans, it seemed, had a habit of getting quickly disoriented in unfamiliar spaces, not being equipped with a cat's superior eyes and noses.

God, it's great to feel the ol' pins moving again, breathed Archie, his nose high in the air as he scooted through the doors of a lift just as they closed behind him. He circled to a sitting position. Above, the lift's sundial floor indicator swivelled anticlockwise, extinguishing the lit floor numbers as the lift plummeted down, down, down. Turning, Archie caught sight of himself in the lift's mirrored wall. His fur sprouted in shock, not because he didn't recognise his reflection (he wasn't one of those daft cats) but because his appearance had greatly altered. It was the first time he'd surveyed himself since spotting his reflection in one of the winches on the *Calypso Spirit,* and seeing his vertebrae protruding in points like a diplodocus skeleton alarmed him somewhat, his scrubby grey skin giving rise to only a sparse covering of grey fur. His whiskers were crooked and his legs, though still muscular, were interrupted by bald patches where the shire-horse fetlocks had thinned to almost nothing.

Blimey, I look like I've got scurvy, he thought.

A voice: 'F deck. Second-class restaurants, Dionysus theatre, and cabins forty-nine to one hundred and fifty-two.'

Oooh, restaurants, this'll do.

The doors parted.

Archie stood flabbergasted. The scene that presented itself was bamboozling. A huge atrium towered above him, crowned with a glass ceiling. Blue under-lighters ran along a set of stairs that parted and rejoined, like the reflection of a snake in a mirror. Everything was gold and brash, the sounds of voices ricocheting across Formica-smooth surfaces. There was something futuristic about it, and under his paws, the floor took the form of endless grey-brown marble slabs.

Ah . . . this is what being on the trot is all about, moments like this, he considered. Silkily, he trod into the atrium's well of light, a streak of LED light crossing his face. The thrill of a recent escape never got old, and something about the cruise liner's lobby filled him with starry-eyed wonder. High-tailed, he lifted his head and gazed up the atrium towards the obsidian night sky. *You've played a blinder here, Archie old boy. Mind you, doesn't sound like you're heading home, does it. Look at this gaff, though! Who needs human company when you've got a gaff like this?*

But the thought was followed with a little backwash of depression. He knew it wasn't true; not any more. Once a cat lets a human in there's no going back, and three of them, over the last months, had slunk their way under the barbed-wire perimeter fence of his heart. He ambled over to a pair of upholstered chairs tucked alongside a giant yucca under the stairs. There he sat and pondered, feeling a little maudlin as the chemical assault of adrenaline subsided. Unlike in London, where such a rush simply gave way to ever-nagging hunger, since being on the *Calypso Spirit*, he had experienced a new phenomenon of simultaneously feeling safe and having a full belly. Initially, it was a wonderful state of existence to be in, but had the habit of leading him into pesky rumination . . . a habit which seemed to have stuck.

He leaped up to the yucca flowerpot to relieve himself on its pebbles. *The thing is,* he thought, staring ahead. *I do need ruddy company. I love moving about, and I'd hate to be a house cat, but I want a human. Oh it's so ruddy hard.*

Finishing his business, he raked over the ornamental pebbles, thinking back to the purr. Had it just been a one-off? The swansong of yet another near-death experience? Sentimentality still felt uncomfortable to him, as if the mere act of experiencing emotions cast him in an unflattering light. Humans like Kev and Mick were firm reminders of why he could never keep his guard down for long. There were wrong 'uns all over the world, who were a threat to all animals, not just cats. And yet Georgie, Hélène and the fisherman had all been *kind* ... deeply kind. Not perfect – indeed there were things about each of them that irked him, but in the time they were together, all three had been genuine and had tried to understand him.

I wish I'd shown them my appreciation sooner, he thought. *Caught them a mouse or something.*

He sniffed the yucca leaf and was transported on its vegetative smell to London; the soft rain and temperate weather; the gasometers, great castle parapets, glinting under a red Thames sunset. *I do miss Old Blighty,* he swooned, the plant's smell unexpectedly kicking up the silt of his homesickness.

A portly man stepped out of the lift. Archie flinched, thinking for a moment it was Mick.

And all this cock-and-bull about me being magic, he pondered. *People have written stories about me, have they? I'm a famous magic cat, am I? Rubbish. Might as well believe there are fairies prancing down the bottom of your garden. I'm no more magic than a rabbit in a hat.*

It was true – the idea that he was influencing the world around him in a physical sense – whether through sailing or merely *existing* – still remained largely blocked from his mind. He refused to give nonsense like that the time of day, as he had sense enough to realise, deep down, that that way madness lies. So notions of the supernatural floated over his mind, like water over oil, refusing to mix. It was enough dealing with the fact that he was gaining the capacity to love.

25

Bermuda

ARCHIE AWOKE TO THE SMELL of paper and ink. To his right, a laser printer had spat out sheets of A4, finally coming to a stop on a final sheet, entitled 'Emergency Customs Arrival Declaration'. Feeling dozy, he propped himself up on his forepaws and stretched his neck so tall and thin that, for a moment, he looked like a Modernist painting of a cat.

He had been curled up on a navy jacket. Encircling the spot where he sat was a little moat of his own grey hair. The jacket had been slung on a pile of ring-bound files and Archie had sought it out as it had still been warm with body heat. Sunlight poured in through a porthole window, and formed little puddles of light on a bureaucratic scene of papers, staplers and hole punches.

Befriending the ship's purser had, in a way, been a strategic decision. A beamy purposeful lady, who walked in big strides (but who had a kindly eye), Archie knew that presenting himself to the purser would mean back-of-house protection for the rest of this trip. He needed to be away – away from the commotion, away from the fracas of cooing passengers and, most vital of all, away from the clutches of Mick and Kev. As a result, he'd spent the last four nights sleeping with his eyes fully closed.

They'll never find me in here, he thought, lapping at a saucer of milk and a peeled-back tin of tuna that had been placed for him at the desk's edge. *Find another pussycat; you ain't having Archie of Stepney Green, magic or no magic.*

Most of the time, the purser wasn't even in her office, allowing Archie the freedom to roam, sniff and peruse the confidential paperwork of passengers aboard. His favourite thing was to claw out the contents of the shredder and chase the little strings of paper until they were torn and soggy with his spit. On the occasions the purser did appear, she eyed him affably with a chuckle, pored over some document, or clicked at her computer before heading out again with a corporal-like air. She didn't seem especially keen to get to know him, but that didn't bother Archie.

Suddenly, as he lifted his leg to clean his nethers, he noticed something out the window. Through the porthole, a dockyard crane loomed its long arm, interrupting the blue Atlantic sky. It was a surreal sight, almost like an alien life form, and seeing it made his heart skip. He had assumed they were still sailing. He surveyed it suspiciously as it rotated its long trussed boom and lowered a shipping container on an abseil of cables. A *ker-thud* drifted through the air as the huge weight met with the ground.

Better see where the hell I am now, then, he thought, rising and padding over to the porthole, raising himself on its frame like a meerkat. *Gordon Bennett. Land-a-bloody-hoy!*

The ship had sidled into a wharf. A little inland was a busy cargo terminal where containers were piled up in colourful mosaic stacks. It was almost beautiful. To one side, lorries idled like obedient cattle, awaiting their loading slot. On an opposite wharf, a tanker sat ugly and brown, orange rust streaking down its great hulking side. Archie's eyes flickered over the scene. Everything was oblong, straight-edged, slow-moving.

Blow me down, that's a Union Jack flag over there!

Archie's eyes had taken him in a circle around the cargo terminal, past a bay, returning again to the stern of the tanker on which there flew the Union Jack. The sight of the flag of his home isles gave him a twinge in his belly. It was the same feeling he experienced when he had smelled the damp earth and the yucca leaf. He looked back at the tanker with new eyes. *Was that boat . . . born in Blighty? Can I finally head home?*

He pawed up and down on the window ledge restlessly. While the last few days in the purser's office aboard the *Athena of the Seas* had been pleasant enough, Archie was beginning to feel hemmed in. The existence, with its lounging and plentiful food, felt a little easy – a little too 'house cat' – and he longed to cut about again as an unenclosed entity. It wasn't good for either his head or his body, the former of which was still locked in a cycle of pesky rumin-ation. He had started to wonder, for instance, whether he wasn't so much magic as *cursed*. The fisherman, the *Calypso Spirit* and the *Zephyrus* had all had good luck with him aboard, but look at how stricken their fates had been in the first place. Maybe he brought *bad* luck and it was jolly good fortune that they all pulled through? So he'd saved a fishing boat from a freak weather event; but who's to say he hadn't caused it? Equally, maybe he'd led the *Zephyrus* to drift into the doldrums, or cursed Georgie into filling the *Calypso Spirit* with the wrong fuel? And even this boat? There had been a fire alarm the other night. Possibly a drill. But maybe … not?

In a way, the *Athena of the Seas* was like a mini-London on water – a huge metropolis of restaurants, shops and people. But unlike in London, he couldn't feel anonymous: he was always the curio; a novelty to be gawped at, and he couldn't abide gawping humans. Perhaps, on some level, the kindness shown to him by Georgie, Hélène and the fisherman was teaching him that he didn't need to *settle* any more; he'd discovered, after all, that it was *possible* to live comfortably alongside humans, so long as they let him be. But that existence was so transient. It kept slipping away, the humans returned to their lives, their commitments, their dreams. *The proof of the milk is in the lapping, mate,* he'd sometimes think. *If they really wanted you, they'd have found a way. They'd have fought that little bit harder.* This glum notion would bury itself deep in his head, like a tick, oozing its poisonous doubt. *Once a stray always a stray. And if you did have powers, you're probably only worthwhile to them as a talisman?*

He recalled the faces of his shipmates. It was true, something had definitely changed in him: the snatched moments of connection he'd experienced in London – the greeting of the imam or the plate of Whiskas left outside Mrs Colwell's door – felt minor compared to the real bonds he'd experienced with the sailors. For so long he had believed that all he was good at was surviving; now he felt he could do human connection too, and part of him was impatient to try it out to check it wasn't all some big fluke. The thought jostled in his head with the desire to get home to cooler climes. He needed to get off the ship.

He lowered himself off the window ledge. Seeing land and the flag of home had lifted his spirits. Disembarking would give him new opportunities and, most importantly, he'd escape the clutches of Kev and Mick for good. *My paws are itching for a dust-up*, he thought as he looked at his claws resting in their sheaths. When the purser next rounded the door, he sprang forward. As with Mick and Kev, feigning a docile demeanour paid dividends. Before the purser could yell 'Hey Mr Cat!', he was sprinting down the corridor.

Eventually, the corridor broke into a junction with a spiral staircase sweeping upwards. He ascended, his little evil eye charm jingling against the metal stair lips. He wasn't quite sure how but he could sense an open door in the change of tone in voices coming from above. He emerged into an oak-panelled lobby, smelling strongly of chlorine. Pictures of pebbles lined the walls at intervals giving way to a reception desk bearing the illuminated words 'Lyceum Wellness Centre'. And sure enough, an open door, where supplies where being loaded aboard. Archie slipped past a set of legs, making a cleaner take a sharp intake of breath in shock. But he was away, and soon he felt the bite of fresh, non-airconditioned air against his fur as he raced down the linkspan.

He was ashore again.

*   *   *

The cargo terminal reeked of oil. Archie edged among the containers, chowing at the occasional weed which spouted through the tar. It struck him that places like these were probably the same all over the world: the messy wastelands that existed between town and countryside. He scanned the litter of drink cartons, bits of shredded tyre and the curved arm of a digger at rest. Every now and again, the earth tremored with earthquake intensity as a shipping container met with the ground. He made a turn past a bank of Portaloos, running headlong at a seagull pecking chevrons into a polystyrene carton. He chanced upon a traffic cone. *What you looking at?* he hissed, swiping it onto its side (one thing the sea clearly hadn't changed was his lifelong 'umpiness towards traffic cones).

Composing himself, he leaped onto a pallet, enjoying the fragrance of sun-drenched creosote. It was hot in Bermuda, but it wasn't the arid heat of Rhodes or the sticky mirage heat of the doldrums. A constant breeze ruffled his fur, carrying with it the appealing whiff of fried bacon. From up on the pallet he could see the tanker again with its British flag hanging from the stern. Men in fluorescent jackets with clipboards were standing alongside it, where a giant arm appeared to be pumping something aboard.

A fair punt it's heading to Blighty, I reckon? thought Archie with a little S of his tail. *Jellied eels. Cor I could go a jellied eel right now. And a nibble round the beer garden of the Prospect of Whitby pub. There ain't nothing like the beery smell of the Prospect at five bells in the morning.*

Automatically, his paws carried him towards the tanker, the draw of home having become a quiet muscle memory. At the end of the linkspan stood a set of Portakabins that seemed to be responsible for the admin effort related to the tanker's departure. As Archie approached the nearest, he could hear the chatter of voices. He ambled over on his way to the tanker, tail low, nosing the ground for bacon until he found himself alongside the first Portakabin.

In the future, he would replay this moment; these few seconds. He would recall that smell of bacon, mixed with cheap instant coffee and hot plastic, and would be instantly here again, in this moment, when everything would change – the first link in a chain that would extend to the end of his days.

26

The Soldier

THE GROUND ALONGSIDE THE CABIN was littered with cable ties and scaffolding joints. A single slab was positioned under its door frame, to act as a step. Archie nosed in and onto the speckled vinyl floor.

He didn't see the soldier at first. He was sitting at the cabin's far end on a plastic seat, hunched over in combats, staring at his phone – so still that even a cat like Archie managed to mistake him for an inanimate object. Instead, Archie was distracted by a man in uniform behind a desk marked 'Immigration' who kept rolling on his swivel chair to and from a metal filing cabinet. Every time he closed one of its drawers, he slung it with force, making it *clang* against the frame. Now and then he whistled and set a printer to work which spat out pages. It was just as Archie turned to leave, disappointed by the officer's lack of bacon sandwich, that he started, suddenly aware of the soldier, who had shifted in his seat.

'Dunno why you're not just getting a plane, buddy,' said the immigration officer.

He spoke curtly, in an accent Archie couldn't place. The soldier – clearly the person he was addressing – didn't respond. Instead he thumbed his phone, eyes frightened and staring. Occasionally, he swallowed – a process made visible thanks to a prominent Adam's apple – and the whole while his leg bounced up and down while his free hand opened and closed, as if trying to clutch something mid-air. Eventually, he slung his phone on the adjacent chair and rested his arms on his thighs, staring hunch-shouldered at the floor as if trying to decode hidden meaning in its vinyl speckles. After a moment, he extracted a lighter from an inside pocket and flinted up a flame. He sucked at his cigarette, his cheeks hollowing out, as the cigarette's tip glowed and crackled. Finally he leaned back, lifted his head and puffed up a column of smoke, the nicotine clearly having an immediate and much-needed effect.

Archie examined his face through the soft focus of smoke: it was angular, with sharp cheekbones and a defined, somehow fox-like nose. This would have given him a fierce look, were it not for his eyes which were wide and frightened, giving him the appearance of a child who had been caught doing something wrong.

'The British Army?' the immigration officer ventured again, hopefully. He still hadn't got an answer. 'They'd pay for your flight back, surely? There's a BA flight leaving for Heathrow at eight, you know.'

'Don't like planes,' came the soldier's final reply. A gravely tobacco-thickened voice.

'Fair enough, man,' said the officer. 'Were you disbanded?'

'Aye, a month back,' replied the soldier. This time Archie detected a Scottish accent.

The officer swivelled on his chair to collect a page from the printer, keeping his eyes, which had become a little wary, on the soldier.

'Where were you fighting, if I may ask?'

'Middle East. Terrorist cells.'

A change came over the immigration officer.

'Oh God, that must be tough. How do you even . . .' He stopped, reconsidered. 'I'm sorry, buddy, that must be hard.'

'Aye.'

The soldier spun the cigarette round his finger.

'You got a girl at home? A wife?'

'No,' replied the soldier, returning to staring at the floor. 'I mean I did have, but . . .' His opened his mouth to speak, but the words dried in his throat. His fingers clenched into a fist, which he tapped against his forehead. 'She . . . I . . .'

The officer looked at him askance. He changed the subject.

'Hey, err. They pay good, the British Army?'

'Aye, no bad,' replied the soldier. 'But I don't know any different, like. It's my first job. Only job, really. But aye, they look after you.'

'That's good, at least?'

'Aye, you get your board, yer pals. I'll miss the boys, though. I was "wee man". They looked out for me.'

'Ah yes, "wee" that's Scotch for small, right?'

'Ha,' replied the soldier. 'Aye.'

For the first time a wry smile flickered across his face, but his eyes stayed scared. Clearly buoyed with his progress, the immigration officer chortled. He threw a stamp up in the air before catching it theatrically behind his back. He then punched two flamboyant stamps on the passport in front of him. 'Well you're a braver man than me, I give you that,' he said.

'I couldn't do that, though – what you just did with the stamp. That was pure class, that.'

'Eh, gotta pass the hours somehow, y'know? Life's plenty quiet for us Bermudans.'

The immigration officer rose and rounded his desk, his black trousers wafting past the nose of Archie, who had ducked behind a water cooler. He offered the soldier his passport and travel documents with a smile, before leaning back on the front of his desk. 'You, sir, fight for your country,' he said solemnly. 'Now *that* is brave. I couldn't do that.'

'They're sending me home, mate,' replied the soldier with a glum downward glance. 'They're sending me home because I'm useless. I lost it out there. Had a breakdown. Nearly topped myself.'

Crikey, this poor bloke's been through the wringer, thought Archie, venturing his neck out beyond the water cooler.

The immigration officer shuffled trying to find the right words. 'Jeez,' he said finally. 'So, how come you're here in Bermuda?'

'I've been "convalescing".' He made air quotes with a snigger. 'It's Cyprus they send us to. When we lose it that is. They stick you on a flight, send you to a hotel, get you bevvied up ... encourage you to get pissed and "clear your head". That's the way they think you deal with it ... with what you've seen and heard and done.'

'I see. And what, it doesn't work?'

'For a bit. It winds you down. You stop jumping at every noise. But you can't live like that forever. Life isn't a holiday.' He sank down a little into himself.

Whatever he's seen, he can't unsee, Archie thought.

The immigration officer cleared his throat. 'So, um, why Bermuda for you? Why not Cyprus?'

The soldier shrugged. 'I was deemed a special case. An MD – stands for "medical discharge". My uncle works at the British base here, so I was considered being "near family". Hardly seen him since arriving. Ashamed, I think. He's one of those types.'

'Damn.' The immigration officer ran his thumb through his belt. 'Are you going to be all right going home on a tanker? I wish I'd known, you know. I'd have introduced you to some good folk here.'

'Ha. I'll survive.'

'I mean, has it worked? Do you feel any better?'

The soldier smiled sadly. 'I'll survive,' he said again. 'Although I didn't like how you slammed those drawers . . .'

'Oh gee, man. I'm so sorry.'

'I'm joking, man, it's fine. Don't fret.'

A squawk of seagulls outside. The two men sat in silence. One thought kept going through Archie's mind: *I know the feeling.*

'Listen, buddy, I don't want to keep you,' said the officer, returning behind the protective rampart of his desk. 'You seem like a good guy. I wish you all the best. Your ship's the *Phaeacian Enterprise* – it's ETD out of here is 15.35 so you might want to think about boarding. That line has been known to leave early. And you're in luck – it's a direct, non-stop transit right into Grangemouth terminal. Grangemouth, is that near – how do you say it – Rose-ith?'

'It's Rosyth,' said the soldier, emphasising the *eye* of the last syllable as he rose and slung his backpack over his shoulder. 'Aye, that's just over the water.'

'Ah I see. There's a terminal there too, ain't there? Is that near Glais-gowe?'

'No, Glasgow's west. Grangemouth is just up from Edinburgh.'

'Ah nice, Edinboro! The whisky and the castle!' The man reclined in his chair, his hands clasped over his belly in a satisfied manner. 'I'd like to visit one day.'

A silence again. Archie forced back a sneeze, his whiskers trembling with the strain. The soldier dawdled as if about to say something. An awkward silence.

'Do you need … assistance getting aboard?' ventured the immigration officer.

'No, I'm fine, mate. This is me. Thanks for the chat.'

He walked to the door and stubbed his cigarette out on the side of the bin.

'They're a good crew aboard *Phaeacian Enterprise*,' said the officer, seeming mildly relieved the soldier was on the move. 'They'll see you right. Danny, the captain, he's a top guy; ace blackjacker too, I hear.'

'Ha, ne'er played, but maybe I'll learn. Cheers mate.'

The soldier hoisted the rucksack higher over his shoulder and turned to the door. In the silence of his wake, Archie emerged from under the table, and trotted after him.

* * *

Walking over the gritty wasteland towards the tanker linkspan, Archie kept his distance. Even though he intended to befriend the soldier, he felt oddly nervous. He noticed a slight limp to the man's walk and a swagger, possibly exaggerated, with both arms swinging in a bumptious way. Occasionally he stopped to look at his phone, before launching forward again. Archie noticed he had a habit of being very still, then moving in sudden jerks, like a lizard along a wall. It was the sort of human body language he would typically be wary of, but for some reason, he wasn't. Eventually, the soldier reached the foot of the linkspan. Archie watched at a distance like a feline spy. *What you up to fella?* he found himself thinking. The soldier took his rucksack from his shoulder, letting it drop to his feet. Pensively, he craned his neck up the rust-streaked tanker's side. He appeared to be thinking. Finally, he spun on the spot, immediately locking eye to eye with Archie.

The little cat slow-blinked and mewed in a quiet voice. For a moment there was silence as the wind tousled Archie's fur and he stood watching, his scraggly tail raised in greeting. He kneaded the weed-strewn asphalt and slow blinked again, and even offered another mew. *Come on, mate, don't mug me off. Give us an 'ello.*

The soldier crouched, hand outstretched. Eye contact with him felt like looking into a fathomless pool. *There we go, that's more like it.* Archie trotted forward and rubbed his cheek along the man's thin, calloused hand, enjoying its gritty, oddly familiar aroma of tobacco. There was a metallic smell to his coat, like coins, a hint of spearmint gum on his breath and his whole scent signature reminded Archie, strangely, of home.

Somewhere deep in his belly, a little purr rumbled to life; his first in the presence of a human.

And that was how Archie met Fraser Drummond.

27

Just Knowing

'JUST DON'T BE A BAWBAG, MAN!'

The soldier's voice echoed along the prefab corridor of the tanker. The walls were painted a mucky white and covered with rubber scuff marks, emergency exit signs and the occasional coiled fire hose. Cold light fizzed out of strip bulbs and a hydraulic whir shook the air, which stank of boiled potatoes – the kind Archie knew, even without seeing them, had been boiled grey. The combination of it all made the little cat feel nauseous as he gazed at the steward who stood square in front of him with a V-shaped hairline, and the self-satisfied air of a jobsworth.

'You're violating carriage rules,' said the steward smugly.

'Oh *am* I?' fired back Fraser.

'Yes. And if you fail to provide the necessary certification, the captain has the right to forcibly offload live cargo at the next port.'

'Does he, aye?'

'He does.'

'Well tell captain Fanny-Danny I dinnae give two monkey's and I heard he's gash at blackjack.'

'Sir, there's no need for rudeness. Unaccounted-for live cargo ...'

'Mate, will you stop saying "live cargo". He's a cat, he's not heading off to market.'

'All the same, he needs to be present on the manifest.'

'He's not a pirate, pal. He's not going to stage a takeover. What do you think this is, *Snakes on a Plane*?'

'Please, sir, don't be facetious,' said the steward flatly. 'It's health and safety and required by international law. What's your name?'

'Ach on yer bike, what's *your* name?'

'I'm Chief Steward Cooper.'

'All right, Chief Steward Cooper. I'm Fraser, and you can shove your health and safety up your arse.'

Fraser jutted his chin threateningly. It did the trick, and the steward backed away. He clamped Archie close to his chest, forcing the cat to readjust his paws, before pushing past the steward who clearly thought better of pursuing the matter.

'I'm asking you politely to obtain the paperwork,' the steward called after them. 'A cat's considered "live cargo" by international law.'

'Aye, and you're considered a bampot by international law. "International law" my arse.'

Yeaaaah! seethed Archie, flashing back a go-to-hell stare. *'International law' his ruddy arse! Now sling your hook!*

Archie snuggled back into Fraser's arms, one paw overhanging his forearm. All throughout the confrontation he could feel Fraser's muscles flinching and twitching – it was a type of expression that Archie understood; the body's coded expression of anger. He recognised the flux of emotion in sinew and flesh – the warning juts, the clenched jaws and lurches; the moves designed to make the enemy skitter. He could smell the adrenaline from Fraser, and feel his emotions seeping between skin and fur like osmosis.

'Your room has Wi-Fi,' shouted the steward in a final bid from the corridor's end. 'You can download the health record form . . .'

'Look at me, mate. I'm returning from war,' shouted back Fraser with a tired voice. 'I've been signed off for my nut. I've no address, no health record and no insurance. And nor does the cat. Just show some empathy and leave us alone.'

Fraser turned and resumed marching away. They reached a T-junction of passageways, and headed up a zigzagging staircase. Eventually, they came to a door locked by a huge horizonal bar, which Fraser lifted, sending a blast of sea air across Archie's face.

It was night. Above, a starless sky. He lowered Archie down onto the deck. 'Jesus, what a daftie, eh cat?' he said. 'Some people! Total jobsworth.'

You're not kidding, mate, agreed Archie inwardly, letting Fraser's hand fall with a tickle round his scruffy nape. His fingers were thin and spindly, a bit like Hélène's but with a softer tickle. He assumed a seat on a metal cabinet of hydraulic controls, Archie coiling round his ankles. Beneath them, the propellers churned through the black water in a low *rd–rd–rd–rd–rd.*

'You've been through the wars yourself it looks like, wee man?' said Fraser, letting Archie paw up onto his thigh for an ear tickle.

Ha, yeah, you could say that pal. Ooh, and that's my favourite tickle spot! How'd you know that? Genius!

On the rare occasions that Archie had accepted a tickle in the past, he'd started an internal countdown timer. The tickler – be they Georgie, the fisherman, Hélène or the purser of the *Athena* – had no idea of the timer's presence. All of them had outstayed their tickle welcome at some point or another, and had been subjected to a dose of flashing Archie anger – two curt swipes and a pugnacious glare. *YOU WANT SUM, THEN?!*

But Fraser was different. Fraser seemed to hear the tickle timer; to sense when the time was up and he should respectfully leave Archie to himself again. More than this, he could anticipate where Archie would want a *new* tickle, before even Archie did himself, thus circumventing the perils of the tickle timer altogether.

Now, mid-scratch, he opened his eyes and looked up at Fraser's face, set against the backdrop of the ship's great bridge. Two enormous floodlights beamed down, and Archie's fur seemed almost silver under their light. It was just past 11 p.m., and the *Phaeacian Enterprise* was already 110 miles due northeast of Bermuda, carrying Archie, Fraser and 20,000 cubic metres of liquid petroleum, at a fifty-degree bearing across the Atlantic to Europe. 'Not the Balmoral is it, wee man,' Fraser said. 'I've had more comfortable nights in a Land Rover, to be honest. Bed's lumpier than Nessie's back.' His finger ran the circumference of Archie's collar until his fingertips came to the pendant. 'Ah, is this your name, wee fella?' he said, cupping the evil eye pendant. 'You're Arabic? No way, it's the evil eye!'

Nah mate, it was put on me by a fisherman bloke. Got any grub?

As if he could hear his thoughts, Fraser produced a cardboard cupful of stroganoff pieces – clearly something he'd smuggled from the tanker's canteen – and emptied them onto the deck. Archie tucked in.

'Givin' me the evil eye!' Fraser sang out with a tobacco-throated rasp. 'You're a good one, pal. We've got the same energy. You and your wee evil eye. What about your eyes, what are they like? Aww nice! Yellow. A tinge of green on that left one, though? A touch of David Bowie about you. He had a mismatched eye ...' He circled his fingers under the string collar that held the evil eye charm, making the little cat purr. Archie had almost forgotten he was wearing the evil eye charm over the last few weeks – his time spent with the fisherman felt like aeons ago, almost another lifetime.

'You like those tickles, Ziggy?'

I'm Ziggy now am I?

'Aye, I'll call you Ziggy. Why not, eh?'

Okay, fine by me.

'Good, good. We'll have fun you and me, Zigs.'

You know what, I think we might, mate.

'Shame we can't see the stars, tonight,' said Fraser, gazing up. 'They're up there, you know. I totally believe it – our ancestors are up there.'

He sighed and rubbed out a flicker of melancholy from his face. Archie circled once, twice, then settled in Fraser's lap. Still a little wary of human laps, he immediately took to Fraser's on account of its tobacco-y, pub-like smell – so homely!

'You and me, we've gotta hide, Zigs. Don't wanna get you turfed off. We'll keep low till we're home.'

Sounds good to me. Watch the tail – bit scabby and sore.

'God knows what we'll do when we hit Grangemouth ...'

Is there anything good there?

'Ach, we could hunt round Edinburgh for a flat share. Get some cash off the tourists. My discharge money's unlocked soon, so we'll be able to get a gaff. We'll figure it out, pal.'

You know what, I think we will.

A gust blew over the deck and set a chain clanging resonantly somewhere out of sight. 'I'm more worried about getting you past immigration back in Scotland.'

Ouch, not there!

'Oh, sorry Zigs, you sore?'

Yeah, sore. Sorry, mate, I didn't mean to . . .

'Don't worry, wee man.'

Rest is fine though, just that bit on my neck.

'I know what it's like. The pain makes you into someone you're not.'

And that's when Archie knew. He knew it deep down already in the way Fraser seemed to be able to read his thoughts. The knowledge hit him as an undeniable truth; a Teflon-coated fact of complete and utter certainty: *He's the one. He's my forever human.*

It was difficult to say quite how he knew this with such certainty. They had, after all, known each less than forty-eight hours. Perhaps it was instinct, but Archie just knew they were the human–cat equivalent of one another: they had been through the same hardships; had been forged by the same flames. Sometimes a bond between human and animal grows – that's how it had been with Georgie, Hélène and the fisherman. But in all three cases, the connection was never *quite* perfect. Yet with Fraser, he just knew.

What's more, he knew Fraser would never desert him.

28

Shipmates

THE NEXT DAY ARCHIE AWOKE feeling magnificent. Things felt different and somehow more vibrant. The sea, the utilitarian hulk of the tanker, even the anodyne art on the walls seemed to glitter with colour. Had the right human finally come along who understood him completely? Or had he – Archie – finally reached a point where he'd learned enough about himself to be brave enough to let someone fully in?

The truth was, both had happened, but neither was the reason why Archie knew Fraser would stay. He knew Fraser would stay because they were both on the same *journey*. He, like Fraser, had been on an unplanned mission into his own selfhood; and he, like Fraser, was returning to an uncertain home. Like two passengers unknowingly boarding and disembarking a train at the same stations, they had been quietly in sync. And the best bit was Fraser didn't even know about his supposed 'magic' – the fact he was a clamoured-for, wanted cat. Fraser liked him for the cat he truly was. Both had been quietly learning and repairing, and both had found each other at the perfect time.

Archie had begun to trot in Fraser's direction whenever he glimpsed him approaching. He had *never* been an 'approach trotter' before, preferring instead to park himself on the spot, or, as he deigned to do with Georgie, amble nonchalantly over. Approach trotting was the preserve of house cats. But when Fraser cupped a pork scratching in his hand, there Archie went … trotting over, tail high; a shadow of the cat he had been but two months ago. His past was now only evident on his body – the topography of scars along his flank; the nips out of his ears. Sometimes his old self would catch up with his newer self and he'd find himself momentarily embarrassed. *Ha, I'd never live this down back in Stepney*, he'd think.

If the longing for Georgie had started to wane over the Atlantic, it had now disappeared entirely. When he did think of her, it was with the sweet aftertaste of nostalgia. The pain of her sudden departure that day had dulled, as had the grief at losing the fisherman before it. These were the wonderful humans who had schooled him in himself; had allowed him to sandpaper down the rough edges of his character, bit by bit, while Hélène had taught him to respect the unassailable truths of his animal nature. If he ever did have pangs towards his former crewmates, they expressed themselves as well wishes; wistful nods of good-will: *I hope they're doing well* – or – *It would be nice to see them again* – or – (thinking of Hélène) *I hope she's not being hounded by those media muppets.*

And for the first time in his life, he felt his mind looking forward, not back. With his current existence on the *Phaeacian* affording him comfort, food and a human whom he trusted to stick around, his default setting of lassitude and depression in quiet moments was recalibrating. He stopped churning through injustices and examining each one with fresh bitterness. Looking back, he realised how addictive this thought pattern had been with each grievance triggering in him a rush of rage which served as a chemical reminder that he was still alive. Now he thought of the UK and of Grangemouth – lovely, magical, halcyon Grangemouth – a fabled place (surely?) of sunlit uplands, fat Scottish mice and perfect temperatures; a place where he and Fraser could commune and build a new life. Grangemouth. Grangemouth, over the water from Rosyth. How could they fail to be fantastic places? Listen to that word: Rossss-ythhh.

But Fraser had troubles. Some nights on the *Phaeacian*, he would wake, gasping, in the gloom of their cabin, his fists balled and his tightly sprung frame trembling over relived horror. In these moments, Archie would let Fraser's inarticulate hand fall upon his head in an aggrieved, clumsy stroke. As for the days, they were long and often characterised by routine. Apart from the morning loudspeaker update on weather and progress, which told of changes in time zone, there was precious little to look forward to. The *Phaeacian Enterprise* inched the endless miles east like a giant metal slug, bringing the sunrise a little earlier each day. The steward with the V-shaped hairline hadn't bothered them any more. *Reckon he's clobbered him one*, thought Archie one evening upon spotting grazes on Fraser's knuckles. *Good*, he thought, knowing full well the type the steward was – the same type as the councillor who got him banned from the library for sitting on the warm printer. Archie soon realised that Fraser wasn't as comfortable with the tedium as he himself was: he fell to eating and drinking at odd times, often returning to the cabin with food items in the early hours. Sometimes, he'd pace around the cabin like a lion in a cage, eventually resorting to a fit of press-ups to direct the nervous energy.

Admin, especially, would frustrate him. One afternoon he came back to the cabin with paperwork, still warm under Archie's paws when he padded over. Archie peered at the sheet on top: Application for Rental – Referees and Guarantors. Picking up the page, Fraser paced the room staring at it, loudly clicking and unclicking a pen, until he eventually swore, balling up the paper and chucking it at the wall. 'Guarantors! I have hee-haw guarantors, Zigs. You wanna be my guarantor?'

Don't have a mouse to my name either, replied Archie with a little chirrup.

One afternoon, back in the cabin, Fraser discovered that taking the laces from his boots and trailing them over the floor was a great thirty minutes of entertainment. Sensing Archie's thirst for a greater challenge, he eventually took to running up and down the corridor outside the cabin, letting Archie career after the shoelace in a flurry of paws. *Bugger, lost it again. All this sea has put you behind on your hunting game, old boy,* thought the cat, pretending sometimes not to see the string so he could steal a moment to lick his paws. The little game of chase became something of a habit and during these moments, Fraser would often fall about laughing and would have to sit down. If someone happened to approach, Archie would hear them first and would zip over to the cabin door – Fraser's sign to hide him. Back in the cabin, Archie would box Fraser's charger cable, knock over his pyramid of cards, or take a little trip to the bathroom sink where he'd let the leaky tap release refreshing droplets onto the crown of his head.

Like Archie, Fraser was half night owl. Once the sun had dropped beneath the horizon, the pair would climb the zigzag staircase to the deck, coming to rest on the helipad just in front of the bridge. Fraser would sit on the painted white 'H', looking up at the stars and warbling lines from rock anthems. Both seemed to find comfort in the dark, becoming bolder, more intellectual versions of themselves. They'd then go on a turn of the long foredeck, dwarfed by the great tanks of liquid petroleum gas. Archie walked obediently alongside Fraser – something he'd never done before with any human, unless begging for food.

After a stint of pull-ups on a balustrade, Fraser would crack open a container and the pair would share a midnight feast on the helipad under a floodlit glow. Processed food tasted all the better in the sea air. Some evenings, Fraser's eyes would become haunted, and take on the frightened look they had when Archie first encountered them in Bermuda. He would start to move in his jolty way again, sometimes even rummaging for pills in his washbag. He'd then devour a handful with a gulp of water before standing in front of the bathroom mirror, his hands trembling on the rim of the sink, staring at his reflection. After one such episode, he lifted Archie onto his shoulders, grabbed a pack of cigarettes, and paced back up the stairs to the main deck. Archie knew immediately something was different. Over behind the helipad a steel pipe leaked dark fluid. Fuel. The odour was subtle; too subtle to break Fraser out of his fretful episode. Just as he poised his thumb over his lighter's flint roller, Archie knew – a spark would set the air ablaze. With a gymnastic leap, the cat swiped the lighter from Fraser's hand, launching it over the side rails and into the sea. The randomness of the cat's goofy acrobatics made Fraser fall about laughing.

Gordon Bennett, you bleedin' muppet, we'd have gone up! What's got into you? Look at that sign – twenty-blooming-foot-high letters: 'NO SMOKING.'

All of this came out in a series of growls and scowls, but Fraser seemed to take it on board: 'Good time for me to stop, eh, Zigs!' he said, bursting with laughter. 'That was my only lighter as well.'

*   *   *

Several days later, the shores of England rose off the port bow. It was with some relief as a storm was thrusting slate-grey waves into the vessel's side, sending it into deep lumbering rolls. All the while, the *Phaeacian*'s anchor clanged the tanker's huge side in resounding, bone-shaking clangs. *Flipping heck, are we coming into Traitor's Gate, or what?* thought Archie who, despite not feeling sick, felt deeply uncomfortable. Unable to sleep, he lifted himself up to the cabin window and peeked out. It was dusk. Rain lashed at the porthole as Archie spotted the first flickering lights of his native land. Lightening speared through the air, momentarily illuminating the peninsulas of Cornwall in stunning white light. They loomed eerily – half-real tongues of land stretching out into a black sea. *Oh, Blighty,* thought Archie. With each bolt of lightning, the land revealed a little more of itself. Now he could see a lighthouse and the sea pounding its banded side, and the long brave sweep of Cornwall disappearing into blackness. Through tiny cracks in the window frame, he felt a cold draught. A cold, wet English draught. He shivered, fluffing up his coat and surveying the scene wistfully. The next day, viewing from a window at the corridor, he and Fraser watched the waves sending their massive towers of spray over the deck. There was a unique smell – a sort of mossy damp aroma. *Why is that smell so damn good?* It was the smell of land all right, much like that he had smelled on the approach to the Caribbean. But rather than undertones of exotic fruit, there was a peaty iron-rich freshness to it.

'C'mon, Zigs, let's get breakfast,' said Fraser. 'Just wait till you see Scotland on Tuesday.'

29

Scotland

'AW THIS IS IT, MAN, YA DANCER! Now we're talking!' The wind blew Archie's fur in ripples. He sat on the edge of the deck, gallantly upright, his forepaws a pair of perpendicular stone pillars. His coat had thickened over the last week and his ankles had regained their shire-horse bushiness. The sea was bluish-grey, now, almost the colour of his coat. It ruched up into angry white horses and slapped the tanker's sides in angry cracks. They were sailing up an estuary with land on both sides, a couple of miles off. In front of them, a long island sat glumly in the water like a crocodile, while above a plane banked into a final approach, its jet fumes streaking blue-grey against the white sky. Off the starboard side, mountains rose in the distance like a crumpled duvet, while in the foreground a double-humped hill protruded from the heart of a scattered city. Everything about the land seemed prehistoric, reptilian; its colours were dull but its contours were jagged and powerful. Archie couldn't help but feel slightly unnerved in its presence.

'This is it, Zigs,' said Fraser, breathing in through his nose, eyes closed. 'This is Scotland.'

He held out his arms in a cup motion. Archie took the signal and leaped into them, and then onto Fraser's shoulders – a trick they had perfected during the weeks of transatlantic tedium. 'Look at that. Well hello, Edinburgh. That's Arthur's Seat there, Zigs. And here's Porty, where we'll be staying with Davy while we find our feet. And that there is Inchcolm Island! Did you know, Zigs, they disguised that as a ship in World War II to confuse the Nazis? Bombed it to smithereens they did and not a sausage died. What do you think?'

Is it up here where the geezers wear skirts? Archie wondered, extending his claws into Fraser's shoulders as he began jigging in a little dance. *The grub's decent, though . . . I've had one of those pies with what-do-you-call-it in them. Bet the hunting's good. There ain't lynx in those hills, are there?*

'And there are wild cats up here, Zigs.'

Oh bugger . . .

'They'll give you a run for your money. Only a few left, though, mind.'

With a chuff, the engines beneath them spooled down. The newfound silence after weeks of droning was blissful. Through the settled air came the squawks of seagulls, tailgating the wake of a fishing boat which trundled alongside. Fraser lifted Archie to his shoulders as he leaned forward on the guard rail and hollered overboard.

'Ahoy there, sailor!'

The fisherman didn't hear. Fraser called again, cupping a hand round his mouth.

'Ahhhoy sailor! I'm comin' home fae war!'

'What?' yelled back the fisherman.

'I'm coming home fae war, mate. Fighting, so you can fish free!'

'Ah top work, ma man!' cried back the fisherman in his yellow oilskin jacket. 'How's it been?'

'Utter gaaaash!' yelled back Fraser. 'Where ye fae?'

'Pittenweem!' yelled back the fisherman.

'Send my love to Anstruther!' said Fraser.

'Anstruther can get tae!' yelled back the fisherman.

Fraser doubled over in laughter causing Archie to extend his claws around his shoulders to secure himself. It was a type of laugh Archie hadn't heard him do, and it felt joyous to feel it taking hold.

'Is that a cat?' called back the fisherman.

'Aye, ma mascot. I got myself a ship's cat.'

'Good on yerself, pal. Take care, eh!'

'You too, ma man, you too!'

They passed between strips of island covered in ruins and under a spectacular bridge formed in a series of red diamonds. Archie craned his neck up as it glided by overhead. *Knocks the socks off Tower Bridge, this does, blimey.* A train clamoured onto the far end in a deafening drumbeat of metal on metal. Archie eyed the livery as it passed through the cantilevers: *ScotRail.* Fraser turned on the spot, grinning. *Coming home's definitely unlocking something in him,* thought Archie, following the push and pull of new emotions upon his face. Suddenly, he felt a pang of worry: *He wouldn't leave me, would he? He ain't going to find a bird and gallivant off into the sunset?*

An announcement blared over the deck: 'Attention crew: approaching Grangemouth. Mooring teams, report to stations. Engine room, stand by for pilot on channel 71. Bridge out.'

Fraser scooped up Archie with a tickle behind the ears and carried him back to the cabin where he purred on the bed as Fraser emptied the wardrobe of his meagre belongings. He only had two sets of trousers and khaki shorts, and a handful of T-shirts. He packed his canvas wallet and passport into a little side pocket of his rucksack, and folded his clothes into sausage-like rolls meticulously. *He must have more than this surely*, thought Archie, kneading a cable-knit jumper, his eyes slow-blinking contentedly. *The army must be sending it back.*

A set of giraffe-like cranes sidled into view. Soon there was a gentle thud followed by the thrumming of hydraulics; the creak of a rope under strain.

'Now, Zigs, Edinburgh's busy. Going to be okay on my shoulders, yes? I don't want you on a lead like those numpty cat walkers. But we got bigger fish to fry, pal. How am I going to get you off and past customs without those fannies confiscating you? Reckon you can get in the rucksack and keep schtum for twenty minutes or so?

Mum's the word. I'll button it.

'I'll sacrifice my Iron Maiden T-shirt for you, Zigs. That's love.'

He turned the bag on its side. Archie sniffed the opening and pawed his way inside.

Gently, Fraser pivoted the rucksack upright, tugging the drawstrings. The muffled voices and joggles of clandestine transit were all too familiar for Archie, and his method, on this occasion as with all others, was to shut off the mind. *And kip right through it*, he thought as he felt Fraser climb the familiar zigzag stairs.

* * *

'Welcome aboard this ScotRail service to Edinburgh Waverley.'

The voice sharpened itself on Archie's ears. He opened his eyes. Beyond the graffiti-etched window was a blurry vision of countryside. Fields, streams . . . bits of stone wall. His head was poking out of the rucksack's drawstring mouth. Above him, Fraser's eyes took in the racing landscape. There was still fear there, but anticipation too. And hope.

'You all right in there, wee man? You're not too hot?'

Ain't going to lie, pal, I'm getting pins and needles down below.

'Edinburgh's not far, then it's a stroll to Portobello. That'll cool you off. Here, I've got some food for us.'

He lifted Archie out of the bag with two hands cupped carefully, one in front of the other. Archie birthed from the bag, like a butterfly from a chrysalis. He felt himself being lowered onto Fraser's lap as his legs prickled with the rejuvenating on-rush of blood.

'Here.' Fraser poured milk from a carton into an empty plastic tray that had held mini sausages. 'It'll wet your whistle, that. Got some pepperoni too.'

Oh my God, diamond geezer! I'm back in the land of Peperamis, yes. Archie lapped at the milk, tinged with sausage remnants. This was the type of culinary experience he was used to – fusion food, flavours overlapping as things mixed in tins and polystyrene tubs behind East London eateries. The very *best* culinary experience. Archie chomped and supped between little grunts.

How does he know? How does he know that this is what I like?

They were in a quiet part of the train, down where the carriages connected and swayed against each other. Archie wondered whether Fraser had chosen the spot so he could talk to Archie and not feel judged by other humans.

He raised his forepaws up to the window. Steadily his pupils tracked the racing fields, the pylons … the odd blue sign of a motorway. *It's definitely the UK, that's for sure*, he thought. Above, the clouds had split following a recent downpour and sunlight was pooling on the damp rooftops of houses. Their slates glistened like the scales of fish. In that ineffable feline way, Archie could sense the calm inhabit Fraser: the *thump-thump-thump* of his heart coming through his nylon T-shirt had a softer insistence than it had before. His legs were relaxed, rather than juddering, and he whistled gently through his teeth.

After several minutes, the train slowed to a gentle clank and nosed through a series of tunnels. Archie pushed his whiskers to the glass. Suddenly a great rock towered up to their right with impressive majesty. And Archie, the little grey London stray, who had travelled half the world in the last few months, settled his lemon-yellow eyes on Edinburgh Castle for the first time ever.

The train stopped, its doors beeping open. Fraser rose, holding Archie under his arm like a rugby ball. Stepping off the train, he lowered him to the ground, letting Archie make paw contact with Scotland for the first time.

'Daddy look, pussycat!' A little boy pointed, hand in hand with his dad.

Oh Christ, not kids, please.

'Ha, so it is,' said the dad. 'Ask the man if you can have a stroke.'

Fraser grinned but drew Archie up again. 'Ahh I wouldn't, mate,' he said. 'He's a bit swipy, wouldn't want the wee man to get a cut.'

'Is he grumpy?' said the boy to Fraser.

'Aye, aye, you could say that, wee man!' said Fraser.

'Grumpy, grumpy, grumpy and lumpy,' chanted the little boy as his dad guided him away.

They headed into a ticket hall, Archie back atop Fraser's shoulders, and up an escalator and set of steps. Fraser strode with the confidence of someone who knew the streets. Sometimes he stopped, his eye lingering on something, before resuming his walk in that sharp, jerky way of his. Archie took in people's varying responses with disdain: some gave a furtive side-eye, smiling out the corner of their mouths; others took out their earphones as if about to say something, before thinking twice as Archie's nose corrugated in a hiss. Some took photos or even engaged Fraser in conversation.

'Aye I've adopted him. What's that? Handsome? Oh he is that, aye!' … 'The collar? You know what, I don't know.' … 'Hard life? Och aye, he has, I ken the feeling!' … 'Oh *no no* don't touch, he might skelp you. Sorry.'

This little spiel was repeated some seven or eight times on their walk to the neighbouring seaside suburb of Portobello, Fraser never seeming to get bored with the retelling. Something about Archie seemed to bring the grin back to his face at just the moment when melancholy started to set in around his features. It struck Archie as a kind, friendly thing to do; an acceptance of people's inquisitiveness while also keeping a distance and a brevity that meant he – Archie – wouldn't feel uncomfortable.

In quieter moments, Archie took in the tenement buildings, which seemed to eye each other ominously either side of the wide streets. Other times, he'd just look down at the crown of Fraser's head where his auburn hair flicked and tossed in the breeze. *I hope he takes care of himself now he's back home*, Archie thought. *And I hope this 'Davy' feller of Portobello has laid on a war hero's welcome.* At one point a drunkard staggered towards them and groped for Archie. The change in Fraser was frightening. Instantly, he yelled '*Oi, get back!*' pushing the man by the chest against the metal shutters of a shop. 'Fanny,' he muttered as he walked away, leaving the drunk bewildered and mumbling something by way of apology. It was a frightening interaction, but only served to strengthen what Archie already knew about the man – they were of the same character, both treading wide-eyed out of a long darkness into a new world.

30

We're Not at Sea
Any More . . .

'DAVY!'
Fraser cupped his hand round his mouth and yelled up the side of the sandstone tenement. Fat droplets of rain fell on Archie's coat, making the hairs on his back twitch.

'Eh Davy, you in there, my man?'

No reply. In the distance, the whir of a train at speed and the drone of traffic.

'Davy, man, it's Fraser? Open the door, pal.'

Archie inched over to some grass in an adjacent front garden and sniffed the shrubs. The walk from Edinburgh Waverley station to Portobello had been long – well over an hour. Fraser had clearly wanted to stretch his legs after weeks at sea, but between joggling on his shoulders, and joggling in his rucksack, Archie felt well and truly joggled out. So it was with some relief when Fraser eventually lowered him onto a piece of gum-freckled pavement where he could sniff out the local feline clientele. *God the tomcats up here mean business*, he thought a little on getting a whiff of cat urine from the base of a rhododendron. And now for the dogs. He followed his nose back out to the pavement and to a dandelion at the bottom of a lamp post. *Hmm, the mutts are bolshy as hell up here, too. There's a terrier who lives nearby who likes a scrap. And I'm getting . . . a couple of dachshunds come through. And a beagle. But nothing bigger than a Labrador.* Archie sank his eyelids in a slow blink of mild relief. *Pah! Child's play. I can handle those little yappers, no bother.*

'Davy, open up, man, I'm freezing my balls off.'

Fraser had taken to throwing fistfuls of gravel up to a window on the tenement where a pair of yellowing curtains hung, half closed.

'M-row?' Archie enquired sidling against Fraser's bare ankle.

'I know, Zigs, I know, I'll get us in soon. Davy, *open up*, mate!'

A moment later, the communal front door opened. A middle-aged woman emerged, clutching an Aldi bag. Fraser bolted to the door and placed his foot in the gap before it shut.

The lady turned and eyed him suspiciously. 'You better not be going in there to shoot up?'

'What? Shoot up?' barked Fraser.

He jutted his jaw – a typical response that often accompanied a flash of anger in his eyes. *Oh here we go, it's going to kick off . . .* thought Archie parking his behind next to the dandelion.

'I'll give you "shooting up",' said Fraser.

The woman stopped in her tracks and clutched her empty Aldi bag towards her protectively. Fraser kept his hand on the door and went to head in, but in that typical way of his, turned back to add an addendum to the confrontational outburst.

'I suppose it's because of what I'm wearing, right? Because of how I look and speak? Is that it?' The woman walked away shaking her head. 'Because I'm just back from war, you know. I've been fighting and dodging bullets so you can ponce off to Aldi for your tea. It's not me you need to jibe at, hen. So stop looking down that wee nose of yours.'

'All right, I'm sorry, I'm sorry,' said the woman. 'It's just we get a lot of trouble in the—'

'Right, apology accepted,' replied Fraser. 'Here, Zigs, *wsssht.*'

They entered the hallway. Ahead, the stairwell was dark, save for one bulb which flickered out of sight. Paint flecked off the walls. Oddly, it reminded Archie not of the East End but of the Victorian theatres of London's West End and their sprawling rabbit warren of backstage passages and stairwells. He had strayed to Shaftesbury Avenue a couple of times, once even begging at the stage door behind the theatre hosting Andrew Lloyd Webber's *Cats*. Lured by the battered cod proffered by the stage-door keeper, he had sneaked past when the keeper's back was turned, eventually finding himself *on stage* for the final dance number of *Cats* – an irony which, unfortunately, was lost on him owing to the terrifying din of laughter coming from the audience.

It feels like I'm backstage, he thought again. *But with more bikes knocking about, and a smell of wee.*

They reached a flat with the number four written on the wall next to it in felt tip pen. Fraser pummelled on the door.

'Davy, what's going on man? I ken you're in there, the light's on, you bampot. Are you all right my man?'

A jangling of locks. The door swung back to reveal a man with dull, unfocused eyes. 'Awwww, Frasey maaaan,' he said nasally, with an uncoordinated raise of his arms. 'Sorry, man, was pure coming down off a big one.'

'For crying out loud Davy, man,' said Fraser, pushing his way in with Archie trotting after, giving Davy's flip-flopped feet a wide berth. 'Thought you were gonna give the gear a rest. What happened to Edinburgh College?'

They entered a large front room, thick with the smell of damp and marijuana. Tins and cigarette cartons lay strewn over the carpet, which was scarred with cigarette burns. A single mattress squatted in one corner under a plain duvet tinged with yellow nicotine; a pillow without a case. Behind the half-closed curtains a fly beat frantically against the panes.

'To hell with the fannies at Edinburgh College, man,' said Davy, his jaw drawn in a dopy grin. He was a tall man with a beard and he didn't so much stand as loll on the spot, like a sunflower in a heavy wind. His arms were spotted with various cuts and a stained singlet clung to his chest in a skim of sweat.

Archie lumbered over to the window with a growling mew, looking at the light beyond and eyeing up the restless fly. *Don't like this gaff,* he thought, a faint panic bubbling in his chest.

On hearing the mew, Davy's head turned stupidly, like a marionette doll's.

'Haw! Haw! Lookie there, a pussycat in here.' He gave another of his ridiculous laughs, not looking at Fraser, who slid his back down the wall, his head in his hands.

He's a ha'penny short of a shilling, this bloke, thought Archie. Davy lumbered forward and Archie spiked up in an arch.

'Davy, man, leave him,' said Fraser, lighting up a cigarette and pinching it between finger and thumb. 'You said I could stay here till my stuff gets back and the pay-off's come through?'

'You can stay here, man, you can!' retorted Davy. His eyes were glazed over and had to scan the room to find Fraser's afresh each time he spoke. 'So what would GI Joe like for tea, eh?' he said. 'His first meal back from war. You gone native, eating all that foreign pish?'

'Don't be an arse, Davy.'

'I'm no being an arse! I got . . . Cheerios?'

'Aye. Sure, Cheerios,' replied Fraser flatly.

'Say please,' implored Davy, enacting a theatrical curtsy.

'I'll have some Cheerios, please, Davy. You're not going to go lording it over me, now, are you?'

Davy padded across the hall to the kitchen cackling with another inane laugh.

'Honestly, mate, look at the state of you,' Fraser shouted after him. 'What you done to yourself? Thought you'd given up the gear. You said you weren't going back to those days.'

'Aye and then . . .' Davy turned, making a swaying attempt at jazz hands. 'Life! Life brought me back to Harry's loving embrace.' He paused and for the first time, spying him from the living room window with his long-focused pupils, Archie saw a serious look come over his face. 'But I'm going to clean up, man. This is just . . . temporary.'

'Your dad still own the flat?'

'Aye.'

'Unbelievable,' said Fraser under his breath. He flattened out his legs so Archie could jump onto his lap.

'Aye, I'm cleaning up, man, I said,' whined Davy from the kitchen. 'And don't go getting on your big high horse, GI. You're back from war – ken how many of the jakeys on the bridges and Princes Street are ex-army skagheads? Dozens, man, dozens. Remember wee mad Kaden who joined us in P4?'

'Aye?'

'A total goner, man. Came back from war last year.'

A sentience seemed to be coming over Davy. He opened a high cupboard and took down a bowl from a mismatched pile of crockery.

'Got his pay-out, paid off his debts. Couldn't get a reference, couldn't get work, couldn't fix his nut and retrain. So he hit up the skag. You got a flat?'

'No,' said Fraser sheepishly. 'Tried on the boat back but I don't have a reference either.'

'Haw! well there you go … ' said Davy, shaking the Cheerios into the bowl.

'There's no way I'm getting into that pish, Davy. I'll stack shelves, I'll go and clean—'

'Stack shelves, aye? Ken how many people want to stack shelves? Ken how hard those jobs are to get?'

'Aye well don't *you* worry about *me*, man. You just sort yourself out.'

'Kitty gonnae see you through is he … ?'

'Actually,' said Fraser, a lilt coming to his voice, 'this wee man's been the best thing that's happened to me. He's my wee ship's cat, Zigs … '

'Haw haw, "Ship's Cat Zigs". Frasey's gone soft!'

'No, seriously,' insisted Fraser, taking the bowl of Cheerios from Davy as the milk slopped over its side. 'This wee dude

and I have an understanding. He's been through it as well,
look how rough he looks. His scarry face and bony back . . .'

*Oh go the whole hog why don't ya and mention my nipped-
out ears.*

'. . . and nipped ears.'

Brilliant.

'Well at least you're not preaching the gospel to me, man,'
said Davy, squatting down on the carpet.

'I reckon he has just as many stories as me. And what's
more,' said Fraser, stroking Archie's back and sending wispy
hairs floating into the air, 'he brings good luck, I swear it.'

'Haw. Well, if you say so,' murmured Davy.

'He does,' said Fraser, gazing into Archie's eyes, the
moment the little cat's brain was struck with the thought:
but we're not at sea any more.

31

Portobello Beach

A STUBBORN RAY OF SUN FILTERED through the filthy windows of Davy's Portobello flat, coming to rest on a threadbare spot of carpet.

Like Davy, Fraser and Archie had slept on a single mattress on the floor. In the top corner of the spare room, a blot of purple mould bloomed down the wall. As well as the mildewy odour, there was a vinegary smell and a mustardy tang; but beyond this was something only Archie's nose could pick up: the legacy of many other human scent signatures having formerly occupied the space.

Archie looked at Fraser's sleeping face. *The fisherman was poor,* he thought. *And he got by. You just have to graft. Things will work out for us . . . surely?*

Fraser coughed, rolled over. Hopeful for his awakening, Archie padded over and sniffed his chest. It smelled unwashed; old sweat, the type that had clung to the skin for a few days. He was unshaven and actually appeared physically worse than when Archie had first met him in the Portakabin in Bermuda. His eyes had a hollow look, somehow giving their naturally scared appearance an added edge of desperation. Awakening, he automatically leaned over the side of the mattress to grab his phone and stare at it.

Oh fine, ignore me then! thought Archie. *I'll just sit here, shall I?*

Several days had passed since they arrived at Davy's flat and Archie had watched, with growing unease, as Fraser retreated more and more into himself. The optimism he'd felt when arriving back in Edinburgh was being slowly replaced with a creeping apathy. He fell into long spells of just sitting with his back against the half-peeling wallpaper and, quite simply, *staring*. What he was looking at, and what he was thinking, Archie couldn't determine, but there definitely seemed to be something on his mind. *Don't go too far down this boulevard*, thought Archie. *'Cause I won't be able to help you out again.* He started to anger more easily: the red flash would come to his eyes, on a daily basis now, sometimes hourly, when Davy said or did something particularly inane. He never lashed out, but Archie knew it was coming.

But more worryingly, his behaviour towards Archie was changing too. When Archie mewed at the door to the flat to go outside, Fraser would tread somewhat begrudgingly, turning the door latch, and slamming it the second Archie's tail had cleared the frame. Once he even punched the floor when Archie mewled hungrily, uttering an 'argh!' as he padded out to the hallway to squeeze out a sachet of food into a dirty bowl for Archie to eat. All in all, it made the little cat feel miserable.

At night, when Fraser slept, he tossed and turned incessantly in bed. Archie had noticed bedbugs; clearly, these were beleaguering the mattress and causing Fraser huge discomfort. A little bald spot had even appeared on Archie's leg which itself was becoming maddeningly irritating. Along with the pinch of hunger in Fraser's eyes, his frame became stooped, his mouth grimacing when he moved. His breath turned foul, his clothes remained dirty and unwashed. *He's becoming a stray again*, Archie thought. He could see the deadly beckon of a life of idleness, and his human slipping into it. But what alarmed him most was that, on this particular morning, when the sun caught the twisting dust, Fraser behaved like Archie wasn't even there.

Archie stared and cried a long doleful mew. *Nah, nah, we can't go on like this mate.* Puzzled and sad, he pushed his little muzzle against Fraser's cheek. But the man just recoiled, squinting at the skim of fur against his eyes, irritated that the view to his phone was blocked. Archie mewed louder as Fraser's eyes sank (*come ON mate, don't go there, come back to me!*), as his furry body flinched with the crash of scaffolding poles being thrown somewhere outside.

Archie meowed again, this time in a mournful wail.

Nothing.

Eventually, Fraser's eyes swivelled to meet Archie's. He exhaled, and kicked his heel down on the floor. 'All right. God's sake.'

Oh! don't get humpy with me! replied Archie in a bassy growl. *We had an agreement you and me, remember? I'm your lucky ship's cat. I gave you hope! Don't go bailing now, this country's too bleedin' cold for me to go it alone.*

Fraser pulled on his jumper with a grimace.

Oh! And don't give me that look or I'll give you what for!

For the second time, a little crack ran down the wrought-iron certainty that he and Fraser would remain together forever. *You wouldn't, you just wouldn't.* His tail sank and spiked as Fraser shoved his wallet into his back pocket and skulked to the front door. He opened it and Archie darted ahead down the dingy stairwell.

Outside, on the street, Fraser would typically sit on a bench on a spot of pavement near the flat and smoke relentlessly – a habit which had returned with a vengeance since moving in with Davy. Sometimes, he would disappear for a bit as Archie sniffed out a rodent under the foliage (*maybe if I catch him a mouse it'll sort things out between us?*) and would return with a fresh packet of cigarettes and a coffee in a takeaway cup. Today, Archie actually did find a mouse – promptly after they emerged from the communal front door. He plopped it at Fraser's feet – in a well-known feline gesture of reconciliation, causing Fraser to lower his fag and offer up the tenderest comment he'd issued in days: 'Oh so you *can* dispatch as well as catch. Nice work, Zigs!'

Buoyed by the exchange, Archie was struck with a thought. *The sea. I've just got to get us to sea. Good things happen when I'm at sea. It'll fix things.*

Archie hadn't visited the sea during his time in Portobello, but his nose told him it was nearby. A chill breeze crept over the rooftops of the adjacent houses laden with the odours of foetid seaweed and wet sand. He trotted away from Fraser to a set of traffic lights at the end of the street, his nose being pulled by the sea's salty aroma. At the lights, he turned back and mewed loudly. Eventually Fraser rose, tossing his cigarette into the undergrowth, and ambled over to Archie, who immediately sprinted over the next street. His coat had already thickened in the short time he'd been living in Scotland and now the air had the faint chilliness of autumn to it. As a result he looked big and bulky with a full face and a more feather duster tail.

Now on the other side of the street he paused. A knot clenched in his stomach. *What if I look back and he hasn't followed?* But Fraser was still following Archie while peering at his phone. 'I'm just nipping in here, Zigs,' he piped up, swinging into a convenience store. Sitting next to the *Edinburgh Evening News* A-frame, the little cat's mind began to twist with unwelcome thoughts. *Check his mug when he comes out. Check to see if he's disappointed you're still here. You watch. He'll be disappointed. He wants rid of you now he's home. He wants you to do the decent thing and take yourself off onto the streets, he just can't admit it to himself. Course he does, you useless ball of fat. You've had your time, and you've done your bit, just like you did for the rest of them.*

The chill air blew through his fur, nipping at the skin beneath. *Leave. Do the decent thing, Archie, and go. Get out of his life. You'll be doing him a favour. You know it's the truth.*

But it's not the truth! Archie heard himself inwardly crying back. *He needs me. He needs help.*

Fraser emerged from the shop doorway, a fresh cigarette pinched between his lips. He caught Archie's eye, and to his relief Archie spied the faintest of grins. *Phew. OKAY.* He rubbed into Fraser's bony leg. *It's the fags he's happy about, let's be honest. But we can work with that. Now c'mon follow me. The SEA!*

They headed down a tightly packed street of terraced houses with handsome frontages, some with lavender spilling out onto the pavement, some sporting huge pompoms of hydrangea flowers. Archie marched purposefully with only the occasional glance back. Arriving at the promenade, Fraser leaped athletically over the sea wall, Archie joining, and the pair trod onto the sand's silky resistance. Down at the water-line seaweed tendrils knitted together the rocks in their vibrant olive-green, like synapses in a brain. Fraser knelt and sunk his finger into the sand and lifted a disorientated crab scuttling up the beach. He lowered it into a rock pool, watching closely as it sank into the limpid waters. Suddenly Archie thought of how the fisherman had done the same thing, way back all those weeks ago.

'Feels good doesn't it, Zigs, being by the water,' said Fraser. *Damn right it does,* gestured Archie, knocking his head into Fraser's palm. The cat thought and thought and thought, willing his thoughts into the air, into the noise of the sea, into the squawk of the birds, and into Fraser's brain: *Please don't throw it all away. We owe it to each other. You've changed me, mate! Before you I was ruddy lost. I've always been lost. I stuck with you because I saw myself in you and thought you were my one proper chance at love. C'mon, mate, we're better as a pair.* He knocked Fraser's head again, craning his neck up his arm in a desperate bid at mute linguistic expression.

'I know, Zigs,' said Fraser.

Phew. Even though Archie's voice was locked in his own head, he sensed at least *something* had come across. He had a flash of hope. They walked a little further along the waterline as Archie watched the damp sand cling to his tufty shire-horse ankles. For a second, it felt like he was gliding sideways as the sea drew back across the smooth sand.

A buzz from Fraser's phone. He unzipped the pocket of his combat shorts.

'Hello? Yes … ? No way, Callum! Calzo, my man, how's it all going?'

Archie rotated an ear.

'I know, man, I know. I saw "international call" and I thought, no way, it cannae be the squad.' Fraser kicked through the sand. 'You using the sat phone? Aye. How's things there?'

A long spiel on the other end of the line. Fraser's eyes flickered as the voice fed through his ear. Gradually his smile faded.

'Aaah no, I appreciate you checking in, man, I really do I, I—'

The caller interjected, cutting him off.

'Ahhhhh no. I have to say I skipped the psych assessments, man. I've just been getting back into things, you know? Chilling, kicking back. Davy? Aye, he's … well he's Davy, you know. I'm staying at his house in Portobello. On the beach right now in fact, I mean how bad can life be, eh?'

Archie swiped at a little minnow in a rock pool, keeping his ear on the conversation.

'Listen, Calzo, listen I appreciate your concern, I really do mate, but—' The caller interjected again, prompting Fraser to clench his teeth. 'Of course I'm not! Why would I get into that shite? No, no, Calz, I'll deal with things my own way.'

Archie jumped as Fraser's voice turned aggressive.

'Oi, you fanny! I'll do what I like, don't you threaten me, man! Bet Sarge put you up to this? Why, what did he say? *"Oh give Drummond a bell, see if he's topped himself yet? Make sure he's taking his meds?"* Sod yous, man, sod the lot of yous.' Fraser swiped an arm through the air. 'What? No I have'nae found any accommodation. Everywhere wants a reference, and I'm on the waiting list for the veteran flats. What am I gonna do with a place to myself anyhow. Share a flat with the posh fannies up in Marchmont? Ach, get tae! There's twenty applications for every flat in Edinburgh anyway. Just leave me alone.'

Archie mewed. Fraser caught Archie's eye. His tone turned a little softer.

'Aye, I was alright on the trip home, because … ' He looked down at Archie again. 'Aye, it was different at sea. Listen, Callum, no offence, but you're chatting at me like a patronising bastard. I'll sort my head out my own way. Leave me alone. Tell Sarge he can tick his daft box.'

Fraser hung up, spitting over his shoulder and digging his heels into the sand. On the *Phaeacian Enterprise*, he'd distract himself with bursts of exercise – press-ups or squats – but here he reached again for another fag out of his pocket, clicking it alight and sucking on the smoke with a decisive air and shake of the head.

Archie drooped his head forlornly. Then suddenly, as if caught by an external force, Fraser straightened up. He plucked the cigarette from his mouth, rubbing it out against a rock.

'Right,' he said, rolling his shoulders back.

He scooped Archie up and headed towards the promenade, tickling just the right spot under the cat's ear.

'I'll sort my own head out, cat. You'll see.'

Archie nuzzled closer, burrowing into Fraser's jacket.

I know you will.

32

Alcinous

'I was just giving him a nudge with the side of my foot.'

Davy's sunken eyes did an unfocussed scan of the kitchen. Pots smeared with dried sauce towered in a dubious pile from the sink, while yet another thrashing bluebottle filled in the silence between voices.

'You kicked him,' said Fraser. He seemed uncharacteristically calm. 'I heard him scream in pain. Fuck you, Davy.'

'Naw, Fraser, man, I didnae,' said Davy with a limp wave of his hand. 'He's just a street cat man, chill out.'

'See ya, Davy. Skag yourself to death, I don't care. You know what, I nearly felt sorry for you back then. I was going to try and get you sorted out. But I've no time for bastards who're cruel to animals.'

'Come on, man!' said Davy, scratching insipidly at his beard.

Fraser turned to the hall, slung his rucksack over his back, and scooped Archie up with a hand under the belly in one crisp movement. He slammed the door behind him, setting the letterbox clattering through the dark stairwell. *Honestly, never a ruddy dull moment, is there?* thought Archie. He licked the edge of his forepaw where his polydactyl thumb had caught the edge of Davy's swinging foot. As Fraser descended, Archie shimmied up his arm, positioning himself atop his rucksack like a sentinel looking out from a fortress.

They headed into the melee of Portobello High Street. Here and there, Fraser stopped to let a passer-by admire Archie, which he allowed, his mood made affable by their untimely departure from Chez Davy. They waited at a bus stop, alone. Seed pods littered the pavement and dandruffed the grass on the front lawns of houses. *What now?* Archie thought, watching them eddy in circles. *What on earth now?*

They boarded the bus and headed up to the back seats of the top deck. Archie's eyes flicked over the roofs of stone houses as the bus trundled its way nearer to the double-humped hill he had first spied from the *Phaeacian Enterprise*. Approaching its humongous gorse-covered haunches, Archie thought how different this city was from his native East London, where the Thames wound flatly past the grey docks of East India Quay. *Gawd knows how the alley cats survive winters up here,* he thought. He had seen so few cats prowling the streets compared to Rhodes and Antigua, and even East London.

They passed along the wide street, a big clock crowning the corner, and down past a row of ancient buildings rearing up on a hill near the castle. *Where the devil are we going?* he wondered, reading the underside of Fraser's chin and Adam's apple for clues. Sometimes Archie got a tickle behind the ear, but beyond that, Fraser's face was vacant, his eyes staring forward in their customary slightly frightened way. Every noise seemed to send a little current through his body, which made Archie uneasy: the parp of car horns, the lumber of the bus through a pothole, and even the *ding!* of the bus's stop bell. At one point Fraser actually leaped from his seat when another passenger's umbrella struck the floor. Soon, Archie could smell the tension – the familiar cocktail of adrenaline, cortisol, and mammalian sweat. He knew he was panicking.

It's all right, mate, Archie insisted, intercepting Fraser's hand with his soft head wherever its bony fingers started to tap. But as they neared the end of the valley-lined street, Fraser was attracting looks – his phone was *tap-tap-tapping* against the seat in front and every few seconds he'd fill his cheeks and blow out a noisy puff of air. A lady got up and walked downstairs, giving him a nervous look as she disappeared down the stairwell. A young man looked over his shoulder; crammed his earbuds in deeper. *It's as if they think they're going to catch his nerves,* Archie thought. He circled on Fraser's lap, enjoying the musty smell of his human's unwashed clothes. Suddenly, whimpers started to creep out of the corner of Fraser's mouth. Archie gazed up and saw tears forming in his eyes. Every sound, every jolt and cough was now sending him trembling. He was splitting between two worlds – his body painfully rigged to the present; his mind reliving the past.

Archie purred. He had now learned how to muster the sound at will. As the rumble took hold, he sank his side into Fraser's belly until he felt his hand run down his bony vertebrae in faltering strokes. It felt tender where the bedbugs had sampled his own blood throughout the month-long sojourn at Davy's flat.

And so the pair of them sat at the back of the bus; oozing their oddness, a pair of misfits, their inconvenient social presence like a malignancy.

We need to get off this and double-lively, thought Archie, feeling no improvement in the situation. He jumped down and careened forward along the steps to the lower deck, making people leap with shock. Dejectedly, Fraser lifted himself from his seat and robotically walked after him.

Outside the pavement was busy. Archie sought refuge in the alcove of a doorway. *Stick with me, pal, come on.* He watched Fraser step off the bus but lost him momentarily among the blur of passing pedestrians – his walk seemed dazed, like he was following Archie, but had forgotten why, and who he even was. Eventually, he joined Archie, who trotted down a busy road called Earl Grey Street before taking a quiet side road to the right where an empty bench sat beside the concertina doors of a fire station.

Sitting on the bench, in newfound privacy, Fraser broke down. Archie watched on, frightened, as his master's face crumpled and contorted with wet, sniffling whimpers.

'I just . . . I just . . .' Fraser locked his bloodshot eyes with Archie's. 'I just cannae go on, wee man.'

Listen, mate, LOOK AT ME. Listen to me, right. You absolutely, absolutely can go on.

Archie placed two paws on Fraser's chest and moved his face right into Fraser's until his whiskers tickled his cheeks and the young man giggled between sobs.

You and me, right, we're survivors. We don't give up. I may have fluff and four legs and be half magic or whatnot, and you may have two legs and skin, but we're basically cut from the same cloth. So we're going to survive, together, okay? I didn't

*bring you all the way back from war for you to give up and . . .
Oh hello . . . hello, hello . . . What's that smell?*

Archie's nostrils flared. Turning away from Fraser, he walked along the bench letting his polydactyl toes grip around its black lacquered bars. He raised his forelegs onto the curled metal handle and breathed the air deeply. He detected an aroma he had not smelled in many months – a strange mixture of urban pungency and – *what would you call that? – damp grass? I'm getting the whiff of rotting stuff, but* [sniff-sniff-sniff] *in a good way. Rotting . . . bread is that? And ducks, lots of* [sniff-sniff-sniff] *ducks. No hang on, that's weed that is. Damp, pongy weed. Water which ain't moving much. Damp as a frog's armpit. Damp wood, diesel smoke. Maybe a hint of rat there?*

Canal! Archie meowed the revelation into Fraser's ear. He had stopped crying, his mind diverted, as was often the way, by Archie's goofy antics. *It's just a tiny bit further, mate. Really close. There's a canal. Let's go have a gander – we're at our best on water remember!*

Fraser rose and followed Archie's lead and after just a few minutes' walk, they had passed down an alleyway and were standing on the banks of the canal. A mallard, asleep under its wing, unfurled and waddled away at Archie's approach. Fraser gazed up the canal's length, wiping his eyes. 'You do like water don't you, Zigs?' he said, with a phlegmy croakiness.

A little coffee stall stood nearby and beside it a trailer selling hot dogs. Archie snaked his tail through the air in a manner Fraser had quickly learned meant, *'I ain't half peckish.'* Shoving his hand down the pocket of his cargo shorts, he jingled up some coins and bought a coffee and a hot dog for him and Archie to share. Archie trotted alongside Fraser, his eyes glued on the frankfurter, until Fraser settled on a grassy spot just beside the canal's towpath. Archie chomped an end off the frankfurter before Fraser had a chance to break a piece off, and ripped into it with over-the-top ferocity.

'It's dead, you know, Zigs,' said Fraser. 'It's not going to spring back to life. It's a sausage ...'

I know, I know, I just like to [rip-tear-grunt-chomp] *make sure it don't go getting no ideas ...*

'Seems that filled a hole, wee man, eh?' chuckled Fraser with a pat on Archie's crown as he flicked a pink tongue around his mouth. 'Just like that sausage, I have no plans on going anywhere, Zigs. You don't have to worry about me running off.'

Damn right, yes! purred Archie, pretending not to hear as he washed his face with a damp leg.

'Here check this gorgeous boat out, Zigs,' said Fraser as a canal boat chugged serenely into its berth. A little gnome-like man stood at the tiller, manoeuvring it with delicate precision against the canal wall. He stopped, stepped out onto the towpath, and twisted a rope around a bollard. Fraser smiled; wiped his eyes dry and called out.

'Nice boat, my man!'

'She's gorgeous, isn't she?' replied the little man in a shy voice. He was shortish, with a cheeky face, and wearing a plain T-shirt over a slightly rounded belly. He pulled the rope taut around the bollard before climbing aboard again and silencing the engine. After this, he turned to Fraser, tapped the boat's flaking green paintwork and said with an impish grin: 'I wouldn't be without my dear old *Alcinous*! Honestly, once you live on water, you can never go back to living on dry land ...'

33

The Union Canal

'AND WHERE'S YOUR BED?'

'It's just behind you, mate. Basically that bench folds out. It's a bit bigger than a single, but not quite a double.'

'Ha, incredible,' replied Fraser. 'Listen mate, I hope you don't mind us taking a look around.'

'No worries, mate, honestly!' said the little man. 'Happy to give you the tour.'

Archie lay cradled in Fraser's arms like a baby, the tip of his tail overhanging and brushing against the canal boat's wall. *What must I look like, eh? I'd never live this down in the East End.* Just above the cat's eyeline, a slit-like window revealed the canal's towpath at ground level – jogging trainers, bike wheels, the occasionally snaffling muzzle of a dog. In the boat's long narrow interior, the air was rich with the scents of hessian and varnish.

'And you can just move off when you like? Sail down the canal?' enquired Fraser. The ceiling was millimetres away from his head, so close that his reddish-brown hair brushed it as he moved about the cabin.

'Yeah,' replied the boat's owner, with his impish smile. His eyelashes stood out to Archie for the perfect rings they made around both his eyes, the lashes spiking out so that each eye resembled a little star. 'So long as you come back to this berth. Or you can stay overnight, down at Ratho, say. But yeah. Don't like your neighbours, then bye-bye, just move.' On 'move' the man swept his arm forward with a grin, like an absurd army officer instructing troops into battle.

'Ha, well that's appealing enough,' said Fraser half to himself. 'Are there any for sale? Or rented out?'

'Yeah, pretty sure there's one up for sale down Polwarth way. No one's been in it for ages. Called the *Penelope* I think? You should check it out ...'

'Aye. Aye, I might just, you know,' responded Fraser thoughtfully.

He ventured towards the stern, running his hand along the headliners that padded the walls. 'Sorry, I didn't catch your name, pal?'

'I'm Gerry.'

'Good to meet you, Gerry.' Fraser extended his hand. 'I'm Fraser. And what do you do for internet?'

'The mobile signal is pretty good,' replied Gerry. 'There's 5G and everything. And there's a house up the back that lets me piggyback off their Wi-Fi. Oh and there's toilet blocks all the way along. Really well maintained. There's a good community round here. People look out for each other.'

Archie wriggled in Fraser's arms. *Let me look around, dammit!*

'Okay, okay, Zigs. Shhh. Sorry, Gerry, mind if I let my cat down to sniff around? He won't be no trouble.'

'Sure, mate, sure.'

Archie felt himself get lowered and immediately set about sniffing; firstly Gerry's ankles – *clean socks, hint of WD40, and bike oil. People who smell of bike oil are always decent to cats,* thought Archie raising his tail with approval. He nosed his way around the miniaturised world – a small fridge, a small chest of drawers, a dinky hob and even dinkier sink. The sun had come out, beating its late-summer warmth through the narrow high windows and drawing out the fragrance in the varnished wooden floor. The boat jostled slightly, as another boat crept alongside, and whether it was the frankfurter hitting his brain, the change in Fraser, or something else entirely, Archie suddenly felt what could quite possibly have been the greatest happiness he'd ever felt.

The narrowboat's inside felt much bigger than the boat looked on the outside. Archie sidled by a chest of drawers, overflowing with trousers and T-shirts, and under a little window flanked by gingham curtains held back with bows. Further along still, two steps led up to a cockpit, the space presided over by a huge wooden tiller pole. Archie lumbered up the steps, sniffed a flowerpot and leaped onto the roof, coming to rest by a squat chimney cowl. *This is the life. I could see myself as a canal cat, y'know.*

He peered over into the water's surface and its stringy green underworld of weed and muck. His tummy lurched as he caught sight of a submerged traffic cone poking up from the murky depths. *Yeah and STAY down there!* he growled, still convinced, as ever, that there was something untrustworthy about traffic cones.

Footsteps pattered from below and Fraser emerged with Gerry at the stern.

'Your cat seems to like it,' said Gerry.

Damn right I do matey, thought Archie with a slow-blink. He collapsed onto the mossy tarpaulin and rolled in the grit and moss, paws hooked in the air. *Nice bloke, this Gerry geezer,* he thought. *And clearly an outcast like us. Just the ticket.*

Stretching like this with his paws in the air reminded him of the *Calypso Spirit* and the luxury suite he'd invaded. And then of course of Georgie. Lovely Georgie. He rolled to his side as her image grew in his mind. *I wonder what she's up to? Should've thanked her, really. Caught her a mouse. First lap I ever sat on! She taught me how to let the love in. They all did, though . . . the fisherman, Georgie, Hélène . . .*

To the boat's side, beyond the towpath, a little bank sloped down into a park, bounded on its far side by a tenement-lined street. On the opposite bank, the water lost itself to a tangle of reed beds and bracken, through which little white-beaked birds turboed their way between rushes. Behind, steep gardens rose up scattered with trampolines, barbecues and gazebos – the joyful expressions of summer. Another narrow-boat glided past, a golden Labrador on its roof gnawing contentedly at a squeaky toy. *All right, mate,* Archie ventured, with a slow-blink. The dog stopped chewing and lifted its head, ears pert, but stopped short of a bark. *Decent manners,* thought Archie. *I like it when a mutt knows how to keep schtum.*

'Thanks, Gerry, really appreciate it.'

Archie turned to see Fraser's hand outstretched to Gerry's.

'No worries, mate,' replied Gerry. 'Like I say, just climb aboard that other one in Polwarth. You'll know it when you see it. No one's been on it for yonks. And if there's no details, get on to the council as they'll have the details on record.

Old woman, she was, must've been like eighty-odd. Doubt she's paid mooring for over a year … if she is still alive.'

'Will do, mate, top man, top man,' said Fraser. 'Here! Zigs! *Wschht*, we're off.'

Nah, I'm staying for a bit pal.

'Oi, Zigs!'

Sorry mate, this roof is the business.

'Oi, Ziggy, c'mon!'

'It's all right, he can stay if he likes,' said Gerry, his head bobbing up from the cabin.

'Ach no, if he stays now, he'll never want to leave,' said Fraser, climbing onto the roof. 'Here, *Zigs, come on.*'

Fraser rustled in his pocket and flung a couple of cat treats onto the towpath.

Get in, my son!

Archie sprang up and leaped ashore from the boat's roof in one clean jump.

'Ha, he likes his food!' said Gerry.

'Aye, this one will do anything for a bit of scran, won't you Zigs.' Archie hoovered up the niblets unhearing before leaping up into Fraser's arms and then onto his shoulders.

'Wow, amazing how he can do that,' said Gerry.

'I know, he's a pure acrobat, eh! Cheers, mate, have a cracking day.'

'B-bye, mate.'

They made their way along the canal, stopping occasionally to let a pedestrian admire Archie on Fraser's shoulders. Archie could even feel a change in Fraser's walk. It was calmer, more relaxed and curious. Now and then he lingered at bushes, cupping the blooms of plants and scrutinising them, passing his thin rough-skinned thumb over their white fleshy petals inquisitively. Something about his spirit seemed to rush forward, like a stream suddenly disencumbered of a log jam.

The canal stretched ahead, widening where little boat sheds clustered, and narrowing under bridges, where pedestrians were squeezed into confrontation with bikes. Eventually, just beyond a meander, they reached a spot where the bulrushes were high and a pontoon bobbed beside a white-clapboarded rowing club.

'Ah, bet that's it,' said Fraser under his breath. Archie followed his gaze. A little mouldering narrowboat sat all by itself, tethered to a pair of bollards. It hung low in the water, its windows cobwebbed and its tiller hanging limply, as if somehow embarrassed by itself. Along its prow, *Penelope* was written in swirling letters, in the style commonly found on traditional gypsy caravans. Its roof was spattered with bird droppings, and the ropes that moored it had turned green and powdery with mildew.

Fraser paused, looked it up and down. A silence fell between them. Archie looked to the opposite bank where indigo-coloured lavender tumbled from the edge of a lawn, accompanied by the constant low-level hum of bees.

'What d'you think, Zigs?' said Fraser eventually. Not taking his eye from the boat, he reached his finger and ran it under Archie's string collar, the evil eye charm glinting. 'She'd scrub up all right, wouldn't she?'

34

Penelope

BLOODY HURRY UP, MATEY, I'm wetter than a seal's hanky here . . .

Archie peered from the hollow of a tree trunk. Night was falling, and a whip-crack of thunder rang out as rain lashed in heavy droplets. Summer had clearly decided to break for good, and the damp, hot air above Scotland was taking its revenge and turning Archie into a skinny, streaky-haired gargoyle of a cat.

Bent over across the rain-washed towpath, Fraser hunched in his cargo shorts, fiddling at the padlock to the *Penelope*, a lockpick clamped between his teeth.

He's been at it ruddy half an hour, thought Archie. *And there's ruddy ice in this rain. ICE. At the tail end of summer?*

Fraser had, in fact, only been working at the lock for ten minutes. In the time that had passed since he and Archie first spotted the *Penelope*, Fraser had taken them on a stroll to the neighbouring district of Slateford to look for a guesthouse. But none of them accepted cats. Increasingly frustrated, with night approaching, and evidently determined not to return to Davy's flat after the kicking incident, Fraser had changed tack, heading to a grocery store for supplies, and a hardware store for a set of lockpicks. He then turned back towards the canal, stopping outside a tenement where a box of items had been placed on the pavement with a note stuck to it saying, 'Free to a good home!' From this, he had helped himself to a table lamp, a kettle, a wooden spoon, a saucepan and a woollen jumper, all of which he plunged into his rucksack and plastic Scotmid bags. *Gosh he don't hang about*, Archie had thought coiling tight around his shoulders.

Now, against the hiss of rain, Archie shivered in the hollowed-out tree trunk as Fraser cursed at the rusted padlock, pulling the hood down over his head each time it blew off. Now and then, a devoted jogger splashed past and Fraser ducked down furtively out of sight.

Oh come oooon, stop making a meal of it! growled Archie from the verge. *You're mugging me off, mate.* A wet cat is always a comic sight, but a scraggy wet cat in a tree, its face fur forming into hemlock-like tendrils, has an almost goblin look to it.

'Yaaaas, ya dancer!'

Fraser fist-pumped the air, letting the padlock drop to the deck. 'Here, Zigs, *wsssht*, we're in.'

Archie galloped his sodden way over. Leaping aboard, he side-stepped over the vestiges of an abandoned bird's nest and a rotten herb planter. The cabin door was painted green with red and black flowers twisting down its length, and reminded Archie immediately of East End pubs. The hinges complained at being awoken, rust seeping out of their spindles, as Fraser yanked at the door in bursts.

Archie's pupils widened in the gloom. The cabin extended ahead, vault-like and forbidding. Rain pattered on the roof. The smell of mildew. A bird carcass. Little by little, Archie decoded the tapestry of odours: sitting among the reek of mould and paint, there was a nutty composite smell Archie couldn't quite place. But underneath these was the subtler smell of rodents, creosote and breakfast cereals. High up along the boat's sides, old curtains lay drawn, their patterns lost to dust and mould. Fraser pulled one set open; the sound of tearing cobwebs.

Riiiiiight . . . thought Archie, taking in the now-illuminated space. *Okkaaaay.*

At large, it was much like Gerry's boat – divided into three parts, with a living space, sided by a lino-covered bench, a kitchen, and a front storage space beyond a pair of saloon doors. A bird had got in at some point, probably the one that lay half rotted, and had deposited its droppings on the age-cracked linoleum. Enamel cups stood on the kitchen counter, one still containing a dried-up tea bag, eerie with a sense of frozen recentness. In the middle of the floor, a fan heater squatted, its wire trailing into a built-in cupboard.

Fraser flicked a switch on the wall. Nothing.

Well, I've slept in worse, I don't know about you, thought Archie, flinching as he sniffed the lip of a bottle of paraffin. Pots and pans hung from hooks, swinging gently as the boat shifted under Fraser's weight.

'Well it's watertight, at least,' said Fraser, whose head had disappeared through a trapdoor in the floorboards. 'What we need, Zigs, is power.'

He stood, letting the hatch drop shut. Whistling, he traced a wire from a light switch up the side of a wall-mounted dresser, over his head, and down behind a built-in cupboard.

Ain't no mice in here, though, thought Archie a little glumly, licking his fur dry.

A scuffling sound as Fraser jiggled something out of the back of a cupboard.

Click.

'No way!'

On flickered the ceiling light.

Excitedly, Fraser traced the end of the fan heater's wire and plugged it into a socket under the wardrobe. It surged with reluctant life, filling the space with an electric-y smell of burned dust. Archie sidled over and let the blast evaporate his wet fur into steam, turning every few seconds, like a rotisserie chicken, as it began to scald.

'Power, Zigs, power!' Fraser cried. 'We can do anything with power. Reckon we're off grid? There's no smart meter here.'

Fraser placed the groceries on the side, and plugged in the lamp and kettle he'd found on the street. Slowly, as Fraser and Archie dried off, their limbs warming under the glow of the yellow ceiling light, the rain still thrashing on the roof, a cosy feeling enveloped the little boat. Archie took to sniffing the kickboards and clutter while Fraser, infused with a new energy, nosed like an otter in and out of cupboards and seat lockers, brushed the dirt off bench cushions, and waded into the miscellaneous junk stored up at the bow. Eventually, he extracted a greasy oblong object from the junk pile which had been coiled in ivy.

'A hob, my boy,' he muttered, a twinkle in his eye. 'I actually cannae believe it.' He set to pulling the tab off a tin of chicken noodle soup he'd purchased earlier, pouring the contents into a saucepan.

'And there's a Scotmid just over that wee bridge, puss. This is absolutely perfect!' He fetched down a dust-skimmed pile of plates, rubbing each one in turn with his jumper. 'It's not much,' he said. 'But I think this will do us just fine.'

And it's all ours!

Fraser gave him a smile, the kind that Archie seldom saw on him – a full smile in eye, face and cheek that seemed to exude its own light. 'And it's all ours, Zigs!'

* * *

Perfection takes a while for a street cat to comprehend: the ideal life, the ideal human and home. Archie felt it initially as little surges of ecstasy that caught him off guard: sitting in Fraser's lap at the *Penelope*'s helm as he steered it nimbly over Edinburgh's Slateford Aqueduct, the Glasgow train clattering beneath; or with the TV on and log burner glowing and a meal blipping on the hob; or, glimpsed for the first time, when he had sniffed around Gerry's boat back in the summer . . . a summer that had turned to autumn, and sent the blackberries fattening on the canal-side brambles.

Ultimately, Archie concluded that perfection wasn't so much a place or even a person, but a feeling that encompassed a whole set of perfect elements. It struck in a golden knot often when he was in the midst of a reasonably mundane moment – a sniff of a new item, or the opportune glance of a bird whirling beyond the *Penelope*'s high curtained windows. He realised that he could be in the present so deeply and absolutely because he had come to terms with his past, and packaged it off in a sort of vault; a vault whose access he had complete control over. The bad moments of his straying life in London, the cruelties and discomforts, became fainter, exerting less of an influence over his moods in the present. They still caused him pain, of course; and sometimes he would be jogged fully back into his straying life, such as one afternoon when he saw a nasty dog fight break out on Harrison Park beyond the canal. But even then, the pain had been muted and inconsequential, like an atomic bomb whose innards had been defused. And when he thought back to the London before his odyssey across the seas, he didn't do so filled with vengeful hate. Instead, he would feel a rising contentment, borne out of the complete and certain knowledge he wasn't in that world any longer. *Thank God*, he'd think. *Archie you jammy git. You escaped it . . . and you didn't even have a pedigree coat, or a knack for tricks and mousing. It was the sea what did it.*

Two months had passed since Fraser first broke into the *Penelope* and Archie would often stare from a little rug-lined bed Fraser had made for him at the sheer resourceful brilliance of his human. Fraser could do it all: he'd made a new kitchen with wood and saws, installed a new log burner, and relined the entire cabin with wood panelling which he'd painted and sealed. Barely a day passed where Fraser did not step into the boat, his cargo shorts flapping around his knees, with a new tin of paint, tube of silicone or bundle of electric cabling. A whole week passed, in September, with the floorboards up and Fraser diligently dismantling the engine, David Bowie crying out in the background on a Bluetooth speaker. Periodically, Gerry would pop down to offer words of encouragement and advice.

'Blimey, the engine, that's brave?' said Gerry one morning.

'The army's got to be good for something, eh?' Fraser had responded with a grin, his body concealed to the waist in the *Penelope*'s bilges.

'I got some crankcase oil and a set of gaskets, if you like,' Gerry had said. 'Want me to get them?'

'The gaskets, if you wouldn't mind, mate, aye. That'd be great.'

The noisy clinks of metal that week saw Archie regularly taking himself off for walks around the park opposite in search of squirrels, or even some fast food from the cat bowls in the ground-floor flats. *Stand back!* he'd retort, with a hiss, as he wolfed down the Felix of a house cat who stood by, back arched but too terrified to take on this fabled cat who had apparently sailed the world and come up from London with his great paws and knotty grey fur. At times like this, he'd play the stray card, for you can take the cat out of the East End, but never fully take the East End out of the cat. *Cheers,* he'd chirrup at the wide-eyed cats, smacking his lips. *Bit harsh I know. Sorry for giving you the 'ump. But your humans are loaded, and I'm but a poor stray. I appreciate it.*

Slowly but surely the little boat turned into a home. Archie grew fatter on the readily available food, strayed into Fountainbridge on the hunt for easy grub, and even found himself as far away as Morningside in hot pursuit of a particularly luscious-smelling Maine Coon. On the occasional hot afternoon, he'd swipe for fish off the bow (*I'll never beat that one I got off the Zephyrus . . .*), now and again swiping up a roach or bream. But the nights were getting colder as summer turned to a crisp-morninged autumn, when the Edinburgh light fell slanted and yellow on the brows of tenements. Skilled tradespeople are hard to find, and word quickly spread of Fraser's skills. He would often rise early, fetch a bike he'd fixed up and kept behind the rowing club hut, and pedal off into town, towing a trailor with his tools. Later, he'd return sweaty and smiling, with a fistful of cash and sawdust around the laces of his boots. After dinner, Gerry would inevitably amble down and Fraser would greet him at the stern, the lit tip of his cigarette a firefly in the darkness. He'd then invite Gerry down to enjoy the glow of the burner, and a glug of amber Scotch. The pair of them would then natter, getting slowly tipsier until the conversation turned wayward.

'Of course it was an inside job,' Fraser would postulate, refilling Gerry's glass.

'Oh my God, *absolutely* an inside job, mate,' Gerry would chime back, sinking his little body deeper into the blanket-covered bench. 'And the moon – don't think for a minute that happened either! The missus used to say I was mad but as I'd say: show me the evidence, show me it *isn't* a Hollywood set.'

And Archie would dose, as the cheers swept over from the stadium at Murrayfield, and think, of all cats, from the present day right back to the lauded felines of Ancient Egypt, it was he, Archie of Stepney Green, who was the happiest of the lot.

35

Hmmm . . .

IT WAS THE MORNING AFTER one such dreamy evening, on a cold night in October, that Fraser first learned something was amiss with Archie.

After heading out for supplies, he returned home to find Archie still snoozing deeply, having skipped both his breakfast and his usual mid-morning jaunt over to Harrison Park. The sky that morning was crisp and wintery, with an avenging streak of red off to the north.

'I'm a bit worried about him,' Fraser had said to Gerry, who'd come along for a catch-up on the previous night's sports scores. 'He seems peely-wally and has been drinking a lot of water these last few days.'

No I bloody haven't, Archie had thought, lifting his head from his doze, a drop of opaque water still hanging on his beard. *Peely-wally. I'll give you peely-ruddy-wally!* In an effort to show he was okay, he got up and sashayed past the men's legs, with a grumpy sense of duty, before resuming his seat on the rug alongside the log burner.

But if he was being completely honest, Archie knew something wasn't quite right. He knew by the way his protestation had backfired in his brain, causing him to feel mildly depressed at its dishonesty. The last few days he had sensed the subcutaneous prickle of a fever. He had shrugged it off and tried to hide it, thinking it was the turn to winter, but really he knew something was afoot. A cat always knows, even if they don't show it.

He curled in front of the coal fire, tight like an ammonite shell. Sitting there he looked delicate, his coiled body giving him an almost kitten-like petite-ness. He'd heard Fraser wondering about his age, telling Gerry he must be getting on now, surely? In the light of the fire, his irises, usually flashing gold with primal energy, had taken on a greyish tinge. His breathing had become a little laboured and his ear failed to flick with its usual quickness when Fraser scrounged the bag of treats.

'If it's not one thing, it's the other,' said Fraser to Gerry in a glum tone. 'Just when I've got the boat all above board and the deeds signed off, the cat gets ill.'

'Yeah,' said Gerry. 'That's life for you, eh. I do love Archie's toes, you know. They're just so great!'

'Yeah,' said Fraser, lightening at the topic change. 'They're polydactyl. He basically has thumbs. Always thought that funny because some cultures think polydactyl cats bring good fortune at sea and ... well ... I got to know him at sea. That's when things changed for me.'

Maybe you're just getting on a bit, old boy, thought Archie, not hearing the men's conversation. He thought of old cats he'd seen: the stoop, the gait, the dim eyes and greasy fur, the slow drawn-out agony of the digestive system decommissioning itself. *A hard nut getting old ain't a pretty sight,* he thought, remembering the ex-gangsters who used to prop up the bar at the Well & Bucket pub; their fading tattoos and beer bellies.

He drifted off to sleep with the gentle rocking of the boat, the smell of coffee on the air comforting and fragrant. And in the thread of half-consciousness he heard a voice, unaware of its place in the world of reality or dream, and completely forgotten by the time he awoke. It was Fraser's.

'The thing is,' it muttered, between sobs. 'I can hardly afford things as it is. If he got ill ... I just couldn't afford to ... Oh, I don't know. And I just think it's bad, mate. I just got that feeling ...'

36

The Gram

'CHEERS, MATE, I REALLY APPRECIATE IT. And I will pay you back – got a couple of jobs next week in Merchiston, should get me a fair bit.'

'Honestly, mate, no worries, I know you will,' said Gerry. 'I've also made a start on the GoFundMe page. I know we all moan about social media, but I really do think the internet gets behind us canal folk.'

They were standing on an Edinburgh street outside a vet's. It was 4 p.m. and turning dark, with splinters of rain visible in the headlamp beams of cars. Archie shivered in his carry box, letting out a drawling meow in protest. *Hurry up, I'm getting real 'umpy, here!*

The vet had felt along his tummy as his great paws trod over the rubber examination table. She had prised open his mouth and peered at the red concertina ridges along its roof; pulled down the corners of his eyes and rubbed his bladder. All that had felt fine. He had growled, sure, but not swiped, knowing well the necessity of these acts. But then the vet's latex-gloved hand had probed a point on his belly and a red-hot pain exploded along his abdomen, his claws immediately extending, and the alley viciousness reanimating in a muscular swipe. It was as if he were a sleeping dragon whose tail had been stamped on. It had caught him off guard. It was a seismic, deep pain.

The vet had said something and Fraser had responded but Archie's ears had blanked with agony. A sample of blood was taken, with the vet screwing the cap on the vial before crisply typing at her computer keyboard.

Now, outside the vet's, they all bundled into the taxi, Gerry ducking his balding head into the rear-facing seat and Fraser placing Archie's carry box between them. Archie heard Fraser sniff, and clear his throat. *What's up? Anything the matter?*

'Jesus Christ,' whimpered Fraser. Above, through the gauze of the carry box, Archie saw Fraser's leg juddering up and down, as it was prone to do in times of stress. 'Five grand? No chance. Just when I was getting back on my feet. And with the money from the army only just covering the boat and now this …'

The taxi lumbered over the potholes with a hiss and splash, the driver silent behind his Perspex screen.

'Honestly,' said Gerry, blinking his little star eyes. 'Hear me out okay? With GoFundMe, we can …'

'No, man, there are weirdos on that …'

'Look, this is the landing page,' said Gerry leaning over with his phone. 'And here are some others I've saved as inspiration. This cat received two grand for its own statue. People will understand … You don't have to say the particulars about your story and your background. Leave the bits about the army vague, if you like …'

A silence fell again between the men, heavy and long.

'You're a good man, Gerry,' said Fraser eventually.

'Us canal folk. We're a community. We stick together,' said Gerry.

'Look, I've got three thousand followers on Instagram with my canal boat page,' said Gerry in a chipper tone, sensing a spark of hope in Fraser. 'That would give it a kick-off. Then there's the canal committee, the Edinburgh forums who'd share it … I'll set up a TikTok, a Facebook page. He's a handsome devil and what with his funny paws, he'll capture people's hearts. And then "bang", before you know it he's viral and you'll be able to pay for the treatment.'

Fraser shot Gerry a rueful look. 'You can tell you're a recovering marketeer, man. No wonder you got out of it.'

Gerry giggled. 'Sure I got out, but this is one *good bit* that I learned during all those years. Us Brits love a personal story, and we love our cats.'

'Oh, I dunno, Gerry. I've done bits and pieces over the years, ya know? Stuff that I'd rather, you know … '

'I'll do it,' said Gerry. 'I'll do it all. I'll be your proxy. You won't even have to *say* who you are. People will see Archie and that's what will make them click … They'll read the story about him being diagnosed with a thing that needs lifelong treatment; they'll see the pretty canal and the thing about the owner having fallen on tough times with his beloved mog. I don't even have to mention the sea and the boats and how he got to be with you. We'll leave all that out, if you like.'

Archie pivoted his ear towards the conversation over the squeak and clang of the taxi's suspension, only able to catch the odd word.

'Let's take some pictures when we get in. And I'll write a thing and send it to you. I'm all right with words, you know. Just see what you think? Even if you raise two grand, it'll get you somewhere. Get you closer, you know? We can do this, mate.'

Fraser unzipped the top of the bag and scratched round Archie's fluffy neck. Archie gazed up glassily and noticed Fraser's eyes, watery and red.

Prrrp?

'Look at you two, for goodness' sake!' cooed Gerry. 'You come as a pair. As if some rich Marchmont woman wouldn't fling you a few quid to get you back on the path.'

'Marchmont women don't use X,' said Fraser flatly.

'It's Instagram,' said Gerry, 'and don't you believe it, mate! They very much do. And it won't just go out to them – it'll go out all over the world. You'll have people in Mexico donating … and Germany … and … hey there's a funny thought …'

Fraser turned and looked at Gerry square. 'What?'

'Well … you might just find out where he originally came from.'

37

A Visitor

GEORGIE'S PLANE BANKED OVER the Firth of Forth. Raising her window blind, she stared at the islands of Inchcolm and Cramond as they broke through the grey sea, vanishing and reappearing through puffs of cloud. She sighed, throwing her head back to the headrest, her big eyes cast upwards. The last few months had not been good ones: not only had her mother become suddenly ill with pneumonia, but her exam results had not been as she hoped. But there had been Callum; he had been a pleasant enough distraction. Decent, loving Callum who doted so much but whose mouth had an annoying habit of twitching at the end of a sentence and who was just a little bit too knowledgeable on the history of the Marvel series. Of course he had said he didn't mind when she said she wanted to use her annual leave from Pizza Express to go and see an old school friend in Scotland. *Of course* he didn't mind. Did he really mind about *anything*, come to that, other than the Marvel comics?

She picked up her phone and swiped to reveal the home screen as the landing gear extended beneath her into the icy Scottish blast. She touched the photo app and a picture of Archie immediately appeared, bright of eye and fluffy of neck. It was him all right. The bitten-out ear alone would have given it away, and the canny yellow eyes, but the polydactyl toe glimpsed bottom left of centre sealed it unquestionably. She scrolled along to the next photo – a screenshot of a GoFundMe page. At the top was written in bold 'Help Ziggy the Canal Cat' and underneath a little caption read: *I'm a veteran and Ziggy saved my life after a tough time on military deployment. he's now very ill and I can't afford treatment. he's my everything. vet note below as proof. any help appreciated, peace, love and mad respect to all. F xxxxxx*

The post was dated late October – nearly two weeks ago. Georgie had donated immediately, when only £95 had been raised; but over the days she noticed to her amazement that the donations counter had gone up and up, reaching £4,370 – touchingly close to the £5,000 target. It all seemed strange and surreal, though somehow checked out with the extraordinary cat she had first encountered on that awful gaudy air-conditioned superyacht, the *Calypso Spirit*, and who had subsequently become her confidant, sage, and mysterious liberator from that horrendous gin palace which had later sunk off the coast of the Canary Islands. She hadn't told Callum about Scruffs the cat: it was still early days – the sort of time when you were scared to tell a partner something you fear they might think strange, even if they, themselves, are evidently strange. To be honest, she was happy to put the whole *Calypso Spirit* episode to bed as quickly as possible – a time which, Scruffs aside, was characterised by stress and misery.

She had told her mum, though, and showed her the GoFundMe page, receiving back a little giggle which her mum seemed to immediately regret after catching her daughter's hurt expression. ('Oh sorry, darling. What I mean to say is there are *loads* of grey cats out there. What makes you so sure it's Scrufferz from your trip? I'm sure the little cat's doing very well down in Cape Verde, catching all those canaries. Now, be a darling, and nip out and pick up half a dozen eggs from Tesco and a GI loaf from Baines, would you?')

So she had dropped it, partly because she didn't want an argument when her mum, who was still recovering, and partly because she didn't want to appear any more ridiculous in front of her parents, who were clearly hoping to glimpse a few more signs of maturity in their ditzy daughter. It can be hard for a human to understand the depth of love felt between a person and a cat particularly when, for all her wonderful qualities, Georgie's mum was a certified dog person, with an allergy to cat hair.

But the little cat from Rhodes had stayed with Georgie and been burned indelibly into the memory of those hot docksides and sun-cream-scented decks. It was the look in its eyes; the way its wiry grey fur tousled in the wind during the night watches on her lap, and the slow, gentle (could you say knowing?) way it turned from stray to lap cat over the weeks she furtively enrolled it as her companion. Sometimes, unbidden, a memory of Scruffs would rise in sleep along with a half-statement (*It was petrol. I one hundred per cent put petrol in that stupid boat.*) or unexpectedly while taking an order from a table at Pizza Express, temporarily throwing her train of thought and making her drop her pen. It was silly, the whole thing. Really silly. But this page was definitely him. And he wasn't well. So she had to visit.

Seeing Rupert in Edinburgh was the perfect cover story for her visit – old Ru-Ru from upper-sixth. Of course her parents approved too – they had hoped for her and Ru to hit it off in his last year of school, Ru being a swot bound for a red-brick university when Georgie had entered the zenith of her daydreamy phase. *Good that she's seeing Rupert Whitmore*, Georgie's mum had said to her husband, climbing into bed one evening. *Lovely boy, that one.* Maybe this time they would hit it off, or at the very least, his studious nature might rub off onto their daughter and give her the kick she needed to take her resits seriously.

'He's welcome down in Truro, *any* time,' Georgie's mum had insisted chirpily, her head out the window of her Nissan Micra at Newquay airport at 6.30 a.m. 'And make sure you pass on our regards, yes? And take your shoes off when you go in his flat, I hear the rug is a Terence Conran.'

'Yes, Mum, heard you the first time,' Georgie had replied, rubbing her large bloodshot eyes and yawning. 'Thanks for the lift.'

But now the plane's engines were spooling down, its nose tilting up as its wheels kissed the tarmac. Georgie thought of the money she had spent on the donation – £500. God, that was a lot. A knee-jerk decision, really, but she didn't regret it. While not working on the *Calypso Spirit* long, she had been paid decently, and her bed and board were covered. That, along with the Pizza Express pay, was enough cash to make someone her age feel somewhat flush, and her bank balance had easily absorbed the donation, the hostel cost and the Newquay to Edinburgh flight. She had no particular plans beyond finding Scruffs. But the Rupert cover story calmed her – its faux agenda was compelling, even somewhat to herself. After all, there was nothing to stop her dropping in on Rupert if things *did* come to nothing. Who would be any the wiser?

A judder along the tarmac. Engines silencing. A chime. Seatbelts clacking. People shuffled into the plane's aisle, lifting their suitcases and rucksacks from the overhead lockers. Georgie thumbed her phone off airplane mode. A message from Marvel Comic Callum: *You arrived yet? Miss you xxxxx.*

Outside, a skim of rain hit her face as she loaded Google Maps to find the Union Canal. She had been to Edinburgh before, a couple of times, to visit her grandma when she was still alive, just outside the city in Dalkeith. She knew the centre, the castle and the Arthur's Seat hill, and had once walked along a canal, though she wasn't sure it was the one she needed to head to. She glided through arrivals automatically, her eyes on her phone and her rucksack bouncing off her back. On the tram, she pulled her hair back into a ponytail, phone on her knee, her scrunchie nipped between her teeth. The GoFundMe page was refreshing – in the last twenty minutes, the funds raised had shot up again. She pinched the image between finger and thumb, enlarging it to the polydactyl toe until it pixelated.

The message bar slid down from the top:

You arrived safe?mumx.

Yes, all good!xx she tapped back.

Remember to take your shoes off on Rupert's rug!!

An eye-roll emoji in response.

Outside the window, the rain had subsided to a uniform greyness, making the pebbledash bungalows look drab and the high-sided stone tenements ominous and looming. She disembarked at Haymarket and threaded her way past commuters and high-rise office blocks following the little blue dot on her phone. It was pulling her towards a point on the canal route which, when she dropped the little yellow Google man, revealed a strip of narrowboats, nose to nose. Other than that she had nothing to go on. But she was emboldened in a crisis, and this did feel like a crisis of sorts. She had travelled abroad after all, and felt confident in asking strangers for directions (so long as they were women). That was the one good thing about the *Calypso Spirit* debacle – it had matured her and made her stand up for herself, for what is right. She wouldn't be a victim, and had the little cat to thank for that. If she couldn't find the gypsy-style narrowboat half-pictured in one of the GoFundMe photos, then she'd simply ask someone . . . or walk further down the canal until she did.

She reached the banks just past 11 a.m. The towpath was wet, the water's surface flecked with wind. Along the bank, reeds sprouted, half-decaying, in the boggy murk. For a moment she stared dumbly at a moorhen as it nibbled at a piece of soggy sliced loaf. Feeling sorry for it, she tossed the corner of her airport sandwich and saw it dart over and begin eating. A bike bell dinged irritably. She stood aside awkwardly, muttering sorry, letting the bike scoot past. On she walked, her mind loose and faint, her footsteps echoing under the bridges where pigeons cooed from their mess-splattered girders. Finally she reached a flotilla of canal boats and her heart began racing. Each one was moored end to end, their bodies long and flat and their noses turned up like pixie shoes.

'Scruffs,' she said nervously, in a quiet pedestrian-free moment. 'Scruffs? I'm so sorry. I didn't mean to go like that. I've been thinking of you the whole time.'

She walked and called, her voice merging with the chattering of coots, until the banks of the canal turned from cityscape to parkland, and a white clapboard hut appeared, cuddling in tight to the banks.

38

Old Friends

ARCHIE'S EAR SWIVELLED, HIS BREATHING laboured and long. He lifted his head more quickly than was comfortable, a move punished with a smart of pain along his spine.

Hang about. What's that?

It was the footsteps that caught his attention before her call, not because he knew they were Georgie's but because they were distinctly different from other footsteps on the towpath and Archie, like all street cats, was acutely attuned to difference. The shoes were tentative, the *slap-slap-slap* of a flat-soled shoe, not the familiar rhythmic *thrud-thrud-thrud* of joggers. They stopped; lingered, their sound becoming momentarily lost under the noise of traffic beyond Harrison Park. It was as if the shoes' owner (*or were they boots?*) was walking warily, unsure of where they were.

Perhaps, on some level, he did know the footsteps were Georgie's – in some deep part of his memory which, like many moments of pain throughout his life, he had sealed

277

off. *Another lost human; no point remembering her step . . . You'll be hearing them everywhere.*

Then the call.

Archie sprang off his bench bed, making Fraser jump as he sat reading alongside, causing the ash to tumble from his cigarette.

THAT'S GEORGIE!

He was certain. More certain than he had ever been of anything. The soft voice, slightly unsure of itself and tinged with a West Country accent. The minor-yet-distinctive huskiness, and the softest hint of a rasp at the back of the throat.

'Hear something, Zigs?' said Fraser as Archie gambolled out to the stern, each movement giving him another smart of pain along his back. Outside, the rain was fine; more of a thick mist. Pulling himself up, Archie advanced stiffly along the roof, tail high, his front half seeming to drag his back half reluctantly along. He stopped at the bow, his sinews smarting with the sudden movement, his tail gradually drop-ping and becoming limp. His eyes searched the towpath ahead, focusing on the point in the middle distance where it met with the canal in the tight meander. Little ruffles of breeze sped over the water's surface which was turning plat-inum, with a break of sun.

It was Georgie, I know it was Georgie. Come on, where are you?

A mallard emerged, gliding in uncanny silence across the channel.

'Scruffs?'

There!

Georgie's voice came from the other direction, her foot-steps soft on the grassy bank.

Flip me it's HER! Archie mewed, feeling his body tremor with pain. He cantered back along the roof as Georgie approached, the distance between them narrowing, narrowing, narrowing.

It's her, it's only ruddy her! Would ya Adam and Eve it?!

He approached the stern, his haunches preparing to leap ashore. But his frame seized, his claws clicking frantically against the tarpaulin roof as he failed to muster the power.

Help me, I need lifting. I can't make the jump!

Georgie placed her hand under Archie's chest and picked him up. His passage up to her face felt slow, almost ethereal, until he met her, eye to eye – the same eyes he had seen crying, laughing and anguished on that faraway sea all those weeks ago. The same big eyes that had given him his first foray in how to love.

'Oh Scruffs, my baby Scruffs!' cooed Georgie between little sobs. 'How did you get here, Scruffs, you cheeky, *cheeky* boy. Are you not well? Oh Scruffs you're purring! I've never heard you purr. Oh my boy!'

Archie breathed in Georgie's sugary odour – the raspberry lip balm and sugary sweets. Her hand fell softly onto his neck, smoothing and tickling it at the same time, just like she used to. He could feel his body trembling, though his head was so full of love for Georgie he couldn't tell whether it was from emotion or infirmity.

How did you find me? he enquired, with a gentle growl, as he pulled his head out from its burrow under her arm to meet again with her damp eyes.

Fraser's voice from behind.

'What's all this, Zigs?'

Fraser, it's Georgie. I met her weeks before meeting you. She taught me to love. Before her, I was angry at the world and at life. She's a great human – be kind to her, let her come aboard. A human was right cruel to her on a boat in the Mediterranean Sea and we helped each other. Let her come aboard, let her come in!

'You better come in, hen,' said Fraser to Georgie with a knowing smile.

* * *

Georgie stepped aboard. Thinking back on this point, later in life, she would reflect on how foolhardy it was of her to board a random man's canal boat in a city she hardly knew; she, who knew well the special claustrophobic fear of being trapped on water with a violent man. The lack of escape routes; the fear of an ever-looming malevolent glare. But she would reflect, too, on how normal it felt and how immediately safe she felt in Fraser's presence – his eyes, bandy legs and gaunt stubbly jaw seeming to convey a thousand axioms of pain and pain's conquest into something peaceful – a victory she knew herself.

'Tell me about yourself,' said Fraser, switching on the hob gas and lighting the flame with a match. 'You go first, because honestly my story of finding him is pure mad.'

'Oh mine's low-key nuts too, I'm not gonna to lie,' responded Georgie. She sat cross-legged on the vinyl side bench while Archie sniffed her sandals and nuzzled her knee. Seeing Fraser's perplexed face, she giggled. 'Sorry, does that chat make you feel old?'

'Oh steady on! I was only born in ' 98, ya know!'

Georgie blushed, the first awkward moment between them. 'Oh I'm sorry, you seemed . . .'

'Older I know,' said Fraser putting her at ease with a smile. 'Don't worry . . . everybody thinks it. It's being Scottish.' He poured hot water into two enamel cups. 'It's cool. Just, you know, living on here, you're a bit cut off from the latest in style and grooming. I've got a radio and the speaker; but then really it's just me, my work and Zigs.'

'You mean Scruffs,' said Georgie with a wry smile.

'Or Scruffs, aye!' said Fraser.

'Scruffs and Ziggy. Scriggy? Scriggy Scar-Fluff.'

'That's ridiculous, but I kind of love it.'

Six of one, half a dozen of the other, thought Archie, slow-blinking on Georgie's lap.

'Sorry,' said Georgie again, looking a little awkward. 'You must think I'm totally unhinged ... some random girl from the West Country coming all this way to see your cat.'

'No it's fine, it's ... ' Fraser shook his head, making an explosive gesture with his hands, the full madness of the situation seeming to dawn on him.

'I just couldn't get that GoFundMe page out of my head,' continued Georgie. 'And I knew it was him from the paw ... the extra toe. I had to come up.'

'Naw, it's fine,' said Fraser. 'And I've been amazed at how much the community's rallied round. I didn't even know about GoFundMe, it was my new pal who's got a boat up at Fountainbridge who told me how it all works. I never thought we'd receive so much. That's his first dialysis and treatment paid for now, pretty much up to Christmas. I'm so grateful, you know?'

'I'm so pleased. Because he helped me out loads.' Georgie turned to stroke Archie's crown. 'I owe him so much. He ... ah, I dunno, it sounds mad, but he probably changed my life.'

'Your *life?*' replied Fraser.

'Yeah. The boat I sailed on sank after I escaped with him in Cape Verde.'

'*What?* So he's ...' Fraser squeezed and lifted out the tea bags before passing a cup to Georgie, who blew over its surface. He squatted down against the opposite wall, tea in hand, his eyes rolling in an attempt to understand the time-line. 'So he must've ...'

'Crossed the Atlantic?' said Georgie.

'Yup!'

'Poor boy, he's been through so much! He really is a survivor. Honestly, he saved my bacon when I was at sea. Couldn't have got through it without him.'

'Same, absolute same. My head was a mess following my discharge from the army. I was heading home via a convalescence stint in Bermuda. That's where I met him.'

'*Bermuda?*' It was Georgie's turn to sound incredulous.

'Uh-huh.'

'How did he get there?'

'I've no idea where he came from. I just thought he'd always been on the island. Mind you, that collar's a weird one, eh …'

Fraser lifted Archie's evil eye collar off a nail, where it dangled like a dreamcatcher between the open curtains.

'No way,' said Georgie. 'He was wearing this when he came aboard our boat in Rhodes!'

'*Rhodes?*' said Fraser. 'Zigs, my God! How far have you travelled?'

I've got about a bit, Archie slow-blinked back.

'He's totally been on his own odyssey,' said Georgie.

'So he must've got across the Atlantic somehow,' said Fraser. 'Wait, where did *you* leave him?'

'I left my crew in Cape Verde after my evil boss *literally* – get this – chucked him overboard.'

'You're kidding me?'

'Nope. I mean what sort of maniac does that to an animal?' said Georgie, throwing her hands in the air. 'So I just got us safely ashore and then I obviously had to fly home. Couldn't take him, of course. I thought about taking him to a centre in Cape Verde – like a cat rescue place; but I don't know, I Googled them and there didn't seem to be any I liked the look of, and he just seemed so *savvy*, you know?

I just knew he'd be totally fine as a street cat. He'd been a stray when he got aboard after all. He never purred with me, though, so this is new …'

'Ah really?' Fraser looked a little smug. 'Aw, you've always been a purrer with me ain't you, Zigs?'

'And he was quite bolshy too. Loving on his own terms, but a definite tom.'

'Aw no,' replied Fraser tickling Archie, who was now climbing into his lap with a purr. 'He's always been a sweetie with me. Once swiped a fag out of my hand, which was hilarious. It was like he wanted me to give up.'

He was about to ignite the whole tanker! thought Archie, shooting Georgie a profound look.

'He's hissed at others who try and pat him, though,' said Fraser. 'But he's always been a softy with me.'

'He's a changed cat, then,' said Georgie pensively. 'Travelling has done something to him. He must hail from an Arabic country originally what with his collar.'

London actually, thought Archie, feeling smug about holding this private piece of the puzzle.

A beam of sun backlit the curtains, casting light across Georgie's forehead. There was a moment's silence as they held each other's gaze and a canal boat passed alongside, sending its wash slurping under the hull.

'And … ' Georgie paused as if the words stalled in her throat. 'And when did you first notice he was ill?'

'Around late summer,' said Fraser, stretching his arm behind a little screened-off space and drawing out a biscuit tin. He popped the lid and offered one to Georgie. 'Wagon Wheel?'

'Oh *nice,* I love Wagon Wheels! Elite biscuit choice, man!'

'I know, they're great, eh.' He placed the lid back on the tin and took a bite. 'He started drinking a lot and got suddenly thinner. I think the kidneys were properly packing up. He was really tender along this bit of his side by the back leg. That was the closest he came to scratching at me, actually.'

'He was always a bit funny about his side with me too,' responded Georgie. 'Poor boy.'

'Oh, no way. So maybe it'd already started then? Anyway, I'd had a small pay-out from the army but burned through it sorting this place out ... and debts and ... just, ach. Long story, I'd started working as a jobbing carpenter and was making a bit, but I didn't have the kind of money he needed for the kidney treatment. My cash in hand could cover the mooring fees and enough to eat, but not much more. I got this boat for an absolute song. That's another story – great guy up the way really helped me out.'

'Ooft, so you're a soldier?' Georgie bit into her Wagon Wheel, holding her palm out to catch the crumbs.

'Was a soldier ... Again, long story.'

'Wow, so we've both had the most chaotic summer all because of this little guy, right?' said Georgie.

'Absolutely mad, eh? It's like something out of a film.'

The pair laughed. It was a different laugh; a laugh Archie hadn't quite heard from either of them before.

'But you've reached the GoFundMe target right? Or you nearly have ... ?'

Fraser glanced at his phone, its screen still bright from a recently received WhatsApp notification. A message from Gerry. A screenshot, next to the words: '*And this just in from someone in France!!!!*'

Fraser grinned.

'Well, we have now.'

39

Iron-Clawed Archie

FTERNOON FELL TO EVENING. The whisky came out. And cards. Later, as Georgie stepped ashore onto the towpath, she lingered for a moment.

Light poured out of the *Penelope*'s windows, illuminating the reeds on the far bank. The air smelled autumnal – of mouldering leaves and the woody smoke coming from the *Penelope*'s chimney as the log burner glowed. Heading out to ankle-brush Georgie, the crisp air on his fur, Archie was struck by the towpath lights – little LEDs mounted in the concrete – which stretched off into oblivion towards the city. It reminded him of the runway lights at Dalaman airport and he thought back to earlier in the year, and its sequence of events. Its wild, strange sequence of events. Could it all *really* have started with him chasing a pigeon aboard a train? Was it all fluke-fluke-fluke? Or was there something else at play? *If the old East End legends are true and there is some crazy cat god in the sky, he ain't 'alf had good fun with me this*

285

year! But why me? he thought, licking round his huge poly-dactyl toes. *Why little old Archie of Stepney Green? I'm just the normalest of normal mogs.*

A minute later, Fraser emerged.

'You okay, hen?'

'Yeah,' Georgie replied softly. 'Was just thinking how lovely it is here. And what a special day it's been.'

'I'm starting to think there is some good at play in the world,' said Fraser.

Archie's tummy did a summersault. Fraser ducked out of the little doorway and climbed ashore to join Georgie on the towpath.

'I feel like I've known you . . . well . . . as long as . . .'

'As long as we've known him?' ventured Georgie.

'Yeah!' For a moment, neither of them spoke. 'Well . . . I'll be seeing you, then,' said Fraser. He leaned in and kissed Georgie's cheek, light and careful. She smiled. As he drew back, her hand brushed his – almost nothing, something that might have been an accident. But then she took his hand properly; passed her thumb over the ridge of his knuckle. *They ain't half standing close to each other,* Archie thought, watching in silence from the boat's edge. The pair looked at him, almost at the same time. When they turned back, the space between them had somehow closed. They were close enough now for their coats to be touching, their soft friction making a little *scritch* through the silent air. And then with a little jut of her neck, Georgie kissed Fraser's lip. *Aw Gawd, I've gone and landed myself a set of parents,* thought Archie with a look to the side. They both laughed, shuffled awkwardly. Georgie reached for her coat zip, fussed with it for a second, then let it go again.

'Well . . . that just happened,' she said.

'Yup, yup . . . yup,' said Fraser, his eyes darting away as he grinned. 'I wasn't expecting that this morning.'

'To be fair you weren't expecting a Cornish girl who knows your cat to rock up this morning,' added Georgie.

'Fair. True.'

Another pause.

'Hey, Fraser!' A voice broke the silence from along the dark towpath. The outline of Gerry formed in the gloom, clutching a fish supper. 'Two hundred quid from Turkey! And something from Greece, too!' There was a pause as he noticed Georgie. 'Oh, oh sorry, mate, I didn't know you had company . . .'

Georgie and Fraser both laughed.

'Don't worry, Gerry mate,' Fraser called back. 'I've got someone to introduce you to at some point . . .'

Gerry raised his hand silently, getting the message, and continued his walk back to his boat.

'I suppose that means I can come back tomorrow?' Georgie whispered.

'I mean . . . that would be grand,' replied Fraser.

'I'll text you,' said Georgie. 'Bye – and bye you, Scriggy Scar-Fluff.'

She tickled Archie and disappeared over the bank towards the park.

'Oh Scriggs,' said Fraser, watching her disappear.

Good for you, old boy, she's a cracker, thought Archie.

* * *

Back in the *Penelope*, the log burner had smouldered to glowing ash. Plates from tea were resting on the draining board, accompanied by a soggy scraped-to-the-bottom carton of Ben & Jerry's ice cream and a dented-in beanbag. A battered copy of *Born to Run* by Bruce Springsteen lay alongside a clump of rugs Fraser had arranged in front of the fire. He knelt and pushed aside *National Geographic* to reveal two sheets of A4 paper, folded in half. They were green-coloured. *From the vet*, Archie immediately thought, eyes widening.

'I couldn't bear to open it while she was here, Zigs. It came yesterday . . .' He turned the envelope over in his hands. And then again. 'It's the initial diagnostic report, to see if it's treatable, boy.'

Fraser slid his finger through the top of the letter. All sounds stopped except the flutter of paper as it un-concertinaed in Fraser's hands. His eyes moved quickly at first, then pinched as he moved the letter closer to his eyes with a frown. He froze.

'Yes!' Fraser fist-pumped the air. 'It's treatable boy . . . !'

Ah jolly good, thought Archie. *Archie the Iron Claw of Stepney Green is going to make it!*

The truth was, over the last fortnight since Gerry accompanied Fraser and Archie to the vets, Fraser had doted on the little cat like a Victorian matron. Each hour, between stints of carpentry on a workbench, he'd come over with fresh water (Archie, like any self-respecting cat, rejected any water that had even the slightest skim of dust on it); offered fresh salmon, purchased from the fishmonger up at Slateford, and special renal cat biscuits. He jostled to and fro, looking up from his work to see if the noise was bothering him, checking the lustre of his coat, and continually readjusted his bedding beside the log burner. It had become almost annoying, particularly when he started to misread Archie's meows as *please, more strokes,* rather than what they actually were: *stop fussing, mate, I'm fine.*

At night, when the owl hooted in the plane trees that spilled their leaves on the *Penelope*'s roof, he'd come up and snuggle with Fraser in bed. *Reckon that food's helping,* he'd think, with slightly forced optimism. *I feel I'm on the up.*

All the while, Fraser had awaited these initial diagnostic results in silent, restless agony. Meanwhile, Archie rebuked himself for his tiredness through weak, self-comforting purrs. (*Look at yourself, Archie old boy,* he'd thought on one particularly depressing day. *Once the fear of the East End. Stepney Green's iron claw! Now you're tired out by swiping a ruddy bookmark.*)

But he'd persevered. And now, as he watched Fraser clean the cabin, singing to himself merrily – now washing up the plates in the tiny sink, now discovering Georgie's scarf squashed behind the beanbag – he found himself ruminating again on his odyssey, but from a different angle: *What saved me? The sea or the humans?* Suddenly, the man came to mind that he'd seen off the bow of the *Zephyrus* as it made landfall. The Caribbean man, who had said: 'He's the Ship's Cat. He's a magic cat, that one.'

I still don't believe I'm magic, he mused, readjusting his paws. He thought of how the fate of each boat seemed to change the moment he prowled their decks. *Although there's magic of some kind going on here.*

The huge expanse of his life stretched behind him, each event, a mosaic granule on a Roman bath floor; the streets of London and this, the great cornerstone, the gold-etched effigy of a marching centurion. He finally recalled his earliest memory – back from when he was a kitten: his mother's fine, full tabby face peering down into the cardboard box that he and his brothers were mewling in on the oil-stained back street in Stepney Green. And the days that followed when, hardly able to walk, he'd been found in a gutter and chucked in the Thames by a hooligan, sending him in a paddling frenzy to the shore, his tiny lungs flooding, before being noticed by the pub landlord of the Prospect of Whitby who happened to be walking the foreshore, and who scooped him up saying, 'Flipping 'eck. Here Tina, you'll never Adam 'n' Eve this; it's a little kitten. Poor little Long John Archie, flung out on the Thames!'

And so he had got his name, and it all began.

If only they knew my story, thought Archie in the weeks that followed, as Georgie and Fraser grew closer, their hands braiding together on the beanbag by the fire. *Like, my full story, ya know? If only they knew all the alley cats' stories — the stories of all the forgotten street cats about the world. What about their lives? Why have I been so lucky? What saved me? The sea or the humans?*

He sank further down into a deep purr, the question fading to obscurity in the back of his head as Fraser placed his collar back on the hook by the window.

He was home, and that was all that mattered.

Epilogue

Twelve years later

IF YOU WALK FURTHER ALONG the Union Canal, you reach the village of Ratho. Walk a further two minutes still, upstream of the old village pub, and you come to a picturesque meadow sloping up to the right. In the spring, the dandelion pom-poms jostle in the breeze, which still has a stab of cold as it eddies up from the Forth between the flagstone walls. On the far side, up a little mound, a row of fir trees stand sentinel-like, as if guarding the field from an unseen invasion. But on summer days, when insects buzz among the cow parsley and the crimson loganberries flower, a quiet falls on the meadow that is unlike any other spot along the canal. It is a sumptuous quiet, interrupted only by the chitter of jackdaws in the high firs or the blackbirds in the thicket on the far side where there stands an abandoned water trough and tap. It is in this furthest corner, beyond the limits of the city, where sheep claim the land and eye the occasional cyclist on the towpath, that an old derelict barn stands, its ribbed interior of rotted beams thrusting up to a sagging roof. Its ancient slates, fallen from the roof long since, gather in little clusters in the tussocky grass. Behind this barn, nestled close to the firs, and beyond the foundation of an old kitchen garden, sits a grave. It is a bleak spot in winter, yet in summer it teems with flickering life; the blue flash of a butterfly, the drone of honeybees, or a lamb shading itself beside the nettles.

It is on one such day, in the year 2038, that four figures will stray off the Union Canal path and into the field, one holding down the barbed wire fence so the others can climb over, and another keeping watch for other passers-by. Seen from behind, as they advance, they seem incongruously different: one is a woman, tall and athletic with short-cropped hair and expensive shoes, and whose arms are skinny and bronzed. Next to her is a smaller woman, her hair in a ponytail and her nut-brown ankles meeting gold-banded sandals. Running alongside her in bright pink shorts is a toddler, just walking, and pointing out the flora and fauna with an intent index finger. Flanking the toddler's other side stands the only man, lean and angular of feature, his T-shirt whipping in the breeze. Eventually, the man breaks ahead, letting the child be taken in her mother's arms, before ducking and disappearing through the old door frame to the ruined barn and emerging around the back, the others ducking in behind him.

Eventually, the three adults form a stately line behind the kitchen garden, while the little girl gambols after a butterfly in the buddleias. Gently, the man leans down and places a loop of string on the freshly turned soil – a black, bitten loop with a pendant hanging from it, bright as day, depicting an Islamic eye – its blue iris flashing in the sun. He steps back, takes his position between the two women, and hooks his arms around their shoulders.

None among the assembled party knows where the collar came from.

The hand that originally threaded the eye charm onto that string never knew what happened to the little cat whose neck he placed it round, returning instead to his life fishing the seas around scorching Turkey. He would die several years later, having spoken often of a little *kedi* who had rescued him at sea (or so he said) in a story that warped and twisted its way around the fishing villages of the Eastern Aegean like driftwood. Eventually it became a misshapen adage; a local fable handed down by mariners – the polydactyl ship's cat who brings good fortune at sea – indistinguishable in truth from the Hellenic myths. The fisherman had once tried to put the story to words, but he was no writer, and the scrawlings ended up being filed in an old logbook, not found or read for many years. When the time came for his funeral, the imam lauded him as '*a good man, who knew his god well, and perhaps should have been a poet. May Allah receive him with mercy and grant him peace.*'

A wind whips through the ruined barn tousling the flaxen locks of the toddler. The tall lady kneels; clears a patch among the ivy, and places an envelope, marked '*mon beau chat*' on the still-soft soil.

The four of them leave and the envelope stays, turning brown and brittle as the days pass, while the stone holds firm its engravings under growing smatterings of lichen, as the surge of days turns to years.

The Ship's Cat

a.k.a.

Mr Lynx
Scruffs
Mon Beau
Ziggy
Scriggy Scar-Fluff

Much loved by us all

Acknowledgements

Firstly, beloved thanks to the constants in my life – my lovely wife Ellie, our little boy Sasha, and my parents, Maria and Michael Howard.

Huge thanks to my brothers, Matt and Rob, for introducing me to East London, Brixton, jazz bars, Massive Attack, and for encouraging their little brother to dip a toe in the turbulent waters of noughties counterculture. Were it not for you, there'd be no Archie of Stepney Green, and the only music I'd have ever listened to would be Andrew Lloyd Webber and *Pan Pipe Moods*.

This book started out as a love letter to the sea, and no single family is more responsible for instilling that love than the Gilsons. To Julia Gilson for inviting twelve-year-old me on your dinghy, *Mambo-Jambo*; to Jo Gilson for making the ostensibly mad decision to call upon unsporty, eighteen-year-old me to help crew a boat across the sea. That trip made me grow in ways I'm still hugely grateful for; I'm indebted to you all, and the kindness of the late Bob Patterson, for making it happen.

Back in Edinburgh, thanks to my fantastic editor, Clem, for attending to things so closely and being just the right amount of scary. This book is much the better for your input. Thanks, as well, to Rachel Morrell for your early input, Ali McBride and everyone at Bonnier Books UK. Gratitude to my lovely agent, Ed Wilson, for being so easy to talk to and for always knowing the answer. Lucy Ribchester: your friendship continues to be as precious as it is inspiring – payment in furniture restoration tutorials simply doesn't seem fitting. Huge thanks to Cecilia Bennett for being so generous in offering up plot thoughts and for getting me into dirty chai lattes; to Emma Granberg, Joy O'Riordan, Bess Ruzich and Jessica Harper for reading early drafts, and to the brilliant Mairi Kidd, Harriet MacMillan and Xa Shaw Stewart for your bookish advice, laughs, friendship and excellent taste in coffee shops.

To my wonderful colleagues at Capital Theatres, for always making me giggle on my 'non-writing days' – I couldn't be without you. Particular thanks to the wit of Pab Roberts, Richard Miller and the Creative Engagement Team. I'm indebted to the kindness and humour of so many here, but special thanks to the camaraderie and support of Kim McKenna, Chris Lindsay, and my late friend, the wonderful Robert Murrell; finally, to Nick Brown, for his encyclopaedic knowledge of Scottish oil terminals.

Thanks, as well, to the dementia-friendly community of Edinburgh, whose tales of Edinburgh past never fail to infuse my writing in one way or another, and to Mark and Ailsa of Cuthberts Café.

Finally, thanks to my brother-in-law, Joe, for letting me use the name of his cat whose former life, prior to his adoption, remains intriguingly mysterious . . .